Malcolm D. Welshman is a retired vet and author of a series of three pet novels and a memoir. His first book, *Pets in a Pickle*, reached number two on UK Kindle's bestseller list and the third was short-listed for The People's Book Prize. He also writes regular features for national magazines including *The People's Friend* and contributes monthly columns to several pet-orientated websites.

Dedicated to my wife, Maxeen, who has had to put up with me disappearing into my study for hours on end to write this book.

Malcolm D. Welshman

PETS ARE A PLEASURE

A Vet's Tale

AUSTIN MACAULEY PUBLISHERS™
LONDON • CAMBRIDGE • NEW YORK • SHARJAH

Copyright © Malcolm D. Welshman (2020)

The right of Malcolm D. Welshman to be identified as author of this work has been asserted by him in accordance with section 77 and 78 of the Copyright, Designs and Patents Act 1988.

All rights reserved. No part of this publication may be reproduced, stored in a retrieval system, or transmitted in any form or by any means, electronic, mechanical, photocopying, recording, or otherwise, without the prior permission of the publishers.

Any person who commits any unauthorised act in relation to this publication may be liable to criminal prosecution and civil claims for damages.

A CIP catalogue record for this title is available from the British Library.

ISBN 9781528977531 (Paperback)
ISBN 9781528977555 (ePub e-book)

www.austinmacauley.com

First Published (2020)
Austin Macauley Publishers Ltd
25 Canada Square
Canary Wharf
London
E14 5LQ

Praise for Malcolm D. Welshman

'His witty take on a young vet's life pet lovers will find endearing.'

– Bel Mooney,
author and *Daily Mail* columnist

'A joyful read full of animals and fun. Guaranteed to delight, though there are some tearful moments.'

– Celia Haddon,
author and former *Daily Telegraph* columnist

'The author has an uncanny ability to paint human as well as animal characters. Any animal lover will adore his writing, of that I am certain.'

– Michael Smith,
editor *Green (Living) Review*

'Everyday adventures are shared with human clients as quirky as the pets treated. A must read.'

– Sue Parslow,
freelance writer and editor

'The writing is funny and full of character.'

– Kate Nash,
literary agent

'It's a pleasure to read this vet's encounters with clients and creatures great and small, which made me chuckle throughout. Highly recommended.'

– Cathy Woodman,
bestselling author of *Trust Me, I'm a Vet*

'The exotic creatures and eccentric characters make for a spellbinding read where the author's love of animals shines through.'

– Jenny Itzcovitz,
editor of Sixtyplusurfers.co.uk

'You'll laugh a lot and thoroughly enjoy reading about the rather hapless Paul Mitchell's escapades. Perfect for animal lovers the world over.'

– Natasha Harding,
Book Columnist, *The Sun*

'These experiences, recounted in a most readable way, illustrate the interesting and challenging situations that can confront a vet.

– Jim Wight,
son of James Herriot, author of *The Real James Herriot*

Table of Contents

Prologue	11
1. When to Draw the Line	13
2. Be My Valentine	25
3. Battles with Bovines	42
4. Seeing Double	58
5. Watch the Birdie	76
6. Feline Frolics	93
7. Fergie the Fox	108
8. Scenes from the Green	126
9. Creeping with Crawlies	145
10. Parrot Patter	164
11. Finding It Hard to Swallow	180
12. Ticked Off	196
13. Knowing Your Neighbour	215
14. A Colourful Life	235

Prologue

Confronted by a pulsating power-pack of muscle, I was instantly turned to a puddle of melted jelly. My bedside manner all of a wobble.

Nothing that St George tackled could compare to this dragon with which I had to do battle. No Basilisk-type reptile with a lethal gaze. No Kraken arising from the sea like some giant squid.

My heart pounded and thudded against my ribcage. My pulse surged, a tsunamic wave that washed through my arteries. The tic in my forehead began to throb. Fear a fist in my stomach.

If the vicious, needle-sharp teeth being displayed – as lips drew back in a rumbling, spittle-filled snarl – weren't enough, the eyes made it worse. Liquid yellow eyes full of venomous intent. Adrenalin surged in them. The instinct to fight had turned the body into a furball of fire, ready to lunge at me. To think, I'd tackled the likes of a lame camel. A gored ostrich. Wrestled with a caiman, struggling to avoid its snapping jaws. Now this – the mother of all challenges. What a monster.

I cautiously circled round, trying to steady my nerves, trying to decide the best way to tackle this without being ripped to shreds in the process.

Words collected on the tip of my tongue.

'Now, now, there's a good lad,' I whispered, speaking in a soft, low and hopefully reassuring tone, even though there wasn't the remotest sign whatsoever that the beast had anything good about its being. As evidenced by a second angry snarl.

'There... There... now. No need to get so upset.'

A third angry snarl indicated my reassurances weren't making the slightest bit of difference.

'Oh, well, if that's the way you feel, then I've no choice.' I stepped forward. There was a flurry of fur. The flashing of teeth. A spurt of blood. My blood – jettisoning from the savage bite inflicted on my hand.

'Oh dear,' cried Mrs Dawson as she scooped her cat into her arms, cradling him to her bosom. 'He's never done that sort of thing before. So out of character.' She bent her head down to kiss the cat's head. 'My poor little Snookie,' she drooled while poor little Snookie continued his stream of rumbling abuse as he prepared to strike again.

My poor little hand, I thought. But there we go. I forced a wane smile and attempted to re-establish what remained of my tattered bedside manner. Attempted to apply all the knowledge and understanding achieved through five years of training. Attempted to show I cared, that I wished no harm. To show empathy – my St Francis of Assisi persona.

That all evaporated when poor little Snookie lunged at me for a second time and I bellowed, 'Why, you little sod?'

1
When to Draw the Line

When my client, Mrs Munday, slipped off her fur coat to stand there naked as the day she was born, it was lucky I hadn't been holding a thermometer in readiness to shove it up the rear of her shih-tzu. Her nakedness would have caused the temperature to rise rapidly, the mercury to soar off the scale, before the thermometer ever reached the dog's bottom.

As it was, the stick of charcoal in my hand snapped in two once Mrs Mundy had stepped forward, baring all before her. The ravages of 60 or so years clearly etched in the sagging contours of her body for all to see, every nook and crevice. Not a pretty sight; not one for sore eyes. But good enough for the eyes of the drawing class of which I was part. Mrs Munday's contours to be put to paper in the form of quick charcoal sketches.

I blamed Beryl for that situation.

I'd just finished expressing a poodle's anal glands. Their contents having liberally sprayed themselves in my face and was feeling as foul as the odious odours still lingering around my nostrils.

'Join an art group,' my receptionist suggested. 'Do something different. Help take your mind off work. Express yourself in a different way (*other than via expressing anal glands?* I wondered). I'm sure it will do you good.' She gave me one of her one-eyed laser-looks which did me no good at all. Other than highlighting my lack of self-confidence even more. As did the art class. After seeing Mrs Mundy in the altogether.

Crystal had observed me flapping around the hospital, flipping through the case notes of in-patients; a bundle of agitation. She called me aside with the curve of a delicate finger and said, 'Try to pace yourself, Paul. Don't let things get under your skin. You'll just get run down. Suffer burnout. And that won't do anyone any good, least of all yourself, would it now?'

I gazed into those wonderful blue eyes of her, observed the delicate earlobes, the copper curls and cast my mind two years back to my first few months at Prospect House. A time when this senior partner was my Julie Andrews. My *Sound of Music*. For her, I could have leapt and bounced across the highest peaks. Now, completely drained of *Odl lay ee*, the best I could have managed was to stumble over a molehill.

Not so, Eric, her husband, the other partner in the practice, who had also noticed my stressed-out state. In stark contrast to me, he always seemed to be in a buoyant frame of mind. With his squat rotund body, he bounded around the hospital like a wallaby on springs, his oversized white coat forever flapping around his ankles.

'I don't know how you keep so cheerful,' I remarked.

'Easy, Paul,' he exclaimed, bouncing up and down on his heels. 'Exercise. That's the name of the game. Helps to boost your metabolism.' He squatted, jumped up. Squatted. Jumped up again. I felt dizzy watching him. 'Just a few easy exercises. Nothing too difficult. Wouldn't want to overdo it.' He threw out his arms, inhaled deeply, dropped to the floor and completed five press-ups. Each one slower than the last.

'There. See? Bob's your uncle,' he gasped, staggering to his feet, his baldpate glowing, his breath ragged. Seeing the state of Eric, if Bob *was* my uncle, he'd have had a heart attack by now.

If that wasn't enough, one coffee break, I was confronted by him flinging balls around the office. I'd gone in to find him scrabbling under the desk, looking for one while a bemused Beryl was perched on a chair, sipping her mug of coffee. I saw his backside sticking out from under the desk well and grimaced at Beryl, placing a finger to the side of my head and twisting it. The action suggested Eric had gone a bit screwy. She raised one of her talons (fingers) and tapped the side of her beak (nose) with a nod of agreement.

Eric emerged with the retrieved ball, a material-covered yellow tennis-sized job and picked two similar balls: one blue, one red, off the office desk.

He threw one in the air and then another and attempted to catch the first as he tossed the third. All three landed on the floor.

'Uhm… Haven't quite got the hang of it yet,' he said.

'So we see,' said Beryl dryly.

'You should give it a go, Paul,' said Eric, tossing the balls up once more. 'It's amazing what juggling can do for you. It's very absorbing.' He paused to search for a ball that had rolled under the desk again. 'Helps you focus on your breathing.' He sighed as a second ball hit the floor. 'And stops unwelcome thoughts from intruding,' adding, 'Bugger,' as he missed catching the third.

'What a load of balls,' I think I heard Beryl mutter.

Certainly, I wasn't impressed. Besides which with the endless stream of dog and cat castrates passing through my hands each week, there were more than enough balls there to handle. Even if I didn't toss them into the air but just tossed them into a kidney dish.

Eric then decided to take up cycling and we found him wobbling into work on a sports bike. The first morning, he'd sprung up the steps of Prospect House and into reception, encased in the full regalia. Cycle hat with yellow reflectors was rammed on his bald head. Yellow Lycra top and black Lycra pants were figure-hugging his portly frame in a very unflattering and revealing way. Imagine jumbo sausage roll squashed in cling film and you'll get the picture.

'What do you think, Beryl?' Eric stood in the centre of the reception lobby, posing, bandy-legged, hands on hips.

Beryl's good eye went into laser-mode and scanned him up and down, only to finally hover at crotch level in a blaze of distaste.

'Everybody to his own,' she uttered, swiftly turning back to her computer screen. Unwilling to be saddled with similar scrutiny, I decided biking was not for me.

A suggestion from Mandy, the senior nurse, came via Lucy, the junior one. As Lucy was now my fiancée, it was less embarrassing for her to put the suggestion to me. 'Mandy wonders if you should try some mindfulness meditation. She thinks it might help reduce your stress levels.'

Ah, yes. Mindfulness. Very much in vogue at present. A way to release my inner bliss. Unlock the engine that runs my life.

'Well, if it makes your engine less cranky, then it can't be a bad thing,' said Lucy, a trifle unsympathetically, I thought.

I tried a few sessions of sitting on the floor of Willow Wren, the practice cottage: with legs semi-crossed, arms, palms up, resting on my knees and a mantra of Ohms going through my brain. No good. It did nothing other than give me a bad back while my pistons of positivity remained seized up.

Hence, those art classes as suggested by Beryl.

I initially reasoned it might be a bit of fun. Mental calmness aside, I potentially could meet some interesting people. Westcott and the neighbouring villages dotted over the South Downs had their fair share of artisans. Many drawn down from London by the prospect of inspirational seascapes and landscapes.

Beryl mentioned one to me. 'Brenda Sudgate. Comes in with her two tabbies. Cat mad. Does those cross-stitch pictures of them?'

'And there's Lucian Boyd,' Eric reminded her.

'Oh, that potter chap,' Beryl shuddered. 'Hopeless man. Churning out shapeless bowls that wobble, teapots that don't pour and mugs with no handles so you burn your fingers trying to hold them. All for the sake of art.' She shook her head sadly. 'Still, I suppose it's better than Colette Symonds and her penises.'

'What?' I exclaimed with a mixture of alarm and intrigue.

Eric cleared his throat and enlightened me. 'She's one of Westcott's more colourful characters.'

'You can say that again,' Beryl butted in.

Eric continued. 'Her forte is the construction of collages depicting...' He paused to give another little cough.

'Oh, for goodness sake, Eric. Since when have you been so coy?' declared Beryl, before turning to me. 'Colette makes papier mâché collages of men's genitalia. She's always on the lookout for new members. So you'd better watch out when she next comes in. She's not the sort to take no for an answer. Isn't that so, Eric?'

Eric's face had turned a deep shade of scarlet and excused himself, hurrying out of reception. Beryl winked at me with her good eye and murmured, 'I've always wondered...'

I suppose it was for the sake of art that Mrs Munday divested herself of her clothes. It may have been her undoing. But it was certainly wasn't mine.

In fact, it was actually her and her shih-tzu, Sophia, that finally helped to reduce my stress levels. Sophia developed diabetes and required stabilisation with insulin injections. So there were many appointments. Each time, Mrs Mundy was always calm. Always collected. Never seemed stressed about Sophia's prognosis and ongoing treatment.

I eventually plucked up courage to ask her how was it she coped so well.

'My dear chap,' she said, 'it's all because of you.' She ran a hand down her shih-tzu's back. 'You've brought life and vitality back to Sophia in a way that no one without a true vocation could do. I've had every confidence in you. And here's Sophia – the living proof.' She gave me a radiant smile. 'I can't thank you enough.'

Her comments rang in my ears as she left. And continued to ring whenever my stress levels rose. Welcome words I could draw on for comfort. Words that would trace the contours of my life as a vet. Without the need for a dropped fur coat.

My life drawing class confrontation with a naked Mrs Mundy was the subject of much banter over coffee for several days.

'Chalk that up to experience,' chortled Eric. 'I'll certainly see her in a different light from now on. Preferably still clothed though.'

Yes, thank you, Eric. Always the funny guy.

As regards Mandy and Lucy, life drawing in whatever shape or size was a lost art as far as they were concerned. A sketch for the two nurses stopped short at one on a TV comedy show. Fork handles – meaning four candles – Ronnie-Barker-style was more to their liking.

'It would put me off sketching for life,' declared Beryl. A decision that the rest of us would have welcomed after being subjected to her attempts at oil painting.

We'd been studying one of her efforts she'd propped up on the office desk while she went and made coffee. In the centre of the canvas was a large swirl of orange with darker orange stripes radiating out from it. At its base were four similarly coloured blobs; and to each side, a bank of unsteadily executed lines in white paint, some thick, some thin.

'What do you think it's meant to be?' said Eric, scratching his chin. 'A bowl of oranges?'

'Looks more like a Bagpuss pyjama case overstuffed with jimjams, if you ask me,' I said. Eric sniggered.

His wife, Crystal, looked up from the computer where she'd been running through the list of appointments Beryl had booked in for her that afternoon. 'Careful now. I daresay she put a lot of effort into painting that. We don't want to go upsetting her.'

There was a sudden hush as Beryl bustled in with a tray of coffee. 'So, what do you think?' She handed each of us a mug. 'Have I caught a likeness?'

'Sorry, Beryl. Caught a likeness to what?' Eric had picked up the painting and was holding it between his hands. 'I'm not quite sure…' He tailed off, his forehead creased in wrinkles as he swung the orange offering from side to side. He was clearly finding it a challenge to express an opinion without hurting her feelings.

I too was finding it difficult to come up with something to say which wouldn't unleash a salvo of laser-looks from Beryl. Was it an allegorical attempt at a sunset? A setting sun sinking in a morass of orange? Or perhaps a surreal effort to depict a bowl of oranges? If so, it had no "appeal" whatsoever. Not that I would dare say so.

Beryl stepped forward with a loud tut, snatched the canvas from Eric and rotated it. 'You were looking at it upside down,' she snapped. 'Now can you see the likeness?'

I could see Eric turning red, his baldpate glowing. I guessed that like me, it made no difference to him whichever way the painting was held. It still depicted a shapeless swirl of orange.

Only now at the top of the ball and slightly to one side, I could see there were two blobs of green encircled in black. Maybe they were meant to be eyes? In which case, the four blobs at the bottom could possibly be paws. Making the straggly lines either side: whiskers.

'Ginger,' I said, hazarding a guess. 'Your cat.'

Beryl beamed. 'Yes, of course. Who else could it possibly be?'

'An alien fruit from Mars,' I thought I heard Eric mutter. But fortunately for him, Beryl didn't.

It was no surprise to me that Beryl had chosen her beloved cat as subject matter for the art classes she's been attending the past six weeks. She was besotted by the fellow ever since he'd strolled in through the side gate to her cottage last summer and resided in her gazebo until the weather started to turn. He then decided to move abode – to Beryl's front room

– where he commandeered a fireside chair with additional bedding provided by her in the form of an overthrow and several feather-filled cushions. A smart move and one which was accompanied by full board.

The effects of that full board were all too evident when Beryl presented him for a check-up and vaccination. He lay contentedly on the consulting table, his rolls of fat rippling towards the edges. I knew anything I said regarding his weight would elicit one of Beryl's brick-bashed-owl looks, her head pivoting from side to side as if sizing up a mouse in front of her – and not one of the computer variety. But taking a deep breath, I took the risk.

'Ginger's a bit on the portly side,' I said, levering up a large lump of fat in his scruff to give him his vaccination. Beryl's head started to pivot.

'Are you suggesting he's overweight?'

'Well, he could do with losing a few pounds. We wouldn't want him to go down with diabetes or problems with his ticker, would we?' Her head pivoted even more. I was going to warn Beryl of the likelihood that Ginger might develop hip problems carrying all that weight but felt it could end up with her head in a spin and her pouncing on what I was saying. So I desisted. And tried another tact.

'Guess he's a hearty eater.'

Beryl shrugged, her feathers settling. 'Only the best for my Ginger.'

Actually, I already knew that. Beryl often popped down the road at lunchtimes, returning to the hospital with goodies for Ginger's tea. Pilchards and sardines were favourites. Invariably accompanied by full cream milk. I dreaded to think of his daily calorie consumption. Huge. And its effects were spread out before me now. Huge rounds of fat.

'You think I overfeed him, don't you?' Beryl was saying. 'But it could be something in his genes.'

No, Beryl, it's in his food, I wanted to say.

Beryl went on, 'Or could be to do with his hormones.'

No… No… No… It's food, glorious food, I wanted to sing out. But it would have been futile. Beryl was never going to listen; and Ginger was never going to lose weight.

The proof of the pudding was in her painting. When Storm Ingrid swept in, talk of art classes and the like was abandoned in favour of discussing the destruction caused by the gale-force winds. Westcott pier took a battering. Roads flooded. Trees blown down. And Westcott A & E was inundated with injuries sustained by flying debris.

In the aftermath of the storm, I was presented with my first canine casualty of the blustery conditions. Arabella. An elderly Saluki. Elegant. Grey-hound-like. Cream-coloured with soft silky ears. She'd been startled by a flying refuse bin, twisted sharply on her lead, and now could scarcely bear weight on her left-hind leg.

I heard a kerfuffle out in reception and walked through to find both Mandy and Lucy helping the Saluki up the hospital steps, supporting her hind legs while Beryl held the door open. It seems Beryl had seen the owner from the reception window, struggling across the car park with Arabella and had run down to the ward to get help from the nurses. All three of them were very eager to be of assistance – almost over-enthusiastic in their support of the dog.

'Probably best if we carry her through for you,' said Mandy.

I thought she was addressing me, but it was the owner she was addressing, her eyelids fluttering like butterfly wings at him.

'That's kind of you,' said the owner.

'It's what we're here for,' said Lucy, her eyelids also in a frenzy of fluttering.

Beryl butted in. 'I'll just take down some details. That's if you don't mind.' Her own eyelids went into similar lash-overdrive as she gazed across at the owner, her red-lacquered talons hovering over her keyboard.

And I could see why. The cause of all that lepidopterous wing-like activity was a lean, muscular, long-legged young man in narrow jeans and loose white T-shirt over tattooed arms. He has dark hair in a gelled quiff, shaved at the sides; neat, dark beard; dark, smouldering eyes – "take you to bed" eyes that would have you flung on a mattress in the time it took to say "King Size". Bathed in an aura of luxurious self-assurance, there was no denying the raw power he exuded. Roberto Mancini is his name. Italian.

'You can call me Rob if you wish,' he said in a low, husky voice.

'Boy, do I wish,' murmured Mandy, nudging Lucy.

'Okay, let's get the dog through then,' I said, my eyelashes stubbornly unmoved. With the Saluki already in the consulting room Mandy offered to stay.

'No, it's fine, thanks,' I told her. 'I can manage.'

'If you're sure,' she said, her doe-eyes sweeping up and down Roberto's whip-thin body.

'Positive,' I replied.

'Well, I'm available if you want me,' said Mandy; and before reluctantly leaving, she gave the young Italian the most "I've the hots for you" face possible, short of asking him to ravish her on the spot. Talk about Juliets hurling themselves off balconies for their Romeos. Mandy would have been the first to jump. No hesitation.

I started my examination of Arabella who had, up to then, been standing and trembling, putting weight on three legs but not on her fourth – her left hind, its toes just touching the ground and her left hip was leaning into Roberto's thigh for support. All suspicious of a problem in that leg. I knew from the history Beryl had obtained that the Saluki was 12 years old and, apart from her annual vet visits for booster vaccinations, had a remarkably free history of problems. Certainly nothing relating to the symptoms she was now exhibiting.

'Okay, old girl. Let's see what you've been up to,' I said, stroking her head. 'We'll check your spine first.' I turned to slide both hands down her back while Roberto held onto her collar. There were no grunts of pain as I prodded her spine, pressing down gently on each lumbar vertebra. At no point did she sit down on me as is so often the case with spinal problems. So, hers was going to be elsewhere. That left leg being the most likely place.

But hips were next.

'We'll ease her down onto the floor,' I said to Roberto. 'We should be able to manage between us.' I hoped so, as I had no desire to have the dog and, in the process, Roberto being man-handled by Mandy.

Once we had Arabella lying on her left side – which we managed very easily as the Saluki was very obliging, bless her – I palpated and manipulated her right hip, easing the leg forwards, backwards and out. I then moved down the leg to test the knee. All sound. No reaction from her.

But a different story when it came to the left leg which I put through the same movements once we'd rolled her onto her right side. As I flexed her left knee, she yelped. There it was in the joint. The diagnosis I suspected confirmed. A rupture of a ligament in the kneecap.

'Sorry, sweetie-pie,' I apologised and looked up at Roberto. 'Seems we've located the problem.'

'We can replace it with an artificial ligament,' I explained, having outlined the damage that had been done. No doubt when she'd made that sudden turn on being frightened by the dustbin lid.

'But at her age?' faltered Roberto. 'After all, she's getting on in years. Coming up 12.'

I nodded. 'Rest is the only other option,' I said, knowing that sounded obvious. 'Coupled with some anti-inflammatory therapy, it might just do the trick.'

A week later, there was little improvement.

'She needs crutches,' said Roberto.

That gave me the idea. Arabella was admitted to the hospital and her right leg put in plaster. 'That should act as a supportive crutch,' I explained. Every week for a month, Arabella stomped in for a check-up. Same day. Same time. A time when Mandy always seemed intent on tidying up the waiting room the moment Roberto and Arabella appeared.

At the final check, all appeared well. Arabella was using her left leg. The plaster could come off.

'Excellent,' said Roberto when he settled his account. 'Means I can get back to the art class now.'

I saw Beryl was immediately all ears. 'Art class? What is this about an art class?'

Roberto explained. He modelled for the life drawing class. The one where the model at the time I attended had been Mrs Mundy. But he hadn't done so while Arabella had been in plaster. Didn't want to leave her on her own in case there were any problems. 'But now I can attend tomorrow's class,' he said, flexing his brawny, tattooed arms.

Beryl nearly fell off her perch. And was quick to spread the word.

Roberto in the buff. A brush with him would be enough to make any Botticelli blush. Can you imagine? Mandy certainly did. As did Beryl and Lucy.

In the office, next day, I spotted three newly purchased sets of charcoal pencils and three large sketchpads, all ready to be used that evening. I didn't need to know why.

Roberto Mancini. He was bound to be a big draw.

2
Be My Valentine

'You know what's coming up this week, don't you?' Beryl posed the question during one of our daily coffee breaks.

Uh-oh… Was Beryl going to be in one of her enigmatic moods here? I wondered. A sudden rash of charades. Something she seemed to do more and more these days. As if there wasn't enough drama going on in the hospital without her adding to it. But then she had recently joined the Westcott's Light Operatic Society. So, I put it down to her need to express herself in more flamboyant fashion than would be expected of a receptionist of mature years, dedicated to ensuring the animals passing through the premises were treated with dignity and respect. Though surely not by bursting out with an aria from *Die Fledermaus* at the sight of a sickly cat – even if the opera did have a whiff of the murine in its title.

I hesitated over my mug. 'Er…' I mentally sped through various ongoing cases of mine. The miniature poodle with otitis. The lipoma removal in Cassie, an overweight Labrador

– stitches were due out tomorrow. Mrs Morrison's incontinent cat.

'Hearts' time,' Beryl continued, her voice oozing enigma. But of what variation?

There was that boxer belonging to Mrs Symonds. Jasmine. She was being stabilised on digoxin for cardiac arrhythmia. Was it a reference to her?

I was conscious of being subjected to one of Beryl's laser-looks. 'So, what will you be giving her?' she said.

I was puzzled. What did she mean? More pills? Higher dose? Additional diuretics?

I considered the situation for a moment. 'Well, I suppose I could up her dose of digoxin if necessary.'

It was Beryl's turn to look puzzled. 'I didn't realise she was on any heart pills. Poor girl.'

'Well, she was getting out of breath just trotting around the Green. Whereas before, she used to have no trouble racing around and have all the dogs chasing after her.'

'Well, I never. Who'd have thought it? I've always considered her to be a quiet sort of girl. Not given to racing all over the place.' Beryl quietly took a sip of her coffee. 'And there was me about to suggest a bouquet of red roses, that being the traditional gift.'

I'd completely lost the thread by now. 'Sorry, Beryl…'

'As a symbol of love. On Valentine's Day.' She took another contemplative sip of her coffee. 'It's good to show that you care for someone. That you appreciate them, warts and all.' She absentmindedly picked at the one on her chin. 'If not roses, I assume you'll get Lucy something?'

Ah. I twigged at last. Nothing to do with Jasmine, the boxer. But Lucy. My fiancée.

I nodded. 'I have been giving it some thought.'

'And… will it be roses?'

Ah, here we go. Beryl in ferret-mode trying to winkle out what I might be getting Lucy for Valentine's Day. That's assuming I'd get her anything. Since we'd hitched up, with the junior nurse moving into Willow Wren with me a year back, I hadn't found it easy to buy anything that suited her. Or more aptly, something that agreed with her.

Take chocolates for example. A nice tray of Belgian truffles or similar. Enough to make your mouth water. 'Sorry, Paul, but I'm actually allergic to dairy produce,' she told me. 'Chocolates make me wheeze.'

Pity that. I quite fancied doing the Black Magic stunt of shinning up the drainpipe into Willow Wren's bedroom with a box of chocolates tucked under my arm. What a wheeze that would have been – in every sense of the word. I'm not that fit and might have found scaling the drainpipe too exhausting.

In the early days of our amour, when lust roamed in my underpants like a mouse in a cheese factory, I did think she might fancy some slinky underwear. Certainly, I fancied her in it. The full works. Red satin and black lace bra and panties.

The look on her face said it all when she undid the wrapping and picked up the bra of the set I'd bought her between finger and thumb like it was a dead rat she'd lifted out of the sewer. She did try to be kind. 'Well, Paul, they're certainly interesting.' But she didn't take the bait. The set lay unworn in her knicker drawer and eventually got thrown out when a mouse gnawed a hole in the pantie's gusset. Hard cheese, Paul.

Undeterred, I did try a baby-doll-style nightie. Nothing too flash. But Willow Wren's central heating system was very erratic and would often leave us freezing during the small hours of the night. Lucy, being a practical sort, would anticipate this happening by appearing at bedtime wearing the nightie but with the addition of thick woollen leggings and quilted bed jacket. Not quite the erotic look I was lusting after. Mind you, I could talk. I'd be in winceyette pyjamas, eyeshade on forehead, ready to be lowered to prevent the dawn light from waking me up too early and wax earplugs already stuffed in to muffle the dawn chorus. Hardly the Casanova of Westcott, the looks of a man preparing himself to spring into action. More those of a resident from the local residential home wandering down the A372 looking for the loo.

Jewellery was another option.

I tried buying her some for her birthday last September. It was a silver lucky charm bracelet. I had this romantic notion that I could buy her a new charm at each successive birthday. Animal-orientated if possible. A little silver dog. A silver cat. A parrot perhaps – like Lisa, the cockatoo we once had before her screeching forced us to find her a new home. Though a silver bunny akin to her pet rabbit, Bugsie, might have been difficult to track down.

'I've kept the receipt,' I said when I gave her the gift. 'Just in case.' Luckily, I did. The bracelet was exchanged for a stout pair of gardening boots. Much more sensible. I should have realised that. Lucy's feet are firmly placed on the ground and she doesn't fight shy of getting her hands dirty. So, a bracelet rattling down over her wrist would have been completely unpractical. My fault.

Another item of jewellery was tried. This time, a thin filigree gold necklace with a pendant. It just happened that Lucy's mum presented her with a family heirloom at the same time. A similar gold necklace with a locket containing a ringlet of her grandmother's hair. So, my gift ended up wrapped around my own neck. Well, at least it went with the gold stud in my ear. Fortunately, I didn't wear fitted shirts unbuttoned to the chest which would have made me a very medallion man. Even so, it precipitated a querying laser-look from Beryl.

On another occasion to celebrate the day Lucy and I first met, I went for a silver photo frame.

'I thought we could build up a collection of family pet photos in such frames,' I said, 'until we start a family of our own.'

'That's a really sweet idea,' said Lucy.

But I sensed hesitancy in her voice.

It was Margaret, her mum, on one of her visits, who spelt it out to me. She went around the living room picking up the various framed photos of Emily, Bertie, Gertie and Queenie that were on the mantelpiece or on the two windowsills. I explained how we intended to expand on them in due course with more silver frames

Margaret grunted. 'Silver tarnishes, you know. Needs constant polishing. Should have chosen frames in lacquered wood.' Ah, good point. I could visualise myself years down the line, a sideboard spilling over with photographs in silver frames, muttering to myself as I repositioned the 20th frame I'd just polished.

There was the obvious choice, of course. Flowers.

Not a bunch snatched up from a petrol station forecourt. Not one of those last-minute efforts. Rather a radiant bouquet of lovingly chosen blooms. A harmonious floral tribute to express my love. I'd tried that last Valentine's Day.

The florist had been very helpful. She suggested red roses complimented by pink Gemini, carnations and lilies set in scented eucalyptus leaves. A dazzling array. Very attractive. Very tasteful. And cost a blooming packet. But I considered it worth every petal.

Not to be sneezed at. But that was just the problem. Lucy did sneeze at them. And continued to do so whenever flowers appeared in the cottage. Along with a pair of red puffy eyes and a red streaming nose. Lucy's hay fever triggered. I gave up giving her flowers last pollen-laden summer. Bless her.

Besides which, she often said, 'I much prefer to see flowers in the ground rather than picked in a vase.' Whoops. Fair point. I should have realised that.

If Lucy had been the sporty type, perhaps there'd have been scope for a present there. Mandy, despite her dumpy appearance, was very much into sports. Always zipping around the tennis court like a sprung chicken, or with her beefy biceps, whacking the living daylights out of a shuttlecock. Quite happy then to be given a new set of balls or coaching lessons as a Christmas present from the practice. Not so Lucy though. Oh, no.

I did try once, paying for a round of golf lessons after Eric, a keen player, suggested we give it a go. 'You never know,' he said. 'You might both really take to it.'

It didn't work out. Lucy never got the swing of things; and the only club I got used to was the one at the end of the course serving drinks.

But there was one thing that Lucy adored. Gardening.

'Well, there you go then,' declared Beryl when I was once discussing the problem with her. 'Plenty of scope there for a decent present she'll like, surely?'

I had to agree there were grounds for thinking that. But not tools. Lucy had got the basics she required. Spade, fork, trowel, etc. All tried, tested and treasured.

In one corner of the back garden of Willow Wren was a magnificent compost heap that she'd created. She was very proud of it, constantly layering it with grass clippings and bags of horse manure she'd cadged from the local riding stables.

That gave me the idea for a Christmas present. I presented her with a large bag of compost accelerator. Oh, dear. That didn't go down too well.

'Not the most romantic of presents, is it?' she said as having given her a tray of tea and biscuits in bed first thing on Christmas Day, I rather spoilt any possibility of a "nudge, nudge, how's your father" *(Father Christmas of course)* by plonking a kilo bag of accelerator on the duvet next to her which made the tea slurp over her cup and splash onto the cover. So, that was a bad choice. As rotten as the compost it was supposed to have been making. I'd have been better off just peeing on the compost heap. Apparently, that works just as well. And would have been a much cheaper option being a free-willie job.

We've done the romantic getaway. The exotic location. The previous autumn, I went on the internet looking for a last-minute deal and found myself with two tickets to the Maldives leaving the following weekend.

'Boom, boom,' I declared. 'We're going on a magical mystery tour.' I waved the e-tickets I'd printed off in the air.

'Don't tell me,' replied Lucy. 'Bognor Regis?'

That was a little in-joke of ours. I'm sure the seaside town has many delightful attractions. We must make an effort and go find them some time.

'No. Not Bognor.'

'Where then?'

Seeing myself fall into the trap of doing a Beryl-style charade, I decided to tell her straightaway. 'The Maldives.'

I waited to see Lucy's face light up with delight. The thought of a sun-kissed tropical beach, fringed with palms. Snorkelling in crystal-clear water, surrounded by a kaleidoscope of brightly coloured fish.

But her face failed to show the slightest glimmer. Her 'Where the hell is that?' reply being the reason for her dimness.

I wasn't too sure myself and scuttled away in search of an atlas.

She still remained doubtful when I told her where it was: a ten-hour flight away down off the coast of southern India.

'We're going for a week, you say?'

I nodded.

She raised her hands. 'What about the animals?'

'I'm sure Eleanor wouldn't mind looking after them.'

'My dears, of course I'd be only too pleased to,' said our neighbour at Willow Wren when asked. 'After all, you both work so hard, you deserve a break.'

'Well, if you're sure,' I said.

'I'm sure,' declared Eleanor with a determined snap of her chin. Though that chin went into up and down overdrive when she read through the list of instructions Lucy typed out for her. Basics for our rescue dogs; Emily, the Welsh springer spaniel; and Bertie, our tan and white crossbreed. No worries. Similar for Queenie the cat. Fine. Bugsie the rabbit. Well, okay. Gertie the goose. Hmm… yes. Lastly, Roderick and his hens. A final consenting thrust of the chin with, I sensed, a click of relief there were no more mouths to feed.

But the trip was good – being able to relax and totally unwind on palm-fringed coral sands. Though Lucy had to stay in the shade of the palms as being fair-haired was liable to get too sunburnt otherwise.

As for the snorkelling, it was truly stunning. To float over banks of coral; at your fingertips, blue and yellow striped angelfish, distinctive white-barred clownfish and the iridescent purples and greens of parrotfish. A watery paradise to die for. Problem was, Lucy would have done just that. Drowned – as she confessed that she couldn't swim. So alas, she remained in the shade of those palm trees all week.

However, it was the return flight which did for both of us. We caught some flu-like bug on the plane, convinced it was due to poor cabin ventilation and vowed never to fly again. Can you blame us? But it did mean another Valentine idea was scuppered.

'Well, you could try somewhere in this country,' Beryl suggested. 'Then you wouldn't have to fly. I'm sure there are plenty of late deals available. Especially at this time of year when hotels are desperate for custom.' She gave me one of her looks. 'What about Bognor?'

We'd already tried that. No, not Bognor. But a last-minute break over in north Somerset. An upmarket country house hotel near Minehead with a five-star rating on the internet.

We discovered the hotel room had central heating you couldn't turn off, sealed windows and winter duvets. Talk about a hot deal. That put us off trying that sort of break again.

Though one good thing did come out of that weekend. The discovery of Culbone church when on a trek along the coastal path. A tiny church tucked into a valley on the edge of Exmoor, near Porlock, hidden in a deep sweep of woods that overlooks the Bristol Channel.

It's the smallest parish church in England, its dark box pews only able to seat 30 people. A jewel. And a jewel that is still in use and which still sparkles. It lies 400 feet above sea level, the track to it snaking two miles along a rugged, wild Somerset coastline where in spring, you walk through soft green mantles of sycamore and larch. The track finally meanders down to a small, stone bridge. Below it, splashes of silver dance as clear cold water from up on the moor, leaps and bounces across the rocks in a cascade that courses down to the shore.

The church is eclipsed by the towering steep woods on either side. Melancholy, dark and brooding on a winter's day. But not that weekend, that Saturday we first caught sight of it. Then, the church was bathed in a warm halo of afternoon sun. Magical in its sylvan setting, we were drawn to it, spellbound.

'So peaceful,' murmured Lucy as we were enticed inside, through the heavy oak door, and stood, slightly awed, in the centre of the tiny nave. Light and airy, the whitewashed walls, simple, unadorned, spelt tranquillity. Under the lofty sweep of the chancel arch lay the altar draped in blue linen. To one side, a pottery vase shone with buttercups.

I stood in the centre of that nave, turned and stretched out my hand to grasp Lucy's, pulling her to me.

'You know what?' I said, gazing into her hazel eyes, 'I think this could be the perfect place for us to get married in.'

She nodded and smiled before I planted a kiss on those sweet lips of hers.

But back to Valentine's Day. Beryl was continuing to ferret right up to and including the day itself. After all, this would be the first Valentine's Day since Lucy and I had got engaged. 'So, something a little special then, Paul?' she said, still digging. If she had been a real ferret, she'd have cleared out the entire rabbit warren by now. 'If a long weekend doesn't appeal, you could always plan a special day-out for this coming weekend. Go visit a National Trust property *(out of season, Beryl – most likely closed)*. Or similar. There are some very interesting places in this part of the world.'

But I'd already tried that. Several day trips in actual fact. All based on a book I'd bought off Amazon, entitled *Far from the Plodding Crowd*. In it were listed attractions throughout the country which were a little off the tourist beat – not so much in terms of location, more in terms of their oddness and, hence, possibly appeal to the likes of me. Someone with a rather warped sense of humour. But of course, that didn't necessarily mean Lucy would find such sites fun. And often she didn't. The list of places sounded intriguing: Rochdale

Pioneers Club, St Peter's Seminary, Pork Pie Pilgrimage, Yelverton Paperweight Centre and Port Logan Fish Pond. We did try the Witchcraft Museum but didn't find it very spellbinding. The Anaesthesia Heritage Centre wasn't a gas. And as for the Clarks Shoe Museum, there wasn't a sole about.

I decided to turn the tables before Beryl's Valentine inquisition became too tortuous and ask *her* if she expected to get a card and present. You should have seen her face. Not the best of visages to scrutinise under normal conditions, grant you. But hers became a picture of acute embarrassment. Her cheeks suffused crimson as a hot flush spread up from her scrawny neck. The wings of her heavily lacquered, coal-black hair flapped like a raven's. The solitary hair on her mole twitched. And the white of her glass eye shone like a scoured lavatory pan. Not a pretty sight. But it was evidence, if evidence was required, that I'd hit the target. 'Well, actually, I am hoping to get something,' Beryl eventually confessed.

And I knew precisely whom it would be from. Ernie Entwhistle, her constant companion since last summer.

He was a client of the practice. I had met him one lunch break during the hot spell of June that year, just after I'd started as assistant clinician. The heat inside Prospect House had been stifling, despite windows and doors flung open everywhere so I was thankful to get out. I headed down past the practice through the tunnel of rhododendrons that had once been part of the house's Victorian gardens and over onto the Green, ever aware of the stream of traffic belting down two sides of it, heading for the centre of town. Despite the exhaust fumes and the roar of cars, the Green was still a popular recreational area; as demonstrated by the office workers who were dotted about the brown-scorched grass, grabbing themselves a bit of tanning time.

A Border collie appeared by the bench I'd sat down on, eyes fixed on the baguette I'd started to eat.

'Oh really, Ben. Do behave yourself,' said a voice. And a gentleman stepped onto the tarmac path to one side of the bench. In his early 60s. On the short side. Cropped, snowy-white hair. Blue, sentimental eyes. And a sweet but weak mouth, nipped in at the corners. His clothes stated "dapper" from the open-necked, crisp white shirt through the light blue blazer to the fawn trousers with razor creases in them. White and blue spotless deck shoes completed the picture of a neat, well-groomed man. Mr Ernie Entwhistle. 'I'm so sorry,' said the gentleman. He stopped a few feet from me and clicked his fingers at the collie, who instantly responded by slinking over to him where, at the double click of his owner's fingers, he sat down. 'Good boy, Ben,' the man murmured, reaching down to pat the collie's head.

'Would you mind?' The man gestured to the empty space I'd created.

'No, of course not.'

The gentleman sat down, the collie coming around to sniff where my baguette bag had been before settling himself between us.

In the ensuing conversation, I learnt that Ben was a patient up at the hospital. Seen by the nice lady vet, Dr Sharpe, for a problem with his spine. Spondylitis. A condition where the vertebrae – the lumbar ones in particular – fuse together. These bridges of bone can then impinge on the nerves supplying the dog's hind legs and lead to pain and difficulty while moving.

At that point I confessed to being a vet at the hospital as well.

'Oh, so you'll know the receptionist then,' he said. 'Beryl Wagstaff. A nice lady. Very sympathetic.'

Hello… hello… Did I detect more than a passing interest in her ability to handle clients?

That handling ability appeared to blossom over the ensuing months. And now I often caught them having very congenial chin wags after Ben's appointments or when Mr Entwhistle came in for repeat prescriptions – the latter seeming to get more and more frequent as time went by.

I once happened to overhear what they were chatting about. Not that I'm an eavesdropper. I just happened to be passing reception on my way down to the ward to check that a dog was coming around from its morning op okay. It was the girlish giggle which made me stop and listen. And the fact that it was Beryl producing it. So unlike her to lose her composure in such fashion.

'I know just how he feels,' Beryl had been saying. I peeped around the door to see her laying a sympathetic hand on Mr Entwhistle's arm as she handed him Ben's tablets. 'With this constant damp weather, we all tend to seize up a bit.' She was attempting to give him a sympathetic look – the effect diminished somewhat by the fishy glaze of her false eye. 'But we keep going.'

Mr Entwhistle beamed. 'Well, we do our best. And you know what they say. If you don't use it, you'll lose it.' He leaned across to Beryl. 'And you, my dear, have certainly not lost it.'

That's when the girlish giggle erupted.

I went on my way feeling slightly sick.

Valentine's Day? Bring it on, man! Especially if the man in question happened to be Ernie Entwhistle.

When the day arrived, there was definitely an air of expectation in the hospital and reached fever pitch mid-morning when a florist's van drew up in the car park. Beryl rushed up to reception, leaving Eric, Crystal and me still having our coffee.

'Now I wonder what all that's about,' said Crystal demurely. 'Is someone expecting flowers?' She smiled sweetly at her husband.

I saw Eric crimson up, his hand twitched as he gulped down another mouthful of coffee. Oh, dear. No prizes for guessing who'd forgotten it was Valentine's Day.

Crystal sighed. Then turned her gaze on me and raised her neatly plucked eyebrows. 'Paul?'

'Lucy's already had hers,' I stuttered, my remark provoking a filthy look from Eric.

Further conversation was abruptly cut off when a scream rang out. The three of us downed our mugs and dashed up to reception as one.

And there was Beryl. Distraught. A large bouquet of bright orange flowers on the counter. She was pointing a shaky finger at them. 'Those flowers… from Ernie,' she gasped.

'Yes. Very exotic,' commented Eric cautiously, still wary of his wife's displeasure.

'Heliconia,' observed Crystal. 'Lobster Claws. An unusual choice. Certainly, a step up from roses. But even a decent bouquet of the latter would have been appreciated. Don't you think, Eric?'

Her husband blushed a shade darker.

Uhm… I think tonight won't be a bed of roses for Eric.

'There was a frog in them,' said Beryl, her breath coming in jerky spasms. She saw our incredulous looks. 'Honest. There was.' She flicked her fingers at the flowers. 'I bent over to take a sniff and it jumped out.'

'Really? A frog?' said Eric, jumping in himself, eager to change the subject from no-show-Valentine flowers.

'Yes. A frog. A black and green job. Looked poisonous. Now it's vanished.' She shook her head and shuddered. 'It could be anywhere.'

'Actually, Beryl…' faltered Eric, pausing to look at me, attempting to stop the smile that was about to break out on his lips as he simultaneously pointed at Beryl's head. 'Don't get alarmed. But that frog's sitting in your hair.'

'What? It's in my hair?' screamed Beryl, her hands shooting up to hover each side of her raven's wings.

Eric stepped two paces forward. 'Hold still. I'll soon get it out for you.'

'Could be poisonous,' snapped Crystal.

Eric stepped two paces back.

'Well, someone, do something,' said Beryl with a shudder. 'Can't just leave it there.' Her good eye swivelled up. Her glass one stared straight ahead.

My suggestion of netting it got a glassy-eyed stare from everyone.

Meanwhile, the tiny frog continued to squat in the parting of Beryl's coiffed cocoon, seemingly unperturbed by the eruptions he was causing around him.

'What about squirting a syringeful of water at him?' Me again. 'It might make him hop off.'

'It would ruin my hair,' moaned Beryl.

'Rather that than having it squirt you with some deadly bodily fluids and finding yourself dead within minutes,' declared Eric bluntly.

Beryl swayed on the spot and clutched the reception counter, her knuckles white.

'That's the last thing Beryl wants to hear,' snapped Crystal.

Beryl swayed even more.

'Well, it *would* be the last thing if it did kill her,' retorted Eric.

Beryl collapsed out of sight.

'Keep your hair on, Beryl,' I said, scooting around the counter to rally her to, in what I hoped was a reassuring voice. 'We'll have it out in no time.'

The latter was an unnecessary comment as the frog had already done that for himself and was now hopping across the floor, heading for the waiting room. Eric and Crystal backed against the reception wall just as Crystal's 12.00 noon appointment – a Mrs Cosgrove with a chihuahua tucked under her arm – entered.

'So sorry, Mrs Cosgrove,' said Crystal, sliding along the wall towards her. 'But you need to be careful.' She pointed at the frog.

'Not to worry. I'm used to having frogs in our pond,' said Mrs Cosgrove cheerily. 'They don't bother me.'

'We think this one could be poisonous,' hissed Eric, back still against the wall.

Mrs Cosgrove fainted. The frog kept hopping.

'What's all this about then?' boomed a voice from the doorway.

Oh, no. Surely not Major Fitzherbert? Why did he always turn up just as an animal had got loose? The fox. The anaconda. He'd been there both times when they'd escaped. Now here he was again.

The major wiggled his white caterpillar eyebrows. His white clipped moustache quivered with anticipation. It was as if he sensed he was in a hunt. A safari echoing those from his days in Africa. He looked around the reception as Beryl and Mrs Cosgrove picked themselves up and Crystal and Eric inched away from the wall. 'Hey ho. Don't tell me you've had another escapee. Let me help catch the blighter.' He strode forward with a determined footfall.

There was a crunch. A splat. The frog stopped hopping.

Ernie Enwhistle was mortified when Beryl phoned him to let him know what had happened when the bouquet had been delivered. He came hurrying over immediately.

'My poor sweet,' he cried, clutching her hand across the reception desk and patting it vigorously. 'It must have been such a shock. My eyes would have popped out of my head if I'd been confronted with such a thing.'

I was in reception when he said it. A rather tactless choice of words I thought, considering Beryl only had the one eye. I showed Ernie the plastic container into which I had scraped the frog's mortal remains.

'Oh, my. That looks frightfully poisonous,' he exclaimed, peering into the container. 'And you say one tiny drop of body fluid from such a beast can kill you on the spot?'

There was a moan. A shuffle. A blur of black. Beryl slowly sank down out of sight again behind reception.

'Oh, lord, now look what I've done,' said Ernie, rushing around to bend over Beryl and haul her up onto her reception stool. 'Are you okay, dear?'

Beryl opened her eyes and clapped her eyelashes at him like the wings of a pheasant at take-off. 'Feeling a bit wobbly. If you could just hold onto me for a bit.'

'Of course, of course, precious.' Ernie slid an arm around Beryl's waist. 'Does that feel better?'

'Uhm… much,' she murmured, resting her head against his chest. 'Just give me a moment.'

'Take as long as you need, sweetie pie. I'm here for you.'

'You're so kind.'

'Think nothing of it, my little honey bunch.'

I crept out with a frog in my throat and the dead one in the plastic container. Yuck.

Once Beryl had fully recovered her composure – which involved inviting Ernie over to her place for a bite of supper later, several cups of sweet tea and a fag by the open backdoor – she contacted the florists. She was told the frog must have been in a flat pack of heliconia flown in from the Ivory Coast. Profuse apologises were given, and the promise of a bouquet of red roses to be sent over as compensation that afternoon.

As for that Valentine's Day present for Lucy. I didn't let on to Beryl that it had already been sorted first thing that morning.

A mug of tea and a couple of biscuits appeared on Lucy's bedside table as they did on most days. Though this time, no bag of compost accelerator accompanied them. She opened one eye. No card. No present alongside. She made no comment.

When nature called, she sprang out as she normally did and dragged the bedroom curtains back. It was a dank, dreary February morning, a moist monochrome barely lifting the darkness of the night. Cats' paws of grey pitter-pattered over the back garden, drenching everything in dew. Watching from the bed, I saw her wipe away a circle of condensation and peer out, commenting, 'Typical February day.'

I observed her as she rubbed at the glass a little more earnestly. Peered out a little more intently.

'Paul, what's that down the bottom of the garden?'

I swung out of bed and padded over to her. 'What's what, Luce?' I said, feigning innocence.

Lucy wiped away an even larger area of condensation. 'Down there. Against the wall.'

I folded my arms around her waist from behind and, chin on her shoulder, peered out. 'You mean that tree with those two red hearts on it?'

'Yes, of course. What have you been up to?'

She was referring to a tree at the bottom of the vegetable patch against the back wall. A newly planted espalier complete with huge red hearts tied to its branches.

My present to Lucy. Her Valentine Day's gift. Surely it was going to be just right for her?

Of course, it had required a bit of forward planning and some help from Eleanor. 'What a splendid idea!' she'd enthused when I told her about it. 'I think it's the perfect gift. Lucy will love it.'

I'd bought the tree earlier in the week and had secreted it in Eleanor's garage. Then last night, while Lucy was at her writing class, the two of us had joined forces to dig the hole against Willow Wren's back garden wall in a spot I'd carefully dug over the previous weekend on the pretence of preparing it to plant some rows of runner beans in early spring.

So here we had it. With my arms still enfolded around Lucy's waist, I whispered that it was an apple tree.

'Your favourite. A Gala,' I said. 'A sweet variety with nice firm flesh. Just like you.' I gave her an affectionate squeeze.

She twisted around to face me, her eyes sparkling. 'Why, Paul, that's so very thoughtful of you. A wonderful present.' Then reached up to plant a kiss firmly on my lips.

I eventually pulled away, looked down at her and murmured, 'Forget the tree a moment, you're truly the apple of my eye.'

3
Battles with Bovines

It was a Monday morning in mid-March. A fairly typical morning's op list. Three cat spays. Four castrates. One bitch spay. A couple of dentals to get my teeth into. Nothing too testing. Nothing too much to worry about. That all changed when the call came through.

Beryl waved the phone at me, her other hand, red talon outstretched, beckoning me over. 'It's one of the Stockwells,' she hissed. 'Wants to speak to a veterinary.'

Oh, dear. I sensed we could have a problem brewing here. The Stockwell twins usually spelt trouble. I took the receiver and took a deep breath before saying, 'Hello. Paul Mitchell here.'

'Veterinary?' queried the voice down a crackly line.

'Er, yes.'

'The one with the big ears and pointed nose?'

I wasn't sure how to answer that but was saved the trouble as the voice went on: 'It's our Petunia's...' The line went dead.

'Hello?' Nothing. I handed the receiver back to Beryl who raised an eyebrow. I shrugged. 'Something about petunias.'

'Petunias?'

Eric breezed into reception at that moment. 'Petunias? Good thinking. We should be getting some for the hanging baskets soon. Brighten the car park up a bit.'

'I don't think it's the right time to be discussing bedding plants, do you?' The words were clipped, clearly enounced in a mid-shires' accent; and uttered by Crystal Sharpe, the other senior partner of the practice, as she swept into reception from the car park and swirled to a halt next to her husband. 'We should be sorting out the morning's visits and ops, shouldn't we?' There was a sweet smile to accompany this, her Cupid's lips parting to show an even row of glossy, white teeth. But the inference was obvious. Get on with it. 'No problems, I hope.'

'We're waiting for a call back from the Stockwells,' explained Beryl as the phone rang again. 'I suspect they've a problem with one of their Jerseys called Petunia.' She picked up the receiver, listened and placed a hand over the receiver to inform us a veterinary was required to visit ASAP. Petunia's uterus had prolapsed.

Crystal gave Eric and me the full-on, penetrating stare of her steel-blue eyes. 'Well, which one of you is going?'

Well, I was the one with the big ears and pointed nose but didn't utter a word for fear of implication.

Crystal switched her attention to the visits' book. She ran a well-manicured, unvarnished nail along the top of the page and within seconds had sorted out the morning's workload, without a murmur of protest from the two of us. Not that we would have dared to do so. She would see the few clients booked in for me. Eric would do my ops. I would visit the Stockwells and see to the prolapse. That seemed to be the best course of action. I'd been to the Stockwells before when they had that cow stuck in the quarry and they'd been impressed by how helpful I'd been then. So, I was to hurry along and see what I could do to help them this time.

'I take it you've no problem with that, Paul?' Another sweet smile.

I shook my head and obediently trotted out to my car, checking I had the necessary calving gown and instruments ready to tackle Petunia's prolapse.

As I drove out of the car park, I realised I needed to get in the right frame of mind to tackle not just Petunia but the Stockwells as well.

Madge and Rosie Stockwell were twin sisters, originating from Yorkshire, but had moved down to Sussex over thirty years ago to take on Hawkshill Farm, secreted away in the side of the Downs between Ashton and Chawcombe; and here, they'd remained ever since, in what could only be described as a time capsule. Little had been done to keep pace with modern advances in farming; and they had ticked along with a motley collection of sheep, the flock now reduced in size; likewise, the herd of Jerseys which now only numbered 12. I had been called out last summer to attend to Myrtle, one of their Jerseys, who had gone down with Milk Fever. Boy, that had been an experience; their slow, unperturbed way of going about things had driven me nuts especially as we'd had an emergency on our hands, but like they'd said on my arrival, 'Doesn't pay to be in a hurry. Nowt gained if vet breaks a leg.' while they watched me rush across their yard and almost do precisely that when I slipped in a cowpat.

Once on the dual carriageway, I headed north over the Downs and dropped down into Ashton where the practice house, Willow Wren, was situated. Taking the road west towards Chawcombe, it was a mile or so before the narrow steep-banked lane on the left wound back up the northern slopes of the Downs and took me to Hawkshill Farm. Though it had been many months since my last visit, I still remembered the Stockwells' instructions at the gate. 'Second one on the right and make sure to close it after you.'

The gate was still there in much the same condition as before. Bleached oak, five bars reduced to four and that fourth one just as loose, though an attempt had been made to prevent it from dropping out of its bracket by some strands of orange bailer twine tied around it and secured to the upright. It was all rather rickety though, and as I prised open the latch, the gate dropped on its hinges. 'When will they ever learn?' I muttered to myself as I lifted it up and dragged it across the chalky track. Someday, chances were that one or more of their livestock would escape. Little did I realise then that it would be someday soon.

The farm, tucked down in a hollow, was picturesque. Very Thomas Hardy. Undulating pitched clay-tiled roof, flint walls set in courses of red brick, tiny lattice windows painted white, oak-panelled front door, weathered grey; and all of this complimented the landscape beyond – a patchwork of fields, hedgerows and the spire of Chawcombe church in the distance. But not today. This mid-March day. Today, the background was a blur of grey as banks of low cloud rolled down and obscured the Downs in droplets of icy mist. The farm's rustic charm was such that I'd half expected a Hardy-esque figure to emerge to greet me – Tess, Bathsheba, or Susan Henchard perhaps – certainly not the gnome-like creatures that shuffled into view when I drove into the yard – Madge and Rosie Stockwell. Identical twins.

They emerged through the mist like phantom goblins from *Lord of the Rings* rather than Julie Christie facsimiles from *Far from the Madding Crowd.* They were dressed identically in brown tweed trousers, stuffed into black wellies and I guessed identical green, army-style pullovers as before, though this time it had to be a guess as their upper halves were obscured by brown rubber capes, buttoned tightly at the neck, stretching down to calf-level, with side vents for their arms which were currently tucked inside. The overall impression was of two overinflated buoys, an impression given more credence by the fact they were standing in a yard immersed under several centimetres of slurry.

As I got out of the car, the two sisters slowly waded towards me.

Never knowing who was Madge and who was Rosie, each having a tomato-soup complexion, hooked nose, mousy and pudding-basin-styled hair, I addressed them as one. 'Morning, ladies.'

'You've come to see Petunia,' said one.

'So I believe.'

'You believe right,' said the other.

'Right. Let's get going,' I said, pointedly looking at my watch. 'In the barn, is she?' I thought it most likely, being warm and dry, out of the rain. The ideal place to have calved down prior to the prolapse.

The twins simultaneously shook their heads, drips of water spraying from the ends of their noses.

'Veterinary thinks she's in the barn, Madge,' said one twin who must have been Rosie.

'She's not though, Rosie.'

'*I* know that, but veterinary doesn't.'

'I know.'

I hastily intervened. 'So where is she then?'

'Fox Meadow,' they chorused together.

My heart sank liked a stone disappearing into that sea of slurry. *Oh Lord. Not Fox Meadow again.*

'Like Deidre was,' said a twin. Rosie?

'When she was calving down in that ditch,' said the other. Madge?

'That's where you'll find Petunia. But not in a ditch,' said Rosie. *(I thought)*

'In the field shelter,' said Madge. *(I guessed)*

'But still in Fox Meadow.' *(I couldn't be bothered)*

The tic in my temple was now starting to throb. A sure sign of my increasing agitation. 'Look, ladies,' I said quickly and a little too curtly, 'we haven't got all day. Your Petunia needs looking at as soon as possible. Let's get over to Fox Meadow without delay. Okay?'

'Rush. Rush. Always in a rush,' murmured the Stockwells in unison. But swivelled around like a couple of ducks and began bobbing across the yard. That's when I noticed each had a backpack over their shoulders. I was to find out soon enough what they had in them.

Despite the difficulties of having to stand on one leg and wobble about in the slurry, I managed to don my boots, overalls and waterproof cape to catch them up just as they were opening the gate into Fox Meadow.

At which point the steady drizzle became a steady torrent.

As we splashed across the meadow, water seeped up my sleeves, crept down my collar, worked into each boot.

Fox Meadow was a small field bounded by overgrown hawthorn hedges – the irregular tops an undulating line of brown spikes in need of cutting back; the grass was poached around the perimeter with patches of mud and puddles leading to a large corrugated-roofed field shelter. Inside, in one corner, huddled ten or so Jerseys, some of which were desultorily snatching mouthfuls of hay from a pile.

In another corner lay a cow. My patient, Petunia, to judge from the bloody mass that was spread out from under her tail. Her prolapsed womb. And the cause of that prolapse lay to one side. Her stillborn calf.

Okay. Time now to step forward. Show some confidence. Show my ability to carry out what was potentially a very difficult procedure. *Er… Right… now what had I written in my finals' exam on the subject?* Sedate cow. Administer epidural. Roll cow over and pull her legs out into frog-like stance. Wash prolapse. Lever onto clean sheet of plastic. Ease back through vagina. With palms. No fingers. Less risk then of perforating uterine wall. All gently done. Very, very gently.

'You're going to wham it back in then?' queried a twin as each of them swung their backpacks off their shoulders.

'In a manner of speaking… yes,' I murmured.

'Rosie will wash it down first for you, won't you, Rosie?'

'That's what this is for.' Rosie held up a large handpump sprayer she'd taken out of her backpack and, after a few vigorous pumps, began to wash the bits of straw, mud and strands of placenta that had been stuck to the inverted wall of the womb.

As she did so, I noticed the engorged mass of red tissue seemed to start shrinking in size. My imagination?

'Sugar solution's doing that,' said Rosie as if reading my mind.

Of course. Yes. Osmosis. Sugar pulling fluids out of the engorged womb. Helping to reduce its size. Helping in the task of getting it back in. I should have thought of that. Well done, Rosie.

Madge, meanwhile, had taken a roll of plastic out of her backpack and had begun easing it under the shrinking womb. Top marks to her too.

Now my turn. I had a horrible feeling I might score rather badly.

What had I said in that exam? Sedate? Clinically the correct procedure. But Petunia looked pretty much out of it already. Surely sedation might tip her over the edge? I decided against it. Next, epidural. Should I? It would stop her straining.

'You're going to jab her in the spine?' Rosie reading my mind again.

Petunia's tail was very floppy even before considering an epidural which would have made it even floppier – an indication the injection had worked and that the cow wouldn't strain against me when I started to push the uterus back in. I had carried over my "bag of tricks" as I called it – needles, syringes, drugs. So, I did clip and scrub the base of the tail just in case I resorted to an epidural. But I'd try without.

'You're not giving one then,' remarked Rosie. *Grrr...*

Okay. Time to set to work.

I knelt down in front of the engorged womb – thankfully now less swollen after Rosie's thoughtful preparation – and splayed my knees, my calving gown looped between them. I then leaned forward and began to push from the sides nearest Petunia. No fingers. Palms. Just palms. The womb felt a dead weight in my lap. No movement. I continued to push. Palms. Just palms. Still nothing. Five minutes became ten minutes. Became 20 minutes. Became… no it didn't become more minutes as I suddenly felt the uterus shift. Yes, it was shifting. Moving. Contracting. Disappearing through Petunia's vagina. My right arm was sucked in with it up to the shoulder. I felt the womb flop over the edge of Petunia's pelvis, falling back into place, everting to normal. I extracted my arm with a huge sigh of relief. Job done.

'Will you be needing this?' Rosie was holding up a wine bottle.

'Only if it's ready to be opened,' I joked. My turn at reading her mind. She was wondering if I'd use it to slip inside Petunia to make absolutely sure the tips of each horn of her uterus were in their rightful positions. But Petunia being a small cow, it wasn't necessary to do that. As if to prove the point, she staggered to her feet with a shudder of her hindquarters, lifted her tail and allowed the accumulation of a very full bladder to be jettisoned over me before I had a chance to get out of the way.

A great relief to her.

As my actions had been to me.

Another start to the week. Monday, April 1st to be precise. April Fool's Day. Not that I would have dared to play a joke on Beryl. It wouldn't have gone down too well. She didn't share my sense of humour. No, not one bit. The episode with the Christmas card was a good reminder of that. An email card I sent her. A Father Christmas on a roof, sack slung over his back, about to descend a chimney pot. You centred the cursor on the sack and clicked, no doubt expecting Santa to go Ho… Ho… Ho… Instead, he squirted a jet of pee down the pot. Beryl was far from amused. 'I do wish you'd grow up, Paul,' was her only comment.

So, a joke played on her on April Fool's Day?

Oh, no… no… no…

Though Eric ran dangerously close to getting one of her laser-eyed looks when he breezed into reception just as she was telling me she'd booked me to see a Cowslip.

'What? What?' he cried, slapping his palms together gleefully. 'A bovine with dodgy hooves?'

I gave him a warning shake of my head, putting a finger to my lips in an attempt to hush him up.

He failed to see the warning. Instead, took it to mean Beryl was talking about a cow's lip.

The laser beam intensified. Flashed dangerously.

'One of the Stockwell's Jerseys,' growled Beryl. 'Requiring a visit.'

'Ah, yes, well. Paul's your man then.' He turned to me. 'Those two have a soft spot for you after what you did for their Pansy.'

'Petunia, actually.'

'Pansy. Petunia. Whatever.'

'What?' The exclamation came from Crystal who had just swept in, all coppery curls as usual. 'Not on about bedding plants yet again?'

'No dear, no.' Eric raised his hands in surrender. 'Honest. Paul will explain.' With that, he dashed out of reception in a whorl of white coat tails.

It was Beryl who did the explanations. The Stockwells were requesting a vet to see one of their Jerseys with a blocked teat. I had a spare hour that afternoon. So she'd booked me the visit.

And for once, I didn't mind one bit.

It was a glorious spring day. And here was a chance to escape from the hospital for an hour or so and enjoy the delights of the Downs as I drove over to Hawkshill Farm. I actually found myself singing 'Oh what a beautiful morning' though strictly speaking, it was afternoon – being around 1.45 pm. And the corn wasn't as high as an elephant's eye, though early shoots were pushing through to cover fields in hazy quilts of green.

As soon as I hit the lane that wound back up to the Downs and Hawkshill, I could feel my spirits lift even further. None more so than on that April afternoon. Sun filtered between the trunks of the beech and birches that arched overhead – peppering the lane with diamonds of light. Either side, the steep banks carpeted with yellow celandine and clumps of primroses, bewitching.

But the spell suddenly got broken when ahead, steaming down the lane towards me as fast as his hooves could carry him, appeared a bull. A Jersey bull. A bull that I knew. The Stockwells' Boris. With no way of him passing me, he ground to a halt just feet away, with a snort of annoyance, a shake of his head, misty clouds streaming from each nostril as the ring between them quivered and dripped with moisture.

I had no doubt as to how he had made his escape. Via that rickety five-bar gate on the chalk track to the farm. And I had no doubt as to his intentions. There may have been an element of the grass-is-always-greener but only if that grass had grazing on it some frisky young heifers eager for a gambol. For Boris was perpetually sex-driven. Always in gear. Always ready for a full-throttled thrust.

And who could blame him? That was his function in life. And he had the good looks to go with it. Plum-coloured eyes fringed with impossibly long, lashes. A solid, beefy-looking dewlap – his equivalent of a brawny lad's biceps. And the tackle that hung between his hind legs was spectacular. One look could have churned a maiden's milk in the wink of one of those alluring eyes of his. There was only one problem. He was rather short in the leg.

'Stumpy,' declared Rosie Stockwell in one of the twins' rare sessions of social intercourse with me. 'Can cause him problems with some of the cows. You know… doing what he wants to do.'

'Getting his end up 'em,' said Madge with remarkable candour, though her look suggested butter – Jersey or otherwise – wouldn't have melted in her mouth.

'Especially with the likes of Cowslip,' Rosie went on, ignoring her sister. 'She's a lanky lass. Very long legged.'

'Very hard to get his end up her.' This was Madge.

'But he's worked out a way to sire her.'

'Get it up her.' Madge again. *(What was it with this woman?)*

'He does it on a hillside. Him, up the slope above her; she, down the slope below him.'

'So, she ends up getting his end up her end.' *(You know who.)*

All a bit confusing, I thought, but I got the general thrust of it – particularly that of Boris's – in the end. *Oh Lord, this was becoming catching. Was there no end to these end games?*

Apparently, not as far as Boris was concerned; hence, his appearance on the lane in front of me, blocking it. An impasse in every sense of the word.

'Right, matey,' I declared, clambering cautiously out of the car to sidle around to the front, almost within touching distance of Boris's ring. I wasn't quite sure if I was doing quite the right thing here. Trusting him in this way. 'We can't be having you going down onto the main road, can we?'

Boris flickered his lashes at me, raised his head and gave a loud bellow. Clearly, his amorous intentions were making him take leave of his senses.

'All that traffic. Dangerous.' I tentatively reached out and grasped the bullring. There was another snort. A pull of the head sideways. A shift of the shoulders. 'You could end up as beef burgers.'

All movement froze. It was as if Boris suddenly realised it wasn't the "end up" he'd set out to seek. Though more likely the effect my tight grip on his bullring was having. 'Okay, let's get you turned around,' I muttered. 'Show you the way to go home, eh?' And much to my surprise, he allowed me to do just that. It was a tight turn between those banks but within minutes – without a mutter of protest from him or me – I had him facing back up the lane. I let go of the ring and hopped back in the car. I gave a toot; he gave a trot. And off we went. I followed the pendulous testicles swaying ahead of me as he trotted faster and faster until we were up to the gate and he went through the gap he'd made earlier. I stopped the car, leapt out to see Boris standing at the top of the field above the farm, surveying his domain, staring down the slope at a cluster of heifers. No doubt working out which angle would serve them best.

I paused a moment to contemplate the scene. The Weald stretched out to the horizon – an undulating patchwork of green and brown fields criss-crossed with hedgerows, peppered white with hawthorn blossom. Tufts of cotton-cloud scudded like winged white balls over the arc of an azure sky in a breeze which cool-kissed my cheeks. And to my ears, the lilting quaver-call of a skylark soaring high up in that blue heaven. Suddenly, the low, lust-filled bellow of Boris brought me rapidly back down to earth and to the job in hand.

Having manoeuvred myself through the gate, making sure I made it secure as possible afterwards, I drove past the thrust-driven Boris and down into the yard. Today, in sharp contrast to my last visit, the yard was dry, devoid of slurry, covered in wisps of hay that danced in the breeze, making it quite picturesque. I could almost imagine two comely milkmaids in mop caps swishing across, yokes straddling their shoulders, attached to pails of rich creamy milk.

But that wasn't going to happen. No way.

Instead, I had the two diminutive twins appear out of the main barn. But there was a certain lightness of foot as they shuffled over. Definitely more of a spring in their steps than usual. Though appearance-wise, they hadn't changed. Green overalls stuffed in black wellies. Tomato-soup complexions, hooked noses, pudding-basin hair fringing their foreheads – today though not squashed under green woollen beanies.

'You've arrived then,' said one twin, shuffling to a halt.

'Bit late,' said the other, stopping next to her.

I explained why.

'Ah, Boris,' declared one of them. *(Rosie, I think.)*

'Looking to get his end up.' *(That had to be Madge.)*

'You've come to see Cowslip,' they said in unison.

I nodded.

'She's just calved down,' said the one that wasn't Madge.

'Boris having had his end up her,' said the one that was. *(No surprise.)*

I didn't need to know the ways of nature. Unnecessary information. But I did need to know where she was. 'Fox Meadow?' I queried, hoping against hope she wasn't. Even though it was a dry day, I really didn't fancy trailing all the way over there.

'No, not Fox Meadow,' I was told.

'The barn?' The building I was referring to was a classic oak tithe barn with exposed beams, infilled with knapped grey flint, linked to the farmhouse by a row of three looseboxes, their walls of similar flint construction.

A shake of two heads.

'Where then?'

Two arms – one of each twin – were raised. A forefinger of each pointed at the first loosebox, its upper half-door open. 'You'll find her in there,' they said.

I yanked on my wellingtons, threw on a brown coat, snatched my black bag from the boot of the car and strode meaningfully over to peer inside. Cowslip was standing quietly, feeding from a hayrack, her calf lying contentedly a few feet from her in a bed of straw. I opened the door and stepped in, pulling it closed behind me. The cow stopped munching and turned to look at me with a slight shake of her head. That should have been a warning. Here we had a heifer who was "calf proud". Potentially, a danger being light on her feet. Quick to turn. I failed to take heed. Meanwhile, the Stockwells stayed outside, two beaky noses peering over the top of the half-door.

I eased myself forward, gently stepping towards her.

'There, there, my girl,' I said softly. 'No need to be frightened.' I stretched out an arm to scratch her back. She shuffled sideways and turned away from me. Then raising a dainty hoof, with deadly accuracy, she kicked me neatly in the nuts.

I staggered back, doubled up, tears streaming down my face, both hands clutching my groin.

'Seems she got him fair and square,' one twin commented.

'A ballseye,' said the other. Both sniggered. 'Shush. Veterinary might hear.'

Veterinary already had.

Twenty minutes later, I'd recovered sufficiently to get to work in a more managed fashion. Cowslip was moved into another box so that being away from her calf, her maternal instinct would be less aggressive. Least that was the idea. And this time, both the Stockwells accompanied me into the loosebox. One had a pair of bulldogs which she fitted across Cowslip's nostrils, the heifer standing there meek and mild as she did so. Once the bulldogs were clamped in place and tied up to the top rail of the adjacent hay rack with several loops of bailer twine, Cowslip became even more settled and allowed the second twin to walk around to her rear end, grasp her tail and pull it up and over her back without so much as a flicker of her long eyelashes.

'There, veterinary. All yours now,' said front-end twin, hand on the bulldogs to steady Cowslip's head.

Indeed, my turn.

'Well, young lady, let's see what the problem is.' I ran my hand along her back and down her left flank. The muscles in her thigh twitched. 'Bit ticklish, are we?' My hand slid down and around onto her udder. I gently tried each teat in turn. Three produced milk. The fourth – her left fore – didn't.

'That's the blocked one,' said the twin holding the tail, peering over my shoulder. 'He's found it!' she called up to her sister holding the bulldogs.

'The one not producing milk?' queried the front-end twin.

'That's the one,' answered the back-end one.

While this rather inane exchange was going on between front and back ends, I'd disinfected the tip of the problem teat, removed a thin metal cannula from the sterile pack I'd brought in with me and was ready to insert it up the teat's streak canal.

'Now, girls, are we ready?'

A 'We're ready' came from both ends.

I eased the canula in. It slid up the canal with no opposition and with no resentment from Cowslip. Only at the top of the teat where it joined the udder did the canula stop. And I knew why. Here, there was a membrane which I needed to pop. Warning the girls, I gave the canula a short, sharp jab upwards. It pierced the membrane. A thin stream of thick, yellow fluid oozed out. Colostrum. An essential requirement for new-borns as it is packed with antibodies – necessary for early protection against disease.

'Finished then?' said back-end twin, still peering over my shoulder, tail still held in her hand though she'd loosened her grip somewhat.

'No, no, I haven't,' I said, scrabbling to my feet. 'I need to make the hole bigger. If I just leave it as it is, it will just close over and we'd be back to square one.'

'Hold your horses, Madge!' shouted back-end twin to her sister. 'Veterinary's got to make it bigger.'

'What?'

'The hole in Cowslip's teat. It's not big enough.'

'How big is it got to be then?'

'A whole lot bigger, I guess.'

I waved the second instrument I'd extracted from the pack in the air. 'Using this,' I explained. It looked a bit like a blunt-ended corkscrew.

'That will make it bigger.' That was front-end.

'Very big,' back-end agreed.

But that was my intention. I needed to tear a much larger hole through the membrane to guarantee a reasonable flow of milk and not have the membrane sealing up again.

'This could be a bit painful for Cowslip,' I warned the twins.

'We're ready,' they chorused again, one gripping the bulldogs tightly, the other the tail.

I removed the canula and cautiously inserted the spiral. It slid up the lumen of the canal easily until meeting the resistance of the membrane; at which point I had to stab the spiral through, rotating it as I did so. I then yanked it down in a short, sharp wrench while stepping away smartly. An action which ripped the membrane loose. As I jumped back, Cowslip jumped up, both hind feet leaving the ground. But tail-holding twin held on making it difficult for Cowslip to attempt any testicle-seeking kicks. However, in the flurry of activity, I'd lost my grip on the spiral and it was now dangling from the cow's teat.

'You'll need to get that out,' said back-end twin unnecessarily.

A few twists on the spiral and I'd done just that.

The first few pulls on the affected teat were going to be heavily stained with blood, but once that had cleared, all would be fine udder-wise.

I was in good spirits as I said my 'Goodbyes' to the Stockwells. I drove up the chalky track, passing Boris who was now down amongst his heifers. Seeing him reminded me that despite the soreness I still felt in my groin, I'd be home later for supper with Lucy. And like Boris, that was sure to have a happy ending.

4
Seeing Double

They say that owners often look like their dogs. I'm not sure it applies to me. I've always been fond of Jack Russells. Short legs. Wiry bodies. Sharp snouts, ready to rat. Well, come to think of it, perhaps there is a certain likeness.

You often see newspaper features showing photos of well-known celebrities alongside pictures of their pooches; or there's a two-page spread where on one side there's a gallery of people's faces, and on the other a similar gallery of dogs' faces. You're then asked to match them up.

'You get the same sort of thing at dog shows,' said Beryl, one tea-break time. 'Isn't that so, Eric?'

'What? What?' Eric had been engrossed in skimming through the weekly edition of the Westcott Gazette. This local paper did have its uses. Allowed you to know what was going on in our corner of Sussex. This week, Mabel Grimshaw of Tamsworth Close had celebrated her 90th birthday by free-falling from a helicopter, landing safely of course, otherwise her name would have been on the obituaries' page instead.

And members of the Chawcombe and Ashton Ladies' Afternoon Tea Group had been entertained by their guest speaker, Cecil Groper, talking about his experiences of meeting a headhunting tribe in Papua New Guinea. Having been spellbound by Cecil's long, lingering close-up pictures of sinewy young men dancing semi-naked around a blazing fire, the ladies adjourned, flushed, for steaming cups of Earl Grey and moist fingers of Victoria sponge.

Eric looked up, startled, when Beryl addressed him.

'Look-a-likes.'

'Looking like what?' Eric clearly hadn't been listening.

'Their dogs.'

'Who?'

Beryl tutted. 'Their owners. Remember that encounter you had with Mrs Nugent?'

'Mrs Nugent? Mrs Nugent?'

'The wife of the High Sheriff of West Sussex. Don't say you've forgotten.'

'Er… no…' replied Eric, apparently wishing he had from the way he began wriggling uncomfortably in his seat.

'Good story here,' said Beryl, leaning across to me and giving me a one-eyed wink. 'Well, go on then, Eric.'

Eric's head was buried back in the Western Gazette. Clearly with no intention to "go on". But with Beryl's laser-look boring a hole through his paper, he had no choice but to surrender, push the paper down and tell me.

It seems he was cajoled into judging a dog show – way back in the early days of the practice. 'Don't do it now. Those clients who don't win anything can get extremely miffed. Not worth the hassle.' So there he was with various categories to judge. Dog with the longest tail. Dog with the waggiest tail. And inevitably, as in all village dog shows, a "Dog Most Like its Owner" class. *Mmm… I could see where this was heading.*

'Actually,' said Eric, 'it wasn't as popular a class as it should have been. So, in an attempt to whip up a few extra entries, I went scouting around the village green. Bad mistake as it turns out.'

He'd bumped into a lady carrying a terrier under her right arm.

'I think it was a Bruges griffon,' Eric said.

'Brussels... actually,' I interjected.

'What? Oh well, whatever. It was a scruffy little thing. Rusty-brown coloured with dark tear stains down each cheek. Undershot jaw. Dribbling. You get the picture?'

I did. It wasn't a very appealing one. 'Don't tell me it looked like his owner.'

Eric explained there had been a certain resemblance. The woman had been wearing some sort of furry-collared coat that matched the dog's. Her eyes had been a bit gummy. And she did have a ragged row of bottom teeth that stuck out.

'And you told her she looked like her dog?' I said incredulously.

Beryl who had been intently listening, head cocked to one side, intervened. 'That's precisely what he did.'

Eric shook his head. 'Not in so many words, Beryl. I merely enquired whether she was entering the class.'

'Boils down to the same thing. And if I remember correctly, you told her she'd win it hands down.'

'Yes, well, perhaps I did put my foot in it somewhat.'

Seemed he did for sure, as the lady turned sharply and stomped off. He later found out she was Dowager Felicity Nugent, the wife of the High Sheriff of West Sussex. She complained to Westcott's mayor, a close friend of hers, that one of the judges at the show had said she looked like her dog. Could you believe the cheek of the man?

Certainly, I could think of several clients who were a good match for their dogs; or vice versa depending which way you wanted to look at them. But bearing in mind what happened to Eric, I didn't ever mention the fact to them. Not face to face. Far too risky. Even if both owner and dog were frisky little bitches.

There was one client in particular that sprang to mind.

Major Marshall and his bulldog, Benjamin.

The major was a classic stereotype. Short, barrel-chested. His arms and legs stuck out like those on a Mr Man character.

A grumpy Mr Man at that. He had a perpetually wrinkled brow. Sagging jowls. Grizzled, hairy upper lip. A description that also befitted his bulldog. Although in addition, Benjamin's jowls were always liberally laced with strings of spittle. Otherwise, the deeply creased forehead, the drooping jowls, and the pouches under the eyes were dead ringers for the major. Though the large pink tongue that lolled out, dripping with saliva when excited, wasn't one of the major's attributes. At least not in my presence. At home with his wife? Well, that was another matter.

Major Marshall would announce his arrival in the waiting room with a loud command to his bulldog. 'Sit BEN-JA-MIN.'

Cats cowered in the back of their baskets. Dogs sank down on their haunches immediately, not a sound from them. Whereas Benjamin stood, elbows out, ignored his master's order and barked; and if given half a chance would cock his leg against the nearest convenient chair leg and liberally spray it, ignoring the 'Stop that AT ONCE!' thundered at him by the major until his vigorous jet of urine had subsided to a couple of drops.

One particular afternoon was no exception.

When it was their turn to be seen, Major Marshall roared 'Heel BEN-JA-MIN,' before being forced to drag the bulldog through to the consulting room. Both were foaming at each end of the lead, both sending spittle flying in all directions. 'Always a good thing to let a dog know whose boss,' declared Major Marshall as Benjamin pulled him across the room. 'Some people have no idea of discipline. Can't control their dogs.'

Benjamin had, by now, wrapped his lead three times around the nearest legs which included two of the consulting table's four and one of mine. A vigorous jet of urine was directed up each. 'Control's the name of the game.'

I smiled wanly. Control of Benjamin's bladder would certainly have been helpful. My warm soggy trouser leg was a proof of that.

Major Marshall fired a 'Sit BEN-JA-MIN'. The dog promptly shot over to sniff at the waste bin while the consulting table, still entangled in his lead, screeched across the tiled floor behind him.

Lucy rushed in, fearful a cat was being emasculated.

Benjamin bounded over, a 'Down BEN-JA-MIN' was being ignored as he leapt up at her. A 'Stay BEN-JA-MIN' also fell on deaf ears when he attempted to follow Lucy as she backed out of the room.

'Always a one for the ladies,' barked the Major.

And gents, I thought, shaking my wet leg.

'So, let's get cracking, laddie. Get Benjamin's vaccination done and dusted before he makes a nuisance of himself.'

'Now do as you're told, BEN-JA-MIN. Behave.' The dog crashed into the consulting room chair. It went flying across the room to hit the instrument trolley; scissors and swabs fell off to scatter across the floor.

I salvaged a syringe to make up the booster and drew up the shot from a vial of vaccine.

The major squared his shoulders. His ponderous jowls quivered. 'Now, BEN-JA-MIN, this won't hurt. So be a good boy and stand still. That's an order.'

Fat chance of it being obeyed, I thought, as I advanced on the dog. The major looked at me. 'Had many jabs during my time in the forces. Took them like a man. Backside, arm, you name it.' The major shuffled his feet. Stood to attention. Stock-still. Benjamin's lead wrapped tightly around his wrist. 'We'll not move. You'll see.'

I patted Benjamin's neck and eased up a pinch of skin as I knelt beside him. 'Steady, boy, steady,' I murmured, slipping in the needle and injecting the vaccine. There was not a sound. No flinch. Not a muscle moved. 'There. All done,' I said, getting to my feet, while the major, having fainted, crashed down on his.

It was decidedly out of order of him.

It wasn't always just a case of owners looking like their dogs. Other pets came into the frame. Two of the practice's clients certainly looked like their tortoises and moved in a similar slow manner too. Harry and Monica Conville.

They owned two Hermann tortoises, Ike and Tina – their names harking back to the Motown sounds of the 60s when these two reptiles were born. Bred in the UK. Thirty years old. Getting on but not that old in tortoise terms. Currently the honour of being the oldest living land creature in the world goes to Jonathan, a giant tortoise who is 187 years old and lives on the island of St Helena. Just think, he's lived under eight monarchs – George IV to Elizabeth II and 52 prime ministers.

'We'll have turned in our shell long before these two do,' said Harry, being remarkably sanguine about the fact they'd be unlikely to outlive their pets.

Ike and Tina were a smart pair. Each carapace yellow-green with black borders to the scutes on the shell. When Harry and Monica emerged from the waiting room, it was impossible to escape the impression that they looked like a pair of tortoises themselves. This was mainly due to the matching cagoules they were wearing that in turn were uncannily similar to the carapaces of their tortoises. Colour-wise in the brown with black blotches. Shape-wise in the bowed backs and ribbed collars turned up at the edges. If this wasn't enough, both Harry and Monica had thin scaly necks and horny-lipped faces. I didn't want to pry. But I did wonder about their dentation – or possible lack of it. Tortoises don't have any teeth.

Even their movements were slow and unhurried like they were the ones emerging from their hibernation box and not Ike and Tina – something the tortoises always did within days of each other, year after year.

'You'll remember Ike, here,' said Harry as his wife pulled one tortoise out of the holdall she was carrying.

'There's no forgetting him,' I said with a smile.

How could one? He was one of my many challenges last year. He'd been brought in with his left leg dangling from his shell, virtually severed.

The Convilles' grandson had run over him on his bike and naturally had been extremely upset.

'Any chance of saving the leg?' asked Harry at the time.

I was doubtful. It looked a mess. 'We'll have him in and see what we can do.'

Mandy flashed me a look of concern when later that morning, I placed Ike on the prep room counter. 'Don't worry, I'm not going to try and anaesthetise him with gas.' We'd tried that on another tortoise; but in the time spent attempting to see whether the vital signs were still evident while ensuring the reptile was sufficiently sedated, we almost slipped into unconsciousness ourselves so long was the wait. 'Different approach this time. I'm going to inject him in his tail vein.'

Again, I was treated to another of Mandy's querulous looks. Those damson eyes of hers had an amazing ability to express what she was feeling; and I could sense they were saying, 'Are you sure you know what you're doing?' I did know. Well, at least I'd read up on the technique and knew how it should be done. The difference of course was that I now had to put it into practice.

Mandy to hold tortoise. Me to pull out tail. Saffan anaesthetic drawn up. 10 mg/kg. Insert 23-gauge needle at 90 degrees until hit vertebrae. Pull back while drawing on the plunger. Blood seen in syringe. Inject the anaesthetic. Tortoise zapped. Surely not too difficult? Damson eyes clearly thought it would be otherwise. Wrong. It all went to plan. I confess to feeling a little smug. A poke-my-tongue-out-at-Mandy moment.

'Mandy, could I just ask you to move Ike's front legs backwards and forwards while I get to work on this left leg of his?'

The damson eyes questioned.

'It's just so it ensures the respiratory compartment is compressed and expanded. Otherwise, Ike won't be able to breath.' *Oh boy. What would I have done without Google?*

The damaged hind leg was irreparable. The tissues too crushed. It couldn't be saved. Amputation was the only answer. I was careful to ensure the stump of the leg did not protrude beyond the shell, otherwise it would have rubbed and become sore.

Ike made an uneventful recovery, warm beneath an infrared lamp. Within 24 hours, he was back to his old self, raring to go – well, at least go at the fastest pace a tortoise could muster. Only one problem. As he moved, he swayed, walked in circles, veering to the left.

'Not so good then,' said Mandy as we watched Ike parade lopsided across the floor, the left-hand side of his shell thumping down at each step.

I felt a bubble of irritation rise up. When she added, 'Pity when the op went so smoothly,' I realised I was being a bit paranoid. But with the addition of 'Much better than anticipated,' I realised I wasn't.

I explained the problem to Harry and Monica. 'I'm afraid Ike is likely to wear away that corner of his shell.'

Harry bit his lip. 'He needs a skateboard like our grandson.'

'A means to keep his shell off the ground,' said Monica. 'Like a wheel of some description.'

'Hey, you could be on to something there,' I declared. 'Excellent idea.'

'We've got a box of our grandson's Lego at home,' said Harry. 'Maybe there's something in there we could use.'

'Well, pop it in and I'll see what I can rig up.'

The following day, Mandy saw me sifting through a box of Lego bricks, doors and wheels.

'Second childhood?' said damson eyes. I continued rummaging.

I managed to find a small brick which fitted under Ike's shell. To this I was able to lock another brick which had two wheels attached. Using some strong epoxy resin, I glued the first brick to the underside of Ike's shell, just to the inside of the leg opening. When this had set, the wheel brick was attached.

'Right, Ike, on your bike,' I said as I eased the tortoise onto the floor and stood back, waiting to see whether my handiwork would be of any use. I was pleased to see the wheels kept Ike's shell at just the right height. He moved into top gear immediately and zoomed across the consulting room floor. There was the added advantage that the wheel brick detached. So, if Ike ever got his wheels stuck when navigating rough terrain, they would spring off and he could move on.

Harry and Monica were delighted. 'Better than our grandson's remote-controlled jeep,' commented Harry.

'And with no fear of Ike's batteries running out,' said Monica, laughing.

Today's problem was with Tina. Monica pulled her out of the holdall.

'We'd like you to check her over for us.'

'She's been out of hibernation a couple of weeks now. Doesn't seem to be much go about her. Whereas Ike has been zooming all over the place,' said Harry, his scrawny neck arching out of the collar of his cagoule shell.

I had to agree. Ike was all for wheeling around and around the consulting table whereas Tina didn't move an inch, head remaining firmly tucked in her shell.

'Not like her, is it, Harry?' murmured Monica, slowly bringing her hand up to run it down the folds of her leathery neck. Her lash-less eyes blinked at me.

'No, it isn't. She's usually zipping about by now. Tucking into the grass on our back lawn.'

I lifted Tina up. She felt reasonably heavy. 'Have you weighed her?'

Harry nodded very slowly. 'We have indeed. Just under three kilograms. Much the same as the past couple of years when she's come out of hibernation.'

'It's just the fact she's not eating,' said Monica with another blink. 'We're wondering if she's got a problem in her mouth.'

I was thinking along the same lines. I was aware that tortoises could come out of hibernation suffering from infected mouths, their lips and tongues gummed up. 'Best if we take a look.'

'You'll find it difficult,' warned Harry. 'We've tried.'

'With no success,' added Monica. Both blinked.

'Nothing like a challenge,' I said breezily, putting on a brave face.

A needle prodded into one of Tina's back legs was my first course of action. She merely responded with a hiss from deep within her shell. Uhm... Another prod. A little harder. Her head jerked out. I went to snatch it. But it shot back in before I had a chance to grab it.

'Right. I'll have to have her in and try a different tactic.'

After morning surgery, I hurried down to the operating theatre where I discovered Tina had been placed under the operating lamp. She was clearly enjoying the bask in the warmth, her head stretched out.

I sprang over. Her head sprang back.

'Okay, Tina, if you want to play difficult, then it's bath time for you.'

Lucy was the duty nurse that morning. She was instructed to fill an instrument tray with warm water. Tina was unceremoniously dunked in it. Water sloshed over the edges. Sloshed up her shell. Out shot her head. Out shot my hand, finger and thumb quickly grabbing her around the base of her skull. I could feel her attempting to retract her head. There was surprising strength there. I could feel my grip slipping. Her head sliding back.

'Oh no, you don't.' I gripped harder. 'Lucy, quick. Forceps please.'

She held up a pair. I quickly pushed the thumb and forefinger of my left hand through the handle. Prised the tip between Tina's horny lips and yanked open the blades, forcing her to open her mouth.

The problem was revealed instantly. Cheesy yellow deposits on her tongue and the roof of her mouth.

'Hydrogen peroxide, Luce.'

I dabbed the affected area as rapidly as I could, all the while feeling my grip on the back of her head loosening. 'Yep. Done it. The tongue's free. Let's have the tubing.'

Lucy handed it over and I slid it down Tina's throat.

'Now the syringe. Thanks.'

The already made up solution of glucose and milk powder was squirted down the tortoise's throat. Just in the nick of time as Tina finally managed to wrench her head free of my grip and sank her head back into her shell.

The next morning, a breezy but bright spring morning, I decided that Tina might benefit from having some fresh grass to explore; and hopefully be tempted to tuck into some. So, I got Lucy to put her in an upturned wire basket, weighed down with a couple of bricks, out on the side verge of the hospital car park in a good sunny spot.

Harry and Monica arrived that afternoon to collect her. I spotted them slowly ambling up the drive arm in arm, stopping by the wire basket still in place on the verge.

I went out to meet them.

'See you've got Tina paying for her keep.' Harry chuckled.

'And in clover too,' added Monica.

We looked down to where Tina, her head now very much out, was methodically chomping, doing a grand job of weeding that patch of lawn.

Tim Hutchinson was another client who had more than a passing resemblance to his pet – or rather pets as he had a fair few of them. We're talking rabbits here.

It was unfortunate that when I first met him, he was dressed like one. The full works. A furry white rabbit onesie. Large pink ears. Whiskers. A bobtail of a scut. His wife, Anna, sported a chicken outfit that had seen better days to judge from the discarded moulting feathers that trailed behind her as she followed her husband into my consulting room. I discovered they were both guides at Wescott Wonderland – the theme park down on the coast – hence the costumes. Donned before going to work.

When Tim pulled his rabbit head off, there was still a striking resemblance to a rabbit in the size, colour and floppiness of his ears, the twitchy snub nose and plethora of whiskers. Then there were his teeth. Long curved incisors that protruded over his lower lip and looked capable of slicing a carrot in two before you could say *Watership Down*. They really did turn him into a lagomorph look-alike. So much so that I had to resist the urge to shout, 'How're doing, Bugs Bunny?'

On that occasion, I was presented with a Himalayan rabbit called Munchkin who hadn't been living up to his name due to overgrown teeth.

Rabbits cropped up again that evening.

'You used to have a phobia about them, didn't you?' Lucy asked the question as we sat, curled up together in front of the TV, watching a wildlife programme about the South Downs. There were several scenes of rabbits bouncing about as rabbits tend to do. Cute, cuddly creatures. Though not many people realise they practise coprophagia – the act of shoving their snouts under their scuts to winkle out droppings and eat them. Worth remembering, when you kiss the cute crinkly nose of your bunny, just where that nose has been.

'I did as a youngster,' I admitted as a Benjamin-bunny-Tim-Hutchinson look-alike hopped across the screen. 'But that was ages ago.'

'Just as well, you becoming a vet.' Lucy gazed up from where she was resting her head in my lap. There was a twinkle in her hazel eyes as she added, 'And the fact I'm a vet nurse with her very own pet rabbit.'

I ran a finger through her fringe. It was true what she said. It wouldn't have looked very professional to suddenly shriek and lurch out of Prospect House when a client's rabbit came in to have his nails trimmed. I suppose it could have been worse. A fear of rabbits is called leporiphobia. But I could have been suffering from ailurophobia – a fear of cats, or cynophobia – a fear of dogs. Even zoophobia – a fear of all animals. If that had been the case, then my veterinary career would never have taken off. And I daresay I wouldn't have been sitting here with my fiancée.

I've searched back to my early childhood days to see if anything traumatic could have instigated my early unease about such creatures. My mother did have a tendency to brandish a constant stream of Beatrix Potter books over my bed at story time. I had to endure endless recounting of the shenanigans of Flopsy, Mopsy and Cottontail, not to mention the exploits of Benjamin Bunny. This was all reinforced a year or so later by the playing of Happy Families, Snap and Pairs with Beatrix's ghastly little friends depicted on the cards. Maybe they were the trigger? But at least it's well managed now. In fact, everyone at the hospital thinks I adore rabbits. That I welcome them with open arms. Particularly Beryl. Every fluffy bundle of angora required to be seen automatically gets shunted in my direction.

'Paul,' she said the other morning as I was scanning the computer screen to gauge how many appointments had been booked in for me. 'I've got Tim Hutchinson coming in to see you. You remember him, don't you?'

Of course, I did. How could I ever forget that lagomorph-look-alike turning up in his rabbit onesie?

Confession time here. I too had once donned such a rabbit outfit. Jo, the manager of the local Red Cross charity shop, remarked she was having a fund-raising event. Would I like to help? She had a rabbit outfit I could wear. Her idea was for me to then undertake a sponsored hop for the Red Cross around Westcott's shopping precinct. Eric and Crystal thought it was a wonderful idea.

'Excellent, Paul,' declared Eric with the customary rubbing of his hands together while his chins wobbled enthusiastically.

'A bit of publicity for us as well,' said Crystal, her demeanour remaining cool, calm and collected as always. Nothing ever seemed to ruffle the feathers of this sassy lady.

As for me, I reasoned that it was all in a good cause and might raise a few bucks for the Red Cross. Which it did.

'It's Hutch today,' Beryl informed me prior to Tim coming in. 'One of his Flemish Giants. A big lad, so he tells me. But I'm sure you'll be able to cope.' Her crimson lips creased in a smile.

Yes, Beryl, I'm sure I'll cope, I thought. No matter how big this rabbit proves to be. However, I must admit that during the surgery's coffee break, I was somewhat preoccupied by wondering just how "big" big could be. A Flemish Giant, huh? A huge beast. Yes?

Eric picked up on my unease. 'All's well, isn't it, Paul? You look a bit on edge.'

'No, I'm fine, really,' I lied.

'Got any interesting patients this morning?'

Beryl intervened. 'Paul's seeing one of Tim Hutchinson's Flemish Giants in ten minutes' time.'

'Well, that could be a bit of a challenge for you,' said Eric. 'They're the biggest breed of rabbits in the world.'

'Thanks, Eric,' I murmured to myself, now decidedly twitchier than a rabbit's nose.

That twitchiness intensified when I was saw Hutch sprawled across the consulting table. Tim Hutchinson had staggered in with the rabbit clasped to his chest, an arm under each end, and with a sigh of relief, had eased the rabbit on to the table. 'He's my biggest lad,' he gasped, stepping back.

I felt a tic in my forehead throb.

'All 20 pounds of him,' Tim went on. 'Solid muscle.'

My tic went into overdrive.

Hutch had a massive head, a long, powerful-looking body with broad hindquarters and huge feet, rounded off with needle-sharp claws. His fur was dense and glossy. The fact it was jet black just added to the demonic qualities that I was conjuring up.

'It's his head, see?' said Tim, tilting his as he pointed at Hutch's.

I could see. The rabbit's head was angled to the right, causing his ear on that side to flop over. Further questioning revealed that it had been coming on gradually. It hadn't affected his appetite; and he was moving about normally with no loss of balance.

'I'll have a quick look down his ears,' I said, reaching into the adjacent glass cabinet for my auriscope.

'Careful. He can bite,' warned Tim.

My tic stepped up a gear and accelerated as I peered down Hutch's ear canals, my cheeks brushing his fur. But at least he kept his teeth to himself. The ears were clean. Nothing in them to cause irritation and precipitate the head tilt.

'So, what's the likely problem?' Tim was asking.

'Could be neurological,' I replied, attempting to sound confident but failing miserably. I didn't have a clue. 'Something affecting the brain,' I tailed off.

'What about that bug that rabbits can get? I Googled it.' Tim pulled a piece of paper out of his jacket pocket and thrust it at me. On it was scribbled "Encephalitozoon cuniculi". 'Apparently that can cause head tilt if it gets into the brain. But you'd need a blood test to see if there are any antibodies.' His nose twitched enquiringly. Minutes later, Hutch and I were down in the prep room with Mandy on hand to get the required sample of blood.

Only now I had a new problem to contend with. This would be my first time at taking such a sample from a rabbit. I started feeling uneasy.

Mandy, as senior nurse, had seen it all before, working with Crystal; as I knew only too well. As far as Mandy was concerned, Crystal could do no wrong. As for me, a junior vet, what could I do right?

Mandy had tightly wrapped Hutch in a towel, everything in place for me to get the sample.

'Crystal uses a 23-gauge needle and two ml syringe,' stated Mandy, pointing to the items she'd laid out in a kidney dish. She didn't bat one of her long, dark eyelashes as she spoke, adding, 'She goes for the marginal ear vein. I assume you'll do the same. So, I've clipped that area for you,' I noticed the shaved edge of Hutch's right ear. Twitch.

'And I've dampened it down. Crystal finds it makes it easier to see the vein.' Twitch. Twitch.

I was about to insert the needle when Mandy said, 'Might be sensible to flick the ear first. Like Crystal does. Helps the vein to stand up better.' Twitch. Twitch. Twitch.

It took me several attempts to get enough blood with Mandy murmuring that Crystal always managed to get sufficient in one go.

It was enough to make me spit blood, let alone taking it.

We just had to wait now for the lab results. See if there were any antibodies to the protozoa. Tim was booked in for the following week to discuss the results and any possible treatment. By then, I'd have searched the internet for therapy regimes and would be able to instigated oral dosing of Hutch with an anti-parasitic drug if required.

The day Tim was due turned out to be my birthday. It was the 14th of March. The day – 25 years back – I'd plopped into this world, kicking, screaming, blue in the face. Not a very happy baby according to my mum. I wasn't too happy this cold, dreary morning as I drove over the Downs to face another day at Prospect House. Mainly because it was a Wednesday when Crystal and Eric took the afternoon off: Crystal to play tennis, Eric to play golf, me left to cope with whatever cropped up that afternoon at the hospital. Talk about birthday blues.

Beryl's antennae picked up on my mood the instant I walked into reception. She gave a hesitant smile as she looked up from applying another thick smear of lipstick to her already crimson lips.

'Morning, Paul,' she faltered as I scanned the computer screen for the appointments' list that afternoon.

'I'm afraid it's nearly full,' verified Beryl. And reminded me that Tim Hutchinson would be coming in to discuss the results of the lab tests on his rabbit, Hutch. 'You know, that big Flemish Giant of his.'

'Rabbit… rabbit…' Eric had sprung in to reception, his bald head glowing. 'Someone having a bad hair day?' He chuckled. 'Bad hare… get it?'

I was not amused. My scowl proof of that.

'Blimey,' I heard him say to Beryl as I rapidly strode out. 'I wonder what's bugging him. Bugs Bunny maybe?' He gave another snort of laughter. Very funny, Eric. Very funny.

I ended the morning, still feeling down in the dumps. A little miffed that no one had wished me a happy birthday. But then, maybe nobody knew. I'd rather hoped Lucy might have mentioned it. At least then I might have got a card from the practice if nothing else.

It was her day off and she'd stayed back at Willow Wren. Mandy organised the ops list with her usual efficiency, conversation restricted to the work in hand. From Crystal, I got a cursory, 'Good morning, Paul,' and a perfunctory smile before she swept past me on her way out to visit Lord and Lady Derwent, her special clients over at Chawcombe Court.

The stack of appointments that afternoon did nothing to cheer me up. Though there was one bright moment when Tim Hutchinson came in and I was able to tell him the results: Hutch did have antibodies to the parasite but that meant anti-parasitic treatment would most likely be effective to stop any more tilting of his head. And that could only be a good thing.

'Ears to a rapid recovery then,' quipped Tim.

'Yes, indeed,' I murmured with a barely audible sigh.

'How much dough do you need?' brought another sigh.

'That's Tim for you,' said Beryl as we watched him breeze out of reception with a cheery wave goodbye. 'He does tend to rabbit on a bit.'

Oh, lord. Beryl was at it as well. What was wrong with everyone today? They all seemed to have gone bunny-hopping mad.

As my last client left, Beryl slid off her stool and slunk down into the office with not so much as a word. I followed her to pick up my jacket and car keys. The office door had swung closed. I pushed it open.

'Ta... rah... It's birthday boy,' chorused the crowd inside. Lined up around the office desk stood the Prospect House team. Crystal and Eric, all smiles. Mandy grinning. Beryl's crimson lips parted in what appeared to be a smile. And of course, Lucy, my gamine-girl, my fiancée, who crossed the room to give me a gentle kiss. The cork popped on a bottle of champagne and candles were lit on the cake in the centre of the desk. A cake festooned with a circle of sugar-sculptured rabbits and prominent in the middle, a large blue one.

'A toast to our Paul here,' said Crystal, once glasses had been filled.

'To Paul,' Beryl, Eric and Mandy echoed.

Lucy slid her hand in mine, the candlelight dancing in her eyes.

'To my very own Benjamin Bunny,' she murmured.

Heartfelt words that immediately bucked me up.

Thanks, Luce.

5
Watch the Birdie

I'm not too sure how my interest in birdwatching first started. Maybe it had always been there. Certainly, as a youth, I used to do weekend trips over to Poole Harbour in Dorset during the autumn and winter. Walk from the ferry along Shell Bay, cut through the sand dunes to the inland sea, and complete my circular excursion back to the ferry along the edges of the harbour; all the while binoculars being raised and lowered as I sought to scan the water for pochard, goldeneye, tufted duck and many other species of birds that were winter visitors to the area.

    I did learn to avoid doing similar trips particularly through the sand dunes during the summer months, as that was the time the dunes became colonised by nudists. Many paraded their bits up and down the humps, possibly with a view to participating in humps of a more physical nature. The sight of a gangly spotty youth stalking silently through the clumps of marram grass encircling those humps, binocular lenses flashing in the sun no doubt raised suspicions as to what else might be flashed in due course. So I thought it sensible to avoid such areas before I was considered to be a dirty old man in youth's clothing.

Not that could have been said of me these days.

Even though I did walk through the rhododendrons that towered over the path down from Prospect House to the Green. Clad in my green op's scrubs – well, they did provide good camouflage – binoculars strung around my neck. And I did prowl between the bushes. Tread carefully. Lurk behind a tree trunk. Wait patiently. But it was with a genuine desire to dabble in a bit of ornithology. My expectations not too high. A robin maybe. A foraging party of blue and great tits in the upper canopies of the three oak trees that still graced the garden. Possibly flush out a couple of wrens skulking in the dense foliage of the rhododendrons, trilling with alarm at being disturbed. I certainly disturbed several human couples as the weather got warmer. Couples from the Green who had sought refuge in the cooler, deeper regions of the hospital grounds. Safe they thought from prying eyes. One flash from me – the glint of my binocular lenses – was enough to make them uncouple, adjust their clothing – or put it back on, depending how far advanced their coupling had been, and beat a hasty retreat back onto the Green.

So, maybe a bit of the dirty-old-man element did lurk in me. But I swear it was completely unintentional.

Beryl was quick to think otherwise. Surprise. Surprise.

'People will think you are a peeping tom,' she remarked, one spring morning as we had our coffee break out in the back garden – the recreation and defecation patch for our in-patients. I had my binoculars trained on the upper branches of the oaks, the buds of which were just bursting through, peppering the trees with green.

'It's surprising what you can spot,' I said, focussing on a tree creeper working its way down the trunk of one of the oaks. A tiny brown bird, its beak furrowing through the bark's crevices. Fascinating to think they work their way down the trunk while the nuthatch seeking similar food sources works its way up. Something I'd learnt in my quest for more knowledge about our feathered friends.

Beryl stuck a fag in the side of her mouth and lit it. 'You can say that again,' she said once she'd had her first drag. She often reminded us of the time she'd been hurrying up the path from the Green, her brolly up, a shower having started, when a scruffy-looking man in a long mac suddenly stepped out of the rhododendrons and exposed himself. We've never pressed her for exact details, but gather she used her umbrella to put a spoke in it.

We continued our morning and afternoon breaks in the back garden whenever the weather was warm enough to allow us to do so. Occasionally, we were joined by Eric. Rather depended on what in-patients we had at the time. Any with severe diarrhoea problems made sitting on the garden bench less desirable as it could mean having to watch the spectacle of a dog stopping to hunch up every few feet and eject a stream of liquid faeces to the accompaniment of loud farts and a rancid smell worthy of any curry-induced human bowel movement.

One morning, Eric hovered by the back door, peering out. He called across to Beryl and me. 'Any squittery dogs around today?'

We shook our heads.

Thus reassured, he stepped out to join us over by the bench.

I saw him look at the binoculars I had dangling from my chest.

'Into birding, are we?' he said, taking a sip of coffee from the mugful he was carrying.

It was Beryl who answered. 'Paul's just put up a food hopper.' She pointed a finger at the nearby oak tree, from a lower branch of which swung a feeder full of peanuts. 'He's already spotted a pair of great tits.'

I saw Eric's lips part, curve at each end – the early indications of a smirk beginning to stretch across his face. *No, Eric, no. Please don't go down that path.* 'I saw two only yesterday,' he said, his face remaining a picture of innocence.

Beryl drew on her fag, puffed out the smoke and studied Eric intently. 'Really?'

He nodded. 'It's surprising how many tits you can see around here if you know where to look. Isn't that so, Paul?' He raised a querying eyebrow. I saw his shoulders begin to shake a little. Mine started too. *No... No... Stop it, Paul.* Such juvenile behaviour. It mustn't happen. I took a deep breath, as did Eric. Both trying to stave off the bubbles of laughter that threatened to pop onto our faces.

'I'm going back in,' Beryl said, pulling her cardigan across her bosom as she stood up and headed for the back door. 'Getting a bit chilly out here.'

Eric and I looked at each other. Two words unspoken between us. "Blue tits." Our bubbles then burst.

Beryl might have reprimanded us for our juvenile sense of humour. Subjected us to one of her disapproving laser-looks. But she wouldn't have got in too much of a flap about it.

Unlike later that day. A very different story.

Beryl came flying in from the garden, her raven-lacquered hair fanned out and her red-clawed fingers gesticulating wildly. 'Paul... Paul!' she gasped, collapsing in an office chair. 'I've just been attacked by some sort of bird.'

Before I could answer, Eric bounced breezily into the office, his bald head glowing.

'It went for my baguette,' said Beryl, turning to him.

'Oh, shame, Bert's baguettes are too good to get wasted like that,' he replied

Whoops. That wasn't too tactful, Eric. Beryl was clearly ruffled. I stepped in to attempt to smooth feathers. 'What sort of bird was it?'

I was told it was big, brownish, with a long white neck. At that moment, Mandy shot into the office and skidded to a halt, breathing heavily. 'The chihuahua I was just exercising nearly got savaged by some sort of bird.'

'Big, brownish with a long white neck?' exclaimed Eric and I. Mandy nodded.

After a few minutes of conferring, we decided we'd better take a look and find out exactly what we were dealing with. Especially when Beryl reminded us all that a Mrs Mugford was coming in with a litter of young rabbits due to have their myxomatosis jabs. One of those could make a far tastier snack than a baguette for a big, brownish bird with a long white neck.

'Can anyone see it?' Eric queried when we were standing huddled together in the middle of the exercise yard, which was originally the Victorian back garden of Prospect House. We were squinting up at the line of three oaks and several sycamore trees whose canopies entwined above the thicket of dense rhododendrons, the sun behind them making it difficult to see anything.

There was a sudden flap and swirl of leaves. Beryl clutched Mandy and both backed into Eric as a wood pigeon flew out of the foliage.

It was closely followed by a scream emanating from the front of the hospital. *Oh no. Not Mrs Mugford's rabbits under attack?*

We tore around to discover Mrs Mugford cowering in her car, another lady quivering in the bushes, clutching a miniature poodle to her bosom, while a man was attempting to hold back a very lively springer spaniel, desperately trying to lunge forward on its lead. The cause of concern was hunched on the steps leading up to reception. Big, brownish, with a long white neck. It looked like some sort of vulture. As I approached, it stretched out its enormous wings and lazily lifted into the air to glide past me and land on the Prospect House billboard that stated "Your pet's health is safe in our hands". A statement at odds with the vulture now perched above it, its white head stretched out, beady eyes surveying the hospital car park on the lookout for prospective pickings.

With the help of Beryl and Eric, we manoeuvred those potential pickings into the safety of the hospital.

'I'll give Mike a ring,' said Beryl. 'He should be able to help us out.' Mike Masters ran a sanctuary for birds called WARS – Westcott Avian Rescue Society – and was an expert in all things avian. He always turned up immaculately dressed in dark blue uniform with shiny buttons; and everything he did was executed in precise military fashion. The capture of the bird – a Griffon vulture as he eventually informed us – was no exception. Mike arrived in his gleaming polished van and out of the back, produced a roll of netting through the ends of which he slid quickly assembled aluminium tent poles.

'Now each of you take hold of a pole, like so,' he barked, lifting one up. Eric and I smartly did as ordered, standing to attention at the far side of the car park, a pole in our hands, the netting draped between us.

'Hope the blighter's hungry,' said Mike as he placed the carcass of a supermarket chicken in the middle of the car park before marching back to join us. All the while, the vulture had been watching the proceedings with hawk eyes. Within minutes, it swooped down on the carcass.

'Charge!' roared Mike as soon as it had alighted. Eric and I sprinted forward feeling like members of the Light Brigade, the net sailing between us to float down over the bird, enmeshing it before it had a chance to flap away.

'A well-executed manoeuvre, gents,' Mike chortled as he untangled the vulture and skilfully eased it into a large carrying crate. 'Homeward bound now.'

'You know where it's come from then?' I asked.

'I sure do. Westcott's Wildlife Park. One of their new acquisitions. I'd warned Kevin Winters, their head keeper, to make sure the aviary was escape-proof. Seems he didn't pay attention.'

Oh, dear. I had a nasty feeling Kevin was going to get a drubbing.

And that feathers were likely to fly.

Another avian encounter, though not so dramatic, nevertheless proved entertaining.

It was thanks to a Mr Grimaldi. An amateur magician. Something he did in his spare time. Otherwise, he was the manager of our local Lloyds bank in Westcott. I could picture him in his office, a client sitting opposite him.

'Now, Mr Jones, I understand you're seeking an easy access account with a high interest? In that case, the Super Saver may be the best for you. For every £100 invested, you'll get £5.00 interest per annum.' At that point, Grimaldi would raise his closed hand, twist his wrist and with a 'Hey, presto,' open his palm to reveal a five-pound note between finger and thumb. 'Whereas with your current account...' He would pause. Then close his palm, twist his wrist back and spread his fingers wide open. 'Nothing.' The note would have disappeared.

With such tricks, he used to delight his audiences, be they ladies of the Women's Institute or children at birthday parties. I too was subject to his skills in the rather bizarre setting of my consulting room.

Beryl reminded me one coffee break out in the back garden as we sat on the wobbly garden bench.

'I've conjured up an appointment with that magician chappie this afternoon,' Beryl informed me. 'You know, Mr Grimaldi.' Now if a pun was intended, she didn't show it as she drew heavily on her customary mid-morning fag.

'Is it to see that rabbit of his? Er...'

'Tzarina. No, it isn't.'

'What then?'

'Wait and let him magic it up for you.' Beryl lifted her mug of coffee to her lips and took a sip. Subject closed. *Grr...* Our Beryl could be *so* exasperating when she chose to be.

But it got me thinking. My previous encounter with Mr Grimaldi has been quite an eye-opener. He's had this sick rabbit he used in his magic show, conjuring her out of thin air. Well, actually out of a top hat. She'd gone down with snuffles and had to be hospitalised. In desperate need of a rabbit for a show that coming weekend, I suggested he could use Lucy's pet rabbit, Bugsie. And persuaded him to do so by dressing up in a magician's outfit complete with hat and cloak to produce Bugsie from a concealed pocket. He went down a storm at the children's party apparently. When Mr Grimaldi returned with

Bugsie, the rabbit was at first nowhere to be seen. Only with a flourish and whirl of scarves did the rabbit suddenly appear on the consulting table. As if by magic. Well, certainly by skilful conjuring by Mr Grimaldi. I now wondered what he had up his sleeve for me that afternoon.

His entrance into reception was as dramatic as if he was stepping onto a stage.

He pirouetted in front of Beryl and declared, 'I've arrived,' in his Italian-accented, sing-songy voice that had undercurrents reminiscent of Kenneth Williams in *Carry on Cleo*. He still had his ginger-brown hair tied back in a ponytail and the enormous, droopy moustache still drooped from the corners of his mouth like tassels on curtain tiebacks. If that wasn't enough to make him stand out from a crowd, then what he was wearing would certainly have done so. Like his last appearance, the silk shirt, baggy trousers, cape and top hat all in shocking pink combined to give him the appearance of a stick of candyfloss. He clearly dressed to impress. In the pink. No question.

Beryl was clearly unimpressed. 'You've an appointment at four,' she remarked dryly, while glancing across at me, eyebrows raised.

'That means... let's see... I'm ten minutes early if I go by your watch,' said Mr Grimaldi, as he skipped up to the desk and swished a pink scarf over Beryl's computer. 'That's assuming it's telling the correct time.' He held up a gold-strapped wristwatch and looked at the dial.

Beryl let out a gasp and clutched her bare wrist.

'No time to lose.' Mr Grimaldi chuckled, handing Beryl's watch back to her. 'But time to be seen, eh, Mr Mitchell?' he went on, turning to me. 'So do lead the way.'

With no sign of any patient, I did feel a little nervous as to what trick Mr Grimaldi would play once he was standing the other side of the consulting table from me.

'How's Tzarina?' I asked by way of a starter.

'Oh, she's in fine fettle. See for yourself.' Mr Grimaldi crossed his arms over his cloak, allowing it to flap over the table and the rabbit popped out to sit quietly, whiskers quivering.

I smiled knowingly, having done similar with Bugsie. Only the smile vanished when a second rabbit appeared. 'She's got a mate now,' said Mr Grimaldi. 'In fact, two,' he added as a third jumped into view. 'But that's not what I've come in about.'

'It's not?' I croaked.

Mr Grimaldi shook his head. Doffing his top hat, he placed it on the table, produced a wand from his pocket and tapped the edge of the hat as he deftly drew another silk scarf – pink naturally – over it. 'It's Bill and Coo here.'

I found myself staring down at two white doves, perched on the rim of the hat.

'Nothing serious,' said Mr Grimaldi. 'They just need their claws trimmed. Getting a bit long and catching in my silks. Can't let them mess up my act, can I?'

With the doves' claws duly trimmed, Beryl and I watched, gob-smacked, as Mr Grimaldi did a final pirouette in reception and swirled out, his animal props once more concealed.

Without question, he'd certainly worked his magic on us.

Feathers featured nearer home when the future of Ashton's pond became a local talking point.

Ashton, the village the other side of the Downs where the practice cottage, Willow Wren, is situated, isn't the most attractive of West Sussex villages. True, it does have the 12th century church of St Mary's, heavily restored by the Victorians. And around the church there is a scattering of 18th century labourers' cottages. Any character it did have had gradually been eroded by infilling of the bypass with an uninspiring housing estate while developers continue to be ever watchful for potential plots – such as the two fields adjacent to Aston Manor – which a canny farmer sold off before buying a villa in Portugal, much to the chagrin of Sandra and John Coles who live there.

For some time, rumours had been flying around that the village pond was now under scrutiny for infilling and development. This was deemed a fill too far and an Ashton group called SOP – Save Our Pond – was set up, spearheaded by our neighbour at Willow Wren, Eleanor Venables. No surprise there. It was just the thing she'd take up the cudgel for. Fight the good fight. Something to get her teeth into – her chomping chin permitting.

'It just can't be allowed to happen,' she declared as she and I stood at the pond's edge, surveying what we were trying to save. 'It's all part and parcel of the village's heritage. It needs preserving.'

To be frank, what we were observing looked almost past preserving. It had been a particularly dry summer and the pond's water had evaporated to such an extent that what was left constituted a cracked pan of dried mud, a few puddles of water smothered in chickweed and a row of forlorn looking reeds, overhung by an equally sick-looking willow tree.

'But we *must* save it,' stated Eleanor with a dramatic flourish of her hand. 'We owe it to the next generation.' I could picture her, Joan-of-Arc-like, standing defiant, not tied to a stake with flames licking around her feet, but tied to the willow, algae-ridden water lapping around her wellies while the bulldozers advanced down the track next to our cottages, intent on gouging out the site.

The campaign, started last year and spearheaded by Eleanor, had been successful. The pond was saved for posterity. Lucy and I banded together with other villagers to dig out most of the silt, dam one end to ensure the pond remained full and plant some additional bulrushes and water marigolds, all of which were now in full bloom. Children from the local school brought in jars of frog spawn. A colony of frogs now resided in the pond. They, in turn, attracting the likes of grass snakes.

This year, in early January, two new residents arrived. A pair of mallards. We named them Donald and Dulcie.

'Do you think they'll nest?' queried Lucy, gazing out of the back-bedroom window of Willow Wren where the pond could just be seen beyond the willow tree.

'Guess it's up to Mother Nature,' I murmured, sliding up to her and putting my arm around her waist.

And to the likes of Eleanor Venables.

'Look, Paul!' she said briskly one early April morning when she was having coffee with Lucy and me. 'We must make sure those ducks have a fighting chance of having chicks.'

I couldn't see how. Foxes, rats, even badgers could snuffle out and scoff any eggs that were laid. But I hadn't reckoned on Lucy's ingenuity. 'We'll get them a floating nesting box,' she said.

'We will?' chorused Eleanor and I, both puzzled.

Lucy showed us a picture on the internet. A wooden ship-lapped-timbered box with circular entrance, sloping roof, constructed on a raft. 'Nothing could be simpler,' she said.

'Except, how do we get hold of one?' said Eleanor. 'Three hundred fifty pounds for one of those is rather expensive.'

'Mike Masters, our bird man in Westcott, is bound to have one. Perhaps we can borrow it,' said Lucy with a shrug. 'Can, but ask.' And she did. Mike apologised that the three he had were all in use. But he was willing to knock one up for us. And he did. Within a week, there it was, floating in the middle of Ashton's pond. Now, would Dulcie take to it? Yes, she did.

Spring Watch had nothing on the excitement that buzzed around the village as Dulcie disappeared into the nesting box, everyone agog as to whether eggs would be laid and chicks hatched.

Lucy and I had been doing some pond dipping one bright April's day, a brisk wind rippling the surface of the pond when we heard a distinct *cheep cheep* coming from the nest box in the centre of the pond. Suddenly, Dulcie's head appeared at the entrance to the box. She eased herself out and plopped down into the water. Closely following her plopped one, two, three then four bundles of yellow and brown fluff. All cheeped furiously as they zigzagged across the water to catch up with mum. While Donald paddled proudly around in circles nearby.

'Wow!' exclaimed Lucy, pushing back a strand of her hair, her hazel eyes twinkling. 'They've made it all seem so easy.'

'Like water off a duck's back,' I said.

For which I got a poke in the ribs.

*

It was inevitable that Lucy and I, both working with animals at Prospect House, both with a passion for animals and both with passion for each other, would acquire a menagerie of our own. And a large proportion of that menagerie consisted of the feathered variety.

In the space of eighteen months, the practice cottage had become awash with animals. Some failed cases, some abandoned pets. All destined to become part of our lives. But there was one proviso. They had to get along with others. Rub shoulders, if only metaphorically. In the case of our feathered friends, it meant not getting in a flap.

Not so when Roderick and friends arrived.

That first started via the appointment booked by Beryl for me to see a hen called Delilah.

Beryl forewarned me what to expect. Done in her customary manner as a loud whisper, hand over her mouth as if divulging some MI5 secret espionage plot. I sometimes wondered if she thought of herself as the Miss Moneypenny of Westcott-on-Sea. But me as her 007? Hardly. What with my bleached hair, stud in left earlobe and tendency to dress in holed jeans when off-duty.

'Sophie and Trudy run a refuge for battered...' Beryl paused in mid-whisper until the two ladies she was referring to had gone into the waiting room.

'Women?' I prompted.

'Chickens,' replied Beryl. She went on to inform me that they ran the Westcott Hen Welfare Trust, rescuing ex-battery hens and rehoming them.

Delilah was one such rescue.

'She's in a bit of a state,' said Sophie, having slid the chicken out of a carrying crate. The bird sank onto the consulting table, reluctant to move. A caramel-brown pile of feathers from which poked a scrawny featherless neck.

'They're often like this to start with,' explained Trudy. 'But their confusion and bewilderment quickly disappear once they taste freedom. It's wonderful to see.'

'But this ex-bat's still poorly,' said Sophie. 'We checked her over on arrival. Clipped her long nails.'

'A common problem due to standing on wire,' interjected Trudy. 'And she'd been pecked quite badly. Hence her scrawny neck.'

I decided I'd better give Delilah the once-over to see if I could work out what was wrong with her. A challenge as these two ladies were experts in their field and probably knew more about hen welfare than I did.

I gently eased my left hand under the bird, running it down her keel bone and lifting her up. 'Uhm… she does seem a little on the light side.'

'She weighs just over 2 kg,' said Sophie.

'About right for a commercial hybrid,' said Trudy.

Okay, I thought to myself. *Point made*.

I prised open Delilah's beak to peer down her throat.

'We couldn't see any white spots when we looked,' said Sophie.

'So, we've ruled out candida,' declared Trudy. There was a tut – or was it a cluck – from both ladies.

Feeling decidedly hen-pecked, I moved onto Delilah's feet. I anticipated a comment and swiftly received it. Sophie assured me there was no sign of bumblefoot. 'We'd have spotted any obvious swelling of the joints or abscesses when we clipped her nails, wouldn't we, Trudy?'

Nevertheless, I felt obliged to take a look. Both legs did appear to be a bit swollen. The scales on them somewhat reddened. I remarked on this. Both ladies peered down to see for themselves.

'We often get traumatised feet,' said Sophie.

'From lying on the wire floors,' added Trudy.

'And scaly leg?' I queried.

'We've never seen a case,' answered Sophie.

'Well, you're seeing one now,' I said, desperately trying not to sound too smug. In between some of Delilah's scales, I'd spotted a couple of tiny mites. These parasites can be responsible for swelling of legs, lameness and even loss of toes. This was causing the hen's reluctance to move and inability to forage.

There was one effective treatment for such cases. An injection of a mite repellent. I have to confess to sounding far too smug as I explained this to the ladies. Very much in the know. Dispensing my expertise with confidence and flair.

But within minutes, I was toppled off my professional pedestal.

'You do know we run a hen rescue centre,' said Sophie.

'And currently have 60 rescues on site,' added Trudy, 'with numbers growing all the time.'

'They'd be all at risk, wouldn't they?' said Sophie.

'Yes, well, they'd most likely be,' I admitted.

'So, you'd need to visit and inject every one,' said Sophie.

'All *60,*' said Trudy, to emphasise the fact that that was an almighty flock-full.

'And as they're free range, they will need catching up,' Trudy continued.

'All *60 o*f them,' Sophie reminded me. 'So, you'll have your work cut out.'

Both ladies pierced me with beady, bright eyes before turning to each other to cackle with laughter.

'We've got Mr Mitchell worried here,' said Trudy.

Her companion turned back to me. 'But really, there's no need to worry. We'll be happy to catch them up.'

'But injecting them?' I queried.

'We can get away without doing that,' said Trudy.

Sophie went on to explain that they had a manual on chicken maintenance and were well briefed on the various ailments that could occur. According to what they'd read, the cure for mites involved a jam jar of surgical spirit and to dunk the hens' feet in it for 20 seconds or so once a week. With 120 such feet involved, it sounded a lot of work to me. But they were both apparently game enough to give it a go.

And I was happy with that.

But not for long. Trudy and Sophie were back in a couple of months' time with one bird that hadn't responded to their surgical spirit dipping. Only it wasn't a battery hen bird they placed on my consulting table but a splendid cockerel that went by the name of Roderick.

Roderick stood on the table with a rather arrogant air. And admittedly, he had every right to assume such an air. He was a massive jungle-fowl sort of bird. Large showy red comb and wattles. Massive cream ear lobes. A mountainous cascade of tail feathers that sailed over his rear in a vibrant question mark of plumes. And which matched the polished sheen of gold, green and black feathers that adorned the sleek contours of his body. A truly handsome bird. Quite the dandy. Very much a cock of the walk.

Only he couldn't walk. Merely hobble. Scaly mites had run amok through the skin and scales of his feet and lower legs despite many surgical spirit dips.

Trudy scooped Roderick up and expertly held his legs between the fingers of one hand while pinning his body between her arm and waist.

'It doesn't look too good,' I said, running my fingers over ridges of cracked raised scales. 'But it could well respond to the anti-mite injection I mentioned last time you were here.'

'I daresay it would,' replied Sophie. 'But there's another reason we've brought him in. Nothing to do with scaly leg.'

'He's being very disruptive with all our rescue hens,' Trudy butted in. 'Making their lives a misery. Constantly harassing them.'

'You know, always after a bit of the other,' said Sophie.

'Doing what cockerels like to do best,' said Sophie.

'Besides crowing, of course,' added her companion.

'Even with his dodgy feet.'

Yes... Yes... I had got the picture.

'So, we were wondering…' said Sophie, pausing to release Roderick who flapped back onto the table.

I had an inkling of what was coming. And was proved right. Seemed that despite their fondness for Roderick, his hen hassling was a step – wonky one or otherwise – too far. He needed to be rehomed. Could I help? In a moment of weakness, I said yes and found myself driving back to Willow Wren with yet another addition to our menagerie.

'Well, you have to admit he is a handsome fellow,' I commented to Lucy as he hobbled around our back lawn.

'Looks as if he needs crutches,' she observed.

I wondered whether I'd need similar support soon as I had yet to confess there were three rescue hens still in the car, Trudy and Sophie having persuaded me to take them on as pals for him. Quite the little hen party.

'So, where do you intend housing them?' questioned Lucy when eventually all four birds were parading around the back garden with clucks of delight.

I didn't tell her that on the way home, I'd stopped off at B&Q and purchased a cheap self-assembly garden shed. That came later, after supper, when I got to work, putting it together at the bottom of the garden.

'There, not bad, eh,' I said, standing back to look at my workmanship once finished. 'I'll bash a couple of hen-sized holes in it tomorrow. And put two hinged trap doors on them. Nice and cosy.'

'If you say so,' muttered Lucy, clearly not that impressed.

By the weekend, there was also a chicken-wire enclosure running around each side of the shed while inside, two perches and a nest box had appeared. The perfect bijou residence for our new acquisitions. Roderick and his cohorts – named by now as Hermione, Drucilla and Cecile.

The three hens settled in well. Not so Roderick. He seemed to resent the confines of his quarters.

'Well, let them out and see how they get on,' suggested Lucy. 'The garden's hen-proof, so they should be safe enough.'

Hermione, Drucilla and Cecile enjoyed their extra freedom and it became a daily routine to let them out first thing. It was good to see them scratch about the flowerbeds and hop onto the vegetable patch especially when we were digging it over. Then three pairs of beady eyes would be on constant watch to snatch a tasty worm or two. Roderick appeared to be disdainful of such activities. Somewhat beneath him. Not something he'd stoop to. And we soon discovered why. His mind was on higher things. The height of the garden fence for one. Was it not too high for him to fly over?

It wasn't. Once his scaly mite infection had been cured, his nifty nimble legs now back in full action, he decided that by taking a running jump at the fence coupled with strong beats of his wings, he could sail over the top of it. And he did. Frequently. To then scuttle off down the lane, at the end of which he discovered a house with a two-acre garden given over to free-range chickens. Here, besides eggs, the hens were laid – succumbing to his furious couplings before he hot-footed it back home for tea, maybe grab another ravish of Drucilla and co before bedding down, shagged out.

With constant repetitions of these fornicating forays, it was inevitable his name would get shortened. Roderick became Hot Rod. The excursions only got cut when I resorted to clipping back his wings. In doing so, I mutilated his resplendent plumage.

A foul move on my part to stop fowl play on his.

But it worked. And Hot Rod became a settled member of Willow Wren's menagerie. Besides which Hermione, Drucilla and Cecile had blossomed, their plumage regrown. Gone were the scrawny necks, the bedraggled tails and bald chests. Now quite alluring. Quite attractive.

Certainly, Hot Rod didn't need any egging on.

6
Feline Frolics

Beryl and I were having one of our regular tête-à-têtes during the morning coffee break. It had almost become something of a ritual over the two years I'd been at Prospect House. In the summer, taking place in the back garden in the morning or lunchtime, munching Bert's baguettes over on the Green. Today, being a blustery, showery April day, we were in the office when the subject of cats came up.

'You're not that fond of them, are you?' she said, giving me one of her customary, one-eyed laser scans, her good one eyeing me up and down intently as if trying to highlight some deadly secret.

'Well…' I faltered, gulping down a mouthful of coffee.

'Go on,' Beryl butted in, her tone of voice hushed, conspiratorial. 'You can tell me. I promise it won't go any further.' She raised the gnarled scarlet talon of her forefinger, and prodded her chest with it. 'Cross my heart and hope to die,' she hissed. 'Honest, not a word to anyone.' She leaned forward, ready, eager, her glass eye glinting.

I shrugged. 'Well, I have to admit to a certain unease in their presence.'

'Ah, there. I knew it,' she replied, leaning back in conquistador-fashion as if triumphant in having dragged some deadly confession from me. Crikey, heaven knows what she might have resorted to should I not have confessed. Nails yanked out? Entrails draped across the office carpet? Head spiked on the Welcome to Prospect House sign out in the drive?

My confession was no big deal really. But obviously not something to tell all and sundry. Especially being a vet. Someone confronting felines on a daily basis. Wouldn't go down too well with cat owners. So I keep mum about it. A sensible thing to do, so I reason.

But yes, that unease is there. Always has been.

I could see that I now had Beryl's full attention. Usually by this time, she'd have excused herself to go and have a fag outside of the back door as smoking is strictly prohibited anywhere inside the hospital. But not today. Not after my revelation. She sensed she was onto something juicy here and like a bird with a worm, she wasn't going to let it go – no doubt relishing the prospect of seeing me wriggle. So, I decided to change tact, go on the defensive and target her. And it worked a treat.

'Not like you, eh, Beryl. You adore cats, don't you?'

Bullseye. Her cheeks flushed. Her lips puckered proudly. And a glint appeared in her good eye to match the glassiness of her false one.

'I do, indeed. I find them such fascinating creatures.'

'And you've always liked them?'

She nodded. 'Ever since I was a little girl. Can you imagine it?'

A picture of a juvenile Beryl sprang into my mind. Face puckered even then with that lopsided look of hers. Wispy strands of hair, not black-dyed as now, tied back in some sort of coarse ponytail. Pouchy cheeks like a hamster that had just stuffed its mouth with pellets. But two-eyed – as the accident where a nail had impaled and destroyed her right one was still to happen. Whatever, one or two-eyed, the picture wasn't a pretty sight. And one I was at great pains to dismiss as quickly as possible.

Needing no encouragement, Beryl went on. It seems it all started when her parents bought her a cat for her sixth birthday.

'Socks, he was called. On account of having four white ones. Otherwise, he was black. Up to then, the only pet I'd had was a goldfish.' Beryl paused to reflect. 'Not that they're really pets as such. Apart from seeing Freddie swim up to the top of the tank when I fed him, I didn't have much affinity with him.'

She went on to tell me she lived just over a mile from school and would walk there daily. Everyone thought it safe enough in those days. I did a rapid calculation. Beryl being 68, those days would have been at least 60 years ago. 'No one ever thought of paedophiles then,' she said. 'So, I never did see a flasher.' *Did I detect a faint air of wistfulness there? No, Paul. Just your imagination going into overdrive. Stick to Socks.*

The cat would meet Beryl on her way back from school every day without fail, sitting on the garden wall of a cottage that was halfway along the lane down which she would walk. Up he'd jump. Stretch. Leap down and trot up to her. A friendly rub against her legs. A meow. All the signs of a 'Hello, where've you been? Pleased to have you back.' This little routine was maintained for over three years. Socks would meet Beryl without fail every day.

Beryl paused. Took a sip of coffee. Then in a voice full of drama said, 'I then changed schools.'

Ah, a change of events – literally.

Of course, Beryl was worried. Concern over the new school. Would she fit in? Would she make friends? Would she cope with the increased amount of homework? Yes, plenty to worry about. But overriding those worries was her concern for Socks. He'd be sitting on that garden wall, waiting, waiting and waiting. And she wouldn't appear because the new school was in the opposite direction. Perhaps once she'd got home, she'd need to run along her old route to find Socks on that wall. Or maybe get her parents to keep Socks indoors. Beryl was indeed a very worried little girl.

She paused again. Took another sip of coffee. Gave me one of her looks to make sure I was still all ears. As indeed, I was. I was worried she'd come to the end of her story and worry me for more details of my cat phobia.

'So, what do you think happened?' she said.

You'll tell me, I thought, *without me having to ask*. And she did.

'Socks found another wall, almost the same distance away from home along the lane to my new school. And was waiting there for me as I returned after my first day.' Beryl had slammed down her mug and raised her arms in a dramatic flourish. 'Wasn't that just amazing? How did he know?'

I didn't have an answer. All I did know was that here was another example of a cat's uncanny instinct for working things out. Just one of the reasons I felt uneasy in their presence.

Having finished her Socks story, I could see Beryl was ready to pounce on my confession again. Eager to drag out some more details. All under the strictest of confidences – as she had already assured me.

And stressed again, 'Honest, Paul, it won't go any further. Mum's the word.'

Just at that point, Eric bounced into the office. 'What are you two up to?' he questioned, having overheard Beryl reassurance. 'You're both looking very secretive.' He smacked his hands together. 'Go on, you can tell your Uncle Eric. It won't go any further.'

'Oh, nothing of importance,' I muttered, glancing sideways at Beryl.

'Paul's just been telling me how he doesn't like cats,' she said, looking a picture of innocence as I threw daggers at her.

'What's this about cats?' said Crystal, bustling in behind her husband.

Eric turned to her. 'Seems our Paul isn't too fond of our feline fraternity.'

'Really?' Crystal's eyebrows shot up, as Mandy hovered in the doorway, her mouth dropping open as she heard what was being said.

Might as well phone the editor of the Wescott Gazette and get a reporter around to do a full-blown expose to hit the front-page next week, I thought miserably.

Talk about letting the cat out of the bag.

I sensed I would, henceforth, get ragged mercilessly whenever a feline encounter proved worthy of a talking point. So, I attempted to play down any such meetings until the novelty factor wore off. But there were several that proved difficult to keep under wraps. Especially as it was usually Beryl who engineered them in the first place. Almost done with a devilish intention – just to see how I would react.

One such episode was a meeting with Madam Mountjoy, our local white witch and pagan. She had a striking aura about her which definitely left you feeling awe-inspired. She'd materialised in the consulting room enveloped in a swirl of white cotton from neck to sandaled-feet. A fuzz ball of grey hair stuck out in spikes as if she'd just been tortured with an electric probe. And she was adorned with a plethora of silver bangles, necklaces, ear and nose piercings that jingled and pinged with every step she made. To complete the mystical effect, she had a black cat by the name of Antac, sitting on her shoulder.

This Antac of hers – an incarnation of an Inca Emperor, so I was told – apparently sensed the spirits of many cats were creating a bad aura in my consulting room. And said as much to Madam Mountjoy by meowing in her ear. Seemed he was suggesting they were failed cases of mine or deaths from botched operations I'd attempted. Thanks, mate. So kind. But I didn't consider myself to be that bad a vet. No moggy massmurderer. Even if Antac thought otherwise. Go back to your Inca trails *(and hopefully get lost)* was all I could say.

My second experience with this cat was on the eve of the summer solstice. 21 June. The longest day.

Beryl's crimson-lacquered talons waved in the air as she bizarrely announced that morning, 'Madam Mountjoy's summoning you to her coven. She can't come in as she's busy getting her rituals ready for tomorrow.'

Rituals? What were they going to be? I wondered. Some sacrificial lamb's throat being slit out on the patio before being skewered for kebabs? Or some steamy spiritual dabbling with wands awash in the hot tub?

'Oh, and she's asked that you take off your wristwatch and leave your mobile phone in the car,' Beryl added. 'They could interfere with her vibes.'

In the event, it was my vibes that got interfered with.

The coven in question was actually Madam Mountjoy's shop, tucked away in a back street of Westcott-on-Sea. The Olde Wicca Shoppe. It sold the paraphernalia associated with witchcraft and the land of the fairies: fauns, elves, incense sticks, scented candles, miniature cauldrons, and broomstick earrings. I had been to the shop last year on a dark, dismal November afternoon. Antac had been behaving very out of character. Madam Mountjoy was convinced a rival witch, Sybil Clutterbuck, had put a curse on him. Revenge for having been ousted as the Supreme Leader of the Order of the Golden Light – a coven of local witches who hired Ashton's village hall the third Thursday of the month for their ritual meetings. However, I discovered the cause of Antac's troubles to be of a more realistic nature. The installation of a cat flap causing unwelcome visits from neighbouring cats. No Clutterbuck jiggery-pokery.

Today, Beryl gave me instructions. 'Go down the side alley and present yourself to Madam Mountjoy in her back garden where she'll be energising her powers in readiness for the solstice.' And without a trace of a smile, added, 'Watch she doesn't put a spell on you.'

So, I set out wary as to what I'd encounter. I parked outside the shop and, as instructed, walked down the alleyway – a dark dank tunnel – until I reached a large solid wicker gate. I opened it, walked in and was instantly bedazzled if not bewitched.

My eyes screwed up against the glare of the sun that was streaming down. I appeared to be in some sort of fairy grotto, beams of light bouncing off grey stone walls and turrets, reflecting from tiny glazed windows that flashed like diamonds. At the same time, my nostrils filled with the vapour of sickly incense that swirled in cloying clouds around me. The combination of the strobe-light effect and heavy perfume made me start to lose track of my senses. Any minute I felt I'd be required to strip naked and plunge into some sort of hallucinogenic whirlpool. To swirl in a writhing orgy of entwined limbs, uttering stanzas of orgasmic chants.

A voice pierced my bathful of Beelzebubs. 'Mr Mitchell, Mr Mitchell? Are you all right?'

From a halo of light, an arm reached out to steady me. There was the tinkle of cascading bangles as another arm joined it. When my eyes became accustomed to the brightness, a white-chiffoned figure materialised to enfold me. Madam Mountjoy. 'The sun can be very strong this time of year,' she purred in my ear as she guided me to a stone bench and sat me down. 'Easy to get overheated. Let me loosen your shirt.' I felt buttons being rapidly undone. A hand hovering over my trouser belt. 'I'll soon have you feeling better.'

'I'm fine. Much better. Really,' I declared, suddenly snapping to. 'What's your problem?'

Madam Mountjoy rose to her feet with a sigh. 'It's Antac. He's gone into a sulk.' She glided forward and turned to point to one of the three turrets that marked the boundaries of her garden. 'He's hidden himself away up in there. See?'

I stood up and peered in the direction she was pointing. A black head was just visible at the top of the turret.

'He refuses to come down. I've tried tempting him with some coley.' She indicated a dish of white fish. Untouched. 'I've even tried this.' She waved a large wand at me. *Blimey. Had she really been trying to magic him down? Would be very tricky,* I imagined.

'I tried shoving it up the turret stairs,' she went on. 'But he wouldn't budge.'

My mind steered to a more practical appliance. 'Have you a step ladder?'

With one in place, I climbed up to the top of the turret to find a very frightened Antac cowering in it. 'Steady on, lad,' I muttered, easing him gently out and climbing back down with him tucked under my arm.

In the house, on the kitchen table, I gave Antac a clinical examination while Madam Mountjoy caressed him and murmured in his ear. It was his shredded front claws that gave me the answer. A sign he'd been scrabbling on the road. 'I suspect he's been hit by a car,' I said. 'But remarkably unscathed. Just frightened. Hence, bolting up that turret. I'll give him an anti-inflammatory injection to counter any shock. And you keep him in for a couple of days.'

'Oh, what a pity. No summer solstice high jinks for us then,' murmured Madam Mountjoy, gazing across at a large broomstick propped up in one corner.

Oooo... er... That could have spelt trouble, I thought as I quickly flew back to the practice.

'I've an unusual house call for you,' said Beryl one morning, having just put the phone down. 'A problem pussy.' Her tone was enigmatic. 'Acting most peculiar.' She peered over her computer, willing me to ask her what it was all about. I obliged. But she just shrugged without elaborating. Which was unusual for her as she was well practised in sussing out problems prior to booking in consultations or house visits, it being helpful to the vet to have some idea of what he or she was going to encounter: a simple vaccination, an upset tum, an ear problem or an itchy skin. But to be told it was a problem pussy was hardly an indication of what I was likely to encounter. But she did remind me it was a cat I'd seen in surgery a few months back.

'It's a cream Persian called Zsa,' she informed me, tapping the computer screen. 'Belongs to a Mrs Volavka. You vaccinated the cat and discussed having her spayed.'

'And?'

'No, she hasn't had it done.'

Mmm... so much for listening to my advice. But I did remember the lady in question. Mrs Volavka. As the name suggested, she was of Russian or Eastern European extraction. One of the breakaway countries you can't quite place: Belarus, Lithuania or Latvia. Quite a striking lady, I recall. Tall. Her height accentuated by ridiculously high black stilettos. It was a wonder she ever managed to totter into my consulting room such was the height of those spikey heels. But they were a testament to her spikey nature and complimented the black midi skirt and jet-black hair, straightened to within an inch of its life, that plunged down her back to her waist. Her eyes, too, were black as coals. And glowed with an intensity that suggested that if I didn't bow to her commands, I'd find myself banished to a Siberia gulag before I could say Cossacks. So quite a lady. Certainly, one who could have rolled a man's roubles with ease. Painful as that might have been.

In contrast, Zsa Zsa was a cream powderpuff. Cute. Skittish. Utterly delightful. That is if you liked cats. Having vaccinated her, I was treated to an icy-blue stare, the arch of a back, a turn-about and a fluffy tail waved in my face accompanied by a squirt of urine. Seemed she had read my mind and acted accordingly. Piss off.

'See?' said Mrs Volavka with the arching of some already very arched pencilled-in eyebrows. 'You have given Zsa Zsa zer shits.'

My eyebrows mimicked hers, arching in puzzlement. Shits? Perhaps she meant to say "frights". Nevertheless, I was in danger of soiling my boxers in similar mode to whatever word she had meant to say, such was my antipathy to her cat. Not that I said as much. Wouldn't do to hang one's dirty linen out in such circumstances. So, I kept my council.

Though I did mention having Zsa Zsa spayed. After all, this is standard procedure. That resulted in an even more skyward-arching of Mrs Volavka's eyebrows.

'No... No...' she exclaimed vehemently. Adding, 'Zer answer is "No",' as if to make sure I knew exactly what she meant.

No doubt about it. I did know what she meant and I didn't dare question it. That gulag exile would have speedily approached had I done so.

But I was puzzled as to why she appeared so anti-spaying. I was soon informed.

'It would spoil her... her...' Mrs Volavka waved a hand, each finger heavily encrusted with rings, like limpets on a reef.

Mmm... her what? I wondered.

Mrs Volavka had suddenly placed her hands on her hips, and begun to sway on the spot. Her balance all the more precarious owing to those high heels of hers. She then tottered towards me, fluttering her girly-glam mascara-laden eyelashes. 'Her... her...' she huffed hoarsely.

Oh dear, I felt I was witnessing a touch of the Beryls here. One of her "guess what I am" charades.

Luckily, Mrs Volavka put me out of my misery by declaring, 'Femininity. Zat's zer word.'

I cautiously shook my head. 'I really do think...'

But Mrs Volavka swiftly cut me short, insisting Zsa Zsa was to remain virgo intacta. Unspayed.

Having noticed several toms in the neighbourhood, I doubted her virgo would stay intact for very long.

Since that consultation, Mrs Volavka had not been in touch. Until now. It seemed her Zsa Zsa was having "zer fits" as she put it to Beryl when she phoned the practice. I was to come immediately. My "immediately" meant after morning appointments. I duly turned up at her comfortable detached house in Central Avenue, Westcott. The same road in which my GP, Dr Merriweather, lived.

I was ushered rapidly into her lounge as fast as her heels would allow her.

'My poor, poor Zsa Zsa,' she exclaimed. 'Behaving in zer most strange way. Look... See?' She waved a hand across the room to where the cat was sleeping, peacefully curled up on a chaise lounge. I approached her with a little quiver of trepidation. Zsa Zsa suddenly sprang awake, blinked, sat up and stretched, her claws digging into the red Dralon in a paddle-action manner. All very normal as far as I was concerned. And I said so.

'No... No... This morning much different. She was for throwing herself around zer room.'

I must have looked puzzled.

'All over zer place,' Mrs Volavka added. For which I was none the wiser. There was a loud tut as Mrs Volavka dropped to her knees, her calves splayed out to end in those wicked heels. 'Like zis.' She leaned forward, her arms sliding ahead on the carpet.

So much for femininity, I thought as Mrs Volavka stuck her bottom up in the air and wiggled it from side to side. I could have pretended to be puzzled by what she was doing in which case I might have been treated to a longer session of butt waving. But for the sake of the lady's dignity, I nodded when she said, 'You gets zer picture?'

'Yes, indeed. Zsa Zsa's in heat.'

There was an arching of those eyebrows. 'She's too hot? I'll turn zer central heating down then.' Mrs Volavka scrabbled to her feet.

'No... No... It's all perfectly normal behaviour. She's wanting a bit of... er...' My turn to hesitate. How did I convey that Zsa Zsa wanted a bit of rumpy-pumpy. A bit of the other. A bit of how's your father. Bad enough explaining the meaning of those phrases to an Englishman, let alone a Russian one.

'Ah, I think I know what you mean,' said Mrs Volavka. 'She wants a fuck.'

Hello, hello, there's more than meets the eye, arched brow or not, in this Russian doll, I thought.

Having established the reasoning behind Zsa Zsa's behaviour – the nature of her call as it were, it was only going to be a matter of time before that call produced kittens.

Six weeks later, Zsa Zsa was plonked on my consulting table.

'She has put on zer weight,' declared Mrs Volavka.

I gently palpated the cat's abdomen. Felt the enlarged womb. The lumps within. Her foetuses. 'I'm not surprised,' I said, 'She's had a night on the tiles.'

'Tiles?'

Here we go again. In the club. Duffed up. A bun *(well several buns actually)* in the oven. And other such euphemisms.

But Mrs Volavka twigged. 'She's pregnant?'

I nodded.

'Oh, my poor, poor baby,' she gushed. 'To think it could have been any of zer Toms, Dicks or Harrys.'

Most likely to have been a Tom, I thought. Though a Dick would have also played a part in the proceedings.

Zsa Zsa went on to produce a litter of five kittens. Three black. Two ginger. Not a white one amongst them.

'Not even one like zer mother,' lamented Mrs Volavka.

Thus, I was instructed to have her spayed at the earliest opportunity before she had the chance to be "zer naughty girl again".

On the home front, one feline did play a part in the Willow Wren household – Queenie, Lucy's grey and white Persian. When Lucy moved into the practice cottage, so did her cat. I was naturally somewhat nervous at the prospect of having a cat under the roof if not one on a hot tin one. But I needn't have worried. She treated me with utter contempt. As far as she was concerned, I was a mere underling not worthy of royal patronage. She kept her distance. I mine. It worked well.

In fact, there was one occasion when her presence was actually beneficial. It was a time when my relationship with Lucy went through a bad patch. Talk about fighting cats and dogs. The spats we had could have outclassed the hisses, spits, yowlings and growls of even the most pugnacious members of the canine and feline fraternity.

It was all work-related of course.

I was a young vet, still in my early days of practice, still anxious to do my best, still acutely aware of my responsibilities to the animals under my care. I'd worry if I'd done the best for Freddie when he came in limping on a hind leg, obviously in pain, but still able to give a feeble wag of his tail. And Flossie, with her right eye all gummed up, unable to see; my responsibility not to miss the cause – an ulcerated cornea.

The same went for Lucy. Forever worrying that the patients she looked after in the hospital were on the mend; fretting that she hadn't put the right instruments in the sterilised packs; was she sure she'd made up the prescriptions correctly? Added to that, Mandy, the senior nurse, was a bossy individual, quick to give Lucy a hard time should she think it necessary, often without justification.

No wonder, the strain we were both under at work eventually spilled over into our domestic life. Who was responsible for the meals when we both arrived home knackered? We did share the cooking. Though when it was my turn, there was a tendency to rely more on the takeaways Tesco had to offer rather than turn out a lamb biriyani with freshly prepared herbs and spices.

Minor niggles became major issues. All blown out of proportion. Usually a sullen silence followed in which you could cut the atmosphere with a knife. Emily and Bertie, our two rescue dogs, would sense it and come slinking up to me, the spaniel's stumpy tail hesitantly quivering, Bertie's long tail pressed down over his rump. Both would push themselves against me. And, of course, I'd respond in a manner designed to goad Lucy even more.

'There, there, you two, don't fret. It's just Lucy having one of her strops.' I'd then stroke their flanks and murmur, 'At least you still love me.' Ouch.

'Oh, for Christ's sake, Paul, do grow up,' was a typical response from Lucy.

'Hark who's talking,' I'd retort. 'You started it. Going on about having pizzas twice in a row. Least I'm getting something in.'

'And so you should. Surely you don't expect me to work AND do all the cooking.'

'Of course not.' I'd glare at her. 'Now you're just finding an excuse to have a go at me. And I quite understand. You must get as tired as I do.'

By now, Lucy's emotions would reach boiling point. And with no safety valve to let off steam, there's be an explosion of emotions. More swear words. Me being accused of being a patronising bastard. Me retaliating in much the same manner.

The effect of these exchanges on Queenie was startling. She hated them. Normally, placid, laid back with a couldn't-care-less attitude, she changed into an agitated, bewildered moggy. She belted around the living room, crying and complaining in loud, shrill meows. It was obvious our arguments upset her.

And it often fuelled the row.

'Now look what you've done,' Lucy would scream, flailing her arms like out-of-kilter windmill sails.

'Me? You're blaming me? You're just as much to blame. Just look at yourself.' I'd mimic Lucy's flailing arms with exaggerated effect. Which of course made Queenie even more upset.

In one particular outburst, we were at each other big time, arms almost being dislocated at their shoulder joints such was the ferocity of our confrontation with each other.

Queenie bolted from her customary snoozing place at the left-hand end of the sofa, shot along to the other end and sprang onto the dining table, skidded across its shiny surface like a drunken ballerina and then sailed up onto the mantlepiece, weaving perilously along it. There was an obstacle to her path along that mantlepiece in the form of a pair of hideous bile-green china frogs – a Christmas present from Lucy's mother. I hated them. And Lucy did too. They were only out now as neither of us had got around to secreting them back under the stairs since the last visit of Lucy's mother. They were large frogs, the size of chickens. And it was their size which brought about their downfall. Queenie careered into one. It toppled down onto the hearth, exploding in a shower of china fragments. To be closely followed by the second one, whose fate was also one of being smashed to smithereens.

This shattering of such loathsome objects stopped us in our tracks, arms still raised. I felt a giggle bubble up in my throat which erupted into a snort of laughter. It was echoed by a similar peal of laughter from Lucy.

We looked at each other, our thoughts as one.

What idiots we were.

We had Queenie to thank for making us realise that we still had a lot in common.

The frogs may have croaked. But our relationship hadn't.

7
Fergie the Fox

I had just arrived at the hospital that morning and was standing in reception, wrinkling my nose at the smell that filled it when Eric breezed in behind me.

'Strewth, Beryl, what the hell's that pong?' he exclaimed.

'Well, don't look at me,' she snapped, bent over her computer screen. 'Maybe something you or Paul have trodden in?'

Eric lifted his left leg and bent his knee at right angles to peer down at the underside of his left shoe. The action was repeated with bending of his right knee. I did likewise. We were both still balancing on our left legs like a couple of wonky flamingos with a bad case of bumblefoot when in stepped Crystal, her dainty feet encased in silver-laced strap-over sandals. No need for her to bend over and check her footwear. A dog's turd would never be permitted to ooze between those dainty toes with their cute pink cuticles.

Nevertheless, there *was* a pungent odour that hung in the air. Of course, we were accustomed to the variety of smells that often permeated the premises. After all, it was an animal hospital. There was always the potential for a nervous dog to evacuate his bowels in the waiting room, or proceed down the corridor to the consulting room with a series of farts along the way. The Jack Russell last Christmas Eve was a good example. He'd scoffed a bowlful of turkey giblets and now had a bowel full of their after-effects. The main one being fermentation and production of the most lethal and odious of intestinal gases. It whistled out of his anus at such speed and high decibel level that he jumped and turned to look at his tail end every time a fart erupted.

The odour filling our lungs today was not of that terrier's ilk. It may have foxed Beryl and co. But not me.

'Fox,' I stated, giving another sniff. 'Definitely fox.'

I was proved right when I discovered down in the ward a small crate tucked away in a corner. On it was scrawled "fox cub".

'It was left by the front door overnight,' explained Mandy, bustling in, all of a crisp and crackle in her starched uniform. My mind zipped back to the time a young vixen had been abandoned here in similar circumstances. On that occasion, despite Eric and I being as careful as possible, she'd escaped out of her crate and caused pandemonium in the hospital. Though in recapturing her in the close confines of the dispensary with the help of Jodie, the Sharpes' daughter, it had given me a few tally-o moments with that young lady of which I still have "fondle" memories.

So, I was going to be ultra-cautious now. No great escape today.

I carried the crate through to the prep room and hoisted it onto the counter. It was wooden but flimsy. Rather like an orange box. Rusty bands held the sides together. A twist of wire over a nail held the top down. Peering through the slats, I could just make out a bundle of brown fur huddled in one dark corner. A closer examination was now required.

'I guess you'll need these, Paul,' said Mandy, handing me a pair of suede leather gauntlets.

Too right. We were dealing with a wild animal here. Every likelihood that being cornered, feeling threatened, it could lash out and attempt to sink its teeth in me. Best to play safe. I donned the gauntlets while Mandy unwound the wire catch on the nail and slowly levered up the lid a few inches.

The bundle of brown fur inside was tiny, no bigger than a kitten. A soft woolly ball. A ball with large ears, deeply cupped, which twitched and twisted to catch the slightest sound; a tail with the characteristic white tip to it; and milky-blue eyes below which were two dark streaks, staining the fur as if the creature had been crying. Which just added to its appealing nature. One to evoke 'oohs' and 'ahhs' and a surge of mothering instincts. But looks can be deceptive. And they certainly were here.

As I eased a gloved hand in, the cub opened its mouth wide and hissed and spat before lunging at the gauntlet, gripping it with surprising strength for such a tiny beast. But at least it gave me the chance to use the other gloved hand to grab it over the shoulders and twist it out of the crate with it still holding onto the gauntlet, still wriggling and squirming. It did finally surrender and released its grip, enabling me to remove that glove while still holding onto the cub with the other. Thus, I was able to give it a reasonable check-over. Ascertained it was a female. In good body condition. Fighting fit in fact. As shown by the spunky performance when she was caught up.

'Okay, Mandy,' I said. 'Let's transfer her to a transport crate and then decide what's to be done with her.'

With her duly installed, we watched through the bars as she slunk to the back and curled into an appealing ball once more. One to be admired by everyone.

'She is rather sweet,' said Mandy.

'Really cute,' said Beryl, appearing from her post-ciggie puff in the garden.

'Cuddlesome,' said Lucy, appearing from her post-poo walking of in-patient dogs in the same garden.

'Who's going to look after her?' said me, unaware of the three sets of eyes that had swivelled on me.

Yes, me it was to be.

The phone call that came through to Beryl later that morning gave us the background.

'Just had Mrs Dixon on the phone,' she informed me over coffee.

'Dixon… Dixon…?' The name rang a bell but I couldn't quite place her.

'She was the one with those impacted anal glands.'

I dismissed the thought of a lady with such personal problems. It would have been her dog. But that was no help whatsoever. One dog's anal sphincter is very much like another as far as me peering under a dog's tail and looking up its arse is concerned. Beryl continued, jumping subject wildly as she suddenly was talking about some local farmer who had shot a vixen in the copse bordering Mrs Dixon's cottage.

I assumed the cottage was also the home of her dog. One that had had impacted anal glands. Totally confused, I let Beryl waffle on.

'Mrs Dixon raced out with Rufus *(ah… him with the anal glands?)* just in time to save one of two cubs the farmer had dug out and was in the process of despatching.'

Beryl held two fingers to the side of her head. 'Bang. If you know what I mean.' I did all too clearly. Ever the dramatist was our Beryl as she banged on. Seemed Mrs Dixon was the saviour of this cub and had persuaded the farmer to catch it up and bundle it into the orange crate. She'd then driven it over the Downs to deposit it on our doorstep before going off to work in town. Profuse apologies for not initially getting in touch. But knew the cub would be in good hands. Especially if it was in the hands of that young vet who'd expressed Rufus's anal glands so ably. Ah. At last I could see the connection. Tenuous though it was.

'So, yet another addition to Willow Wren's menagerie,' declared Lucy when, once back at the cottage, I'd carried the travelling crate into the hallway and dropped it on the floor. Her tone suggested she wasn't that enthusiastic. But Emily and Bertie were. Wildly so. Out they rushed from the sitting room, tails wagging, to immediately sniff the crate and push and shove it across the floor. The effect being to provoke a series of hisses and growls from within.

'So, how are you going to cope with this then?' Lucy again. Still wildly unenthusiastic.

'No problem,' I replied, the two words expressed in such a way that they screamed "big problem, haven't a clue".

'No?' Lucy arched an eyebrow.

'Obviously, we need to keep the dogs and cub separate for a bit. Until they get used to each other. As I'm sure they will.'

'Really?' Lucy's eyebrow remained arched, joined now by her other.

'Yes, really,' I replied, two fingers crossed behind my back.

I did realise it wasn't going to be really easy. But surely not that impossible? Why, only recently there'd been that feature in the Sunday papers about how foxes are finding an increasingly warm welcome in people's homes. A couple in Cornwall had hand-reared a cub from one week old. It quickly bonded to them and more importantly, bonded to their terrier as well. So, it could be done.

'We'll have to shut Emily and Bernie out in the garage,' I explained.

The eyebrows remained arched.

'To allow Fergie to explore the house. Get used to her surroundings.'

'Fergie, is it?'

'Well, unless you can come up with something better.'

Lucy had named an orphaned squirrel Cyril and a mallard Lucky Ducky. Since Lucy seemed less that animated by this cub, I feared she might suggest Poxy Foxy. But she seemed to accept Fergie. And also the idea of the fox cub's sortie around the cottage. Well, sort of.

So, with the dogs shut away in the garage and Queenie snoozing up in the bedroom, I did the honours. Opened the door of the crate. At first, there was no reaction. Fergie remained curled up at the back. Then she slowly got to her feet and padded forward. Stopping when she got to the door. She poked her head out. Raised her snout. Sniffed the air.

Tested it. The foxy air around her was certainly testing us. Whiffy, being a word for it. Though foul as a fetid fart was more descriptive.

'Go on, girl,' I urged. 'There's nothing to be afraid of.' *Nothing ventured, nothing gained,* I was thinking. In Fergie's case: venture out, confidence gained. She tentatively put a paw on the tiles, then another. 'That's it. Well done,' I murmured as she crept out. Just then our eviscerated-grasshopper doorbell erupted. Then too did Fergie.

She emitted a high-pitched hoot and bolted across the hall as the front door inched open and the head of Eleanor peered round it.

'Hope this isn't a bad time,' she said apologetically while the fox cub shot between her legs and out into the garden.

Uproar ensued. Pet pandemonium.

Gertie, the goose, honked in her pen and beat her wings savagely. Roderick, in mid-mate, tumbled off Cecile, all of a flap, while her companions, Drucilla and Hermione, tore around in circles, feathers flying and vocal cords at full screech. Only Bugsie, the rabbit, seemed unperturbed, munching away contentedly in his run on the lawn. Of course, Emily and Bertie, hearing all the commotion, added to it in the way only canines can. Their baying and barking thundered out of the garage where I had temporarily installed them.

'Oh dear, seems I may have upset the apple cart somewhat,' tittered Eleanor, nervously. *Hmm... an understatement if ever there was.*

I rushed out just in time to see Fergie scrabble up over the chicken fencing and disappear into the hen house. I ground to a halt when Lucy shouted, 'You'll need gloves.'

Yes, of course. Silly me. A quick dash to the boot of the car to retrieve a pair and then back to the hen house. I slid down the covers on the entrances to the nest boxes and opened the side door to cautiously peer in. Yep. Fergie was still inside. But in a very strange position. Having retreated as far as possible, she had backed up against one wall, doing a handstand – her hindquarters up the wall behind her. I was to read later that this is an instinctive stance adopted by a fox that has been trapped in the back of a tunnel when under attack by terriers. Despite her torrent of abuse, it wasn't too difficult to grab one of Fergie's front legs and drag her out to the travelling crate which Lucy had hurried over with.

'I did wonder what that furry thing was between my legs,' mused Eleanor, peering at Fergie once back in the crate. Suppressed grins from both Lucy and me. *No comment, Eleanor. No comment.*

Further excursions, between legs or otherwise, were better managed. Fergie gradually gained confidence and became surer of her surroundings. And surer of me. By the end of the first week, she allowed me to bum-shuffle up to her without her shying away; and permitted me to stroke her back without her cowering too much. The big breakthrough was when she plucked up sufficient courage to climb onto my lap and let me tickle her ears. I grinned like a Cheshire cat. Wonderful.

However, there was still the problem of introducing the dogs to her.

'You'll need to think it through carefully,' warned Lucy.
Yes, dear. Thanks.

Up to now, Emily and Bertie had spent most of their time stuck in the garage. But with Fergie now having gained so much confidence, it was time to get introductions over and done with.

'Dogs in the sitting room. Fergie in the kitchen. Door closed between the two?' suggested Lucy.
Yes, dear. Thanks.

With that set-up in place, we witnessed Emily and Bertie going berserk. A frenzied sally around the settee and armchairs, chasing the scent left by Fergie in her meanderings around the room. Tails flicking backwards and forwards. Noses to the ground, side-to-side, sniff, sniff, sniff, sucking up that scent like manic vacuum cleaners. Eventually ending up at the living room door to the kitchen, snorting at its base, desperate to have it opened so they could charge through and meet this dog-like creature in their midst.

'We'll have to introduce them soon,' said Lucy.
Yes, dear. Thanks.

'Probably best if we introduce them one at a time. Smallest first – Bertie. Fairer on Fergie that way,' pointed out Lucy.

Yes, dear. Thanks.

So, that's what we did.

All thanks to Lucy.

Not only was Bertie the smaller of our two dogs, he was also the more docile. Far less boisterous than the springer spaniel. A gentle soul, who liked nothing better than to tuck into a large bowl of food, finish it off with a loud burp and then retire to curl up in front of a roaring log fire and snooze the evening away. Even better, if there happened to be a lap spare for him to jump onto and do his snoozing there – with an occasional ear or tummy tickle thrown in. Pooch paradise. Absolute bliss.

Even so, I was still a touch apprehensive of how the meeting with Fergie might go.

'We could light a fire,' said Lucy. 'Bertie's bound to curl up in front of it especially if we put a blanket down as well. Maybe Fergie will join him.'

Really? Why hadn't I thought of that?

'It's the middle of July. We'd all roast,' I declared. 'Besides, Fergie could well get spooked by the flames and crackle of the logs.'

'Well, then, we could try feeding them at the same time. They're both food-mad.'

Really? Why hadn't I thought of that either? Was I thoughtless?

I shook my head. 'Can't see it working. Bertie's such a piglet, he'll polish off his and try to snaffle Fergie's before she's finished hers.' I could see sparks flying there without a fire in sight.

'In that case, we'll just have to let them meet up while keeping a careful eye on them both.'

Now I *had* thought of that. And that's what we did.

Though I did feed both Fergie and Bertie first – but separately – to ensure they had nice full tummies. And I did fold a blanket up in front of the hearth but didn't light a fire.

Opting for a convector heater instead. See? I do listen to Lucy. Sometimes.

And so to the meeting.

Bertie first. Having gobbled his dinner with an ensuing loud belch, he trotted into the sitting room and made a beeline for the blanket in front of the convector heater. No surprise there. He fussed around a bit, rucking it up with his paws, going around and around in circles. Eventually, he lifted one corner with his snout and buried under it, out-of-sight, going around one final time, before settling with a loud sigh. Moments later, he was snoring.

Next, Fergie. Now confident of her surroundings, she came bounding in, saw the snoring lump of blanket and put her brakes on suddenly. In doing so, she somersaulted to land spread-eagled in front of the blanket, dragging its top off Bertie.

I felt Lucy squeeze my arm.

'Okay. I'm ready,' I whispered. Ready to dash across and separate the two of them should a skirmish break out.

Bertie stopped snoring. An eye was opened. The other eye followed. There was an effort to focus on Fergie only inches from his face. Bertie yawned. Startled, Fergie leapt back. Only to creep forward again and give Bertie a tentative sniff. She circled around him as the eyes closed and he began snoring again. Then Fergie gently eased herself down close to him, snuggled up, and fell asleep too.

'Well, would you credit it,' I whispered in a hushed tone, barely believing what I'd just witnessed.

'Just goes to show what a full belly and a nice warm fire can do for you,' remarked Lucy softly, the merest hint of "I told you so" in her tone of voice.

It now left Emily.

And, as expected, that proved far trickier.

We left it a couple of days to allow the bond between Fergie and Bertie to really bind.

As with Bertie, Emily took a great interest in food. Only trouble being, it didn't have to be on a plate, dished out of a tin. It could still be alive on two feet or four. Pheasant. Rabbit.

Squirrel. The occasional blackbird fit for her eye rather than a pie. She wasn't fussy. After all, it was in her breeding. That gun-dog element. To go after things like a bullet. Only in Emily's case, a bullet need never have been fired for her to give chase. So, what better game than to aim for a juicy bundle of fox cub?

For the initial meeting, Emily stood in the middle of the sitting room, restrained by a lead Lucy held. In I came, Fergie gambolling beside me.

Immediately, Emily strained forward, eyes gleaming, coat quivering and tail wagging like an overwound metronome. Fergie dashed behind my legs, desperate to distance herself from this terrifying monster.

'Now, Emily, that's enough,' warned Lucy. 'Be a good girl. Calm down.' She yanked on Emily's lead and pulled her back. The spaniel's eyes continued to bulge, saliva dribbling from her jaws, choking as she pulled against her collar, her sights still clearly set on the cub who had now shot out into the hall and into her crate. Her safe haven.

'Okay, that's enough for now,' I declared. 'We'll have another go later.'

It was many attempts later, spanning a week, before the two touched noses without a riot ensuing. And then, with Bertie brought in and his laidback attitude brought to bear, Fergie eventually became Emily's friend rather than a potential food item. All was now well. All three were now buddies. They slept, walked, played and ate together.

Feeding in particular was fascinating to watch. Especially with the hierarchy that was established.

There had been no problem in getting Fergie onto solid food. A couple of cursory sniffs of a bowlful of dog meat and then, "woof", it was gone.

'I have to say,' started Lucy one morning.

Uh… Uh… Warning bells began ringing. Never did like it when she said that since whatever it was she had to say, she said it. And *I* have to say it was usually never anything to my liking.

I paused in the doorway from the kitchen, breakfast tray in hand: orange juice, cereal, bacon, fried egg and toast to be eaten in front of the TV – part of my morning ritual before heading off to the hospital.

'That's one of your more unsavoury habits,' continued Lucy, pouring herself a cup of tea to have with her low-fat yoghurt and sliced melon at the breakfast bar in the kitchen.

One of? I thought. *Did I have that many unsavoury habits then?* Surely not. After all, I didn't pick my nose in the car while waiting for traffic lights to turn green. No leaving the toilet seat lid up. No overt scratching of my arse when it was itchy. And since my digestive problem had developed, I now made sure I masticated better and more often – chewing each mouthful as many times deemed necessary for the type of food I was attempting to eat. And doing so with decorum. Making sure to keep my mouth closed. Unlike Lucy's cousin. Whenever he came over for a meal, he'd sit opposite me and plough through his food, chewing everything with his mouth wide open so that I could see mashed meat and vegetables churning between his teeth before being swallowed.

Lucy elaborated as she took a sip of tea. Seems she was referring to my habit of breakfasting on the settee while watching morning TV. Since my fry-up was getting cold, I merely shrugged and went through without comment. She might not have liked it but Emily and Bertie – now joined by Fergie – certainly did.

It had become part of their routine. To join me the other side of the coffee table; the three of them sitting, lined up in a row, watching every morsel pass between tray and mouth. Hoping I would eventually pass one or two of those morsels their way, having succumbed to three pairs of pleading brown eyes. Only Fergie's were more watchful, sharper and cunning. On several occasions, distracted by some news item, I'd turn back to my plate to find a rasher of bacon had disappeared and Fergie licking her lips.

'I have to say…' Oh dear. Lucy was at it again. Only this time, in reference to Fergie. 'She does need a new home.'

'What?' I exclaimed a little too loudly. I was enjoying the fox's company. Surely, she didn't need rehousing? Well, not yet, at least.

'I'm talking about her crate,' she explained, a little exasperated. 'She's outgrowing it. Besides which, it's taking up too much space in the hall.'

Lucy did have a point. Fergie had been using it as her sleeping quarters. Her retreat. But now was finding it difficult to curl up in. She had investigated other alternatives to use as her base. The washing machine being one of them. She'd slipped into it when the door had been left open, dragging in with her some dirty towels due for washing and making herself a cosy nest.

Of course, that simply wouldn't wash.

I had intended hauling her out wearing my thick gauntlets knowing she'd buck and scream and swear.

'No, no, don't,' said Lucy. 'You'll break her trust doing that. I've a much better idea.'

She opened the fridge, took a sliver of ham from a pack on a shelf and dangled it in front of the washing machine. There was a flash of brown as Fergie shot out to snatch the ham and I slammed the machine's door shut behind her. An action that stopped us all from getting in a spin.

I turned to Lucy and found myself saying, 'I have to say...' before saying it had been a good idea of hers.

Next, Fergie tried the under-stair's alcove, burrowing through an assortment of household items. That wouldn't have been a problem except that we were liable to get bitten every time we reached for a tin of polish, duster or clothes pegs.

'What about the cupboard next to the boiler?' suggested Lucy. 'It's nice and warm and we only use it for wellies and buckets.'

'You don't think the noise of the boiler would frighten her?'

'Worth a try, surely?'

So, we did try. And it did work.

I replaced the kitchen unit front with a wooden panel in which I'd cut a hole near ground level to enable Fergie to slip in and out as she would have done in a natural earth. She seemed pleased with my efforts and needed no persuasion to make the adapted cupboard her new home. Often, she'd lie with just her head sticking out, ever on the watch for a possible titbit to come flying her way.

As to letting her out in the garden, we resolved that issue without her whizzing between Eleanor's legs to get out there. With its flint and brick wall down one side and strong fencing panels down the other, we thought the garden secure enough to risk letting Fergie have the run of it. Of course, we made sure Gertie and Bugsie remained securely pen-bound and Roderick and co. hen-coop-bound when we did so. No need to tempt a fox's wild instincts. Better to play safe.

Fergie's first foray into the garden, other than that initial escape, had her tear around looking for a bolt hole, shear panic of the unknown territory making her dive-bomb in and out of the shrubs and zigzag at speed through the rows of runner beans and clumps of Brussel sprouts. In a final spurt of panic, she shot back indoors and disappeared into her bolthole next to the boiler.

'I'm sure she'll soon adjust,' said Lucy. 'Just give her time.'

She was right of course. Fergie did adjust. And soon. Often, we'd find her sunning herself on the patio wedged between a dozing Emily and a snoring Bertie. Very much a case of letting sleeping dogs lie. As they did on those lazy, hazy days of summer.

And over that period, Fergie gradually matured. The milky-blue of her eyes lost early on, now amber. Distinctive, the two-tone coat, a clear demarcation between light underparts and brown flanks and back. Here, through the woolly coat, longer, coarser, reddish guard hairs were beginning to poke out. Below the hocks and knees and the back of the ears, the hair remained short but dark, almost black in colour. A petite attractive vixen was beginning to blossom.

But she remained a skittish girl. Playful. Ready to pounce on wiggling fingers spread out on the carpet. She'd sit bolt upright, her brush arched so that only the tip touched the carpet as she fixed on my hand. Then up she went on her hindlegs, sway, make a dance step or two forward before swooping down. I had to be quick to clear my fingers from her claws.

During that summer, she endeared herself to us. Stole our hearts. Utterly. So, all the more difficult with the dilemma we knew we'd have to face. A decision we'd have to make. What would be her future?

'Are you thinking of letting her go?' asked Lucy.

I dithered.

'After all, she is a wild animal,' continued Lucy.

'I'm not sure that would be wise. Could she cope? Would she be considered a pest? Get shot by one of the farmers around here?' My mind was racing with all the possibilities. All the dangers that could confront her. 'I daresay we could track down a wildlife centre willing to take her on,' I added. 'That would be a safer bet.'

'The sooner, the better then,' said Lucy.

'Okay, I'll get something sorted.'

Only I didn't get it sorted soon enough.

Fergie vamoosed. I should have recognised the signs earlier. Anticipated what could have been the consequences well in advance. But I didn't. Perhaps in part due to a reluctance to let her go. So, she did it herself. Went.

The tell-tale signs were there for a few days. Up to then, her normal daily routine was to be active during the day, retire to her den at night. Sleep through. One evening, she was reluctant to come in for her evening meal. Almost as if she didn't want to be shut indoors overnight.

'You're just imagining things,' said Lucy when I mentioned it to her as we got into bed. With the lights switched off, I lay in the semi-darkness of a summer's night, still doubtful. But in the morning, there was Fergie, tucked up in her den, still fast asleep. So, maybe Lucy was right. I *was* just imagining things. Only it happened again the next night.

And the night after that. Fergie prowled around the garden in the gathering dusk, only persuaded indoors by the offer of a meaty titbit.

It was the scrabbling in the kitchen that woke me in the early hours a few days later. Followed by what sounded like a plate smashing on the floor. And the barking of the dogs. Burglars?

Lucy half-woke and murmured, 'What's going on?'

'I'll go take a look,' I answered, now fully awake.

Switching on the kitchen light, I discovered a broken plate on the floor and several plates that had slipped off the draining board into the sink. Cutlery scattered everywhere. And a half-open window. No sign of Fergie. Her den empty. The call of the wild had been too much for her. She'd answered it. The faulty window latch I'd been meaning to fix for ages the key to her freedom. She was never to return.

Of course, I fretted for days afterwards. How would she cope? Where would she go? What would she feed off? When Rev. James lost a couple of chickens, was it her? A car roaring down the by-pass. Had she been run over? The sound of gunfire over at the farm one evening. Was she being shot?

'Rabbits more likely,' Lucy reassured me.

Every prolonged cackle of our hens made me race out to see whether it was because Fergie had returned. But no, it was only because Roderick was giving them another prolonged banging.

'Oh, for goodness sake, get a grip, Paul,' declared Lucy as, startled, I dropped my spoon in my soup when a car backfired outside. 'There's nothing you can do for Fergie now. She's on her own. But I'm sure she'll be okay. They're very resilient creatures.'

But that was scant consolation. I felt responsible for having reared her. Maybe making her too tame. Too reliant on me feeding her. Lacking skills to survive on her own in the wild. I dreamt of her padding up to the farmer who had killed her mother and sister. To stare him in the eyes. Only to be shot between hers.

I took to taking the dogs out for early morning walks across to the woods, the sun barely risen. Not too sure what I was hoping to achieve. The sight of her trotting up one of the many paths criss-crossing the glades maybe. Pushing her way through the dewy grass of the meadow. Pouncing on a mouse. Digging into a molehill. Proving she was okay. Doing well. Enjoying life. All wishful thinking. I saw nothing.

I was expressing Mrs Dixon's dog's anal glands during a consultation in early September when she told me.

'In confidence, you understand,' said Mrs Dixon.

'Of course,' I replied, having finished and wiped Rufus's bottom.

'Well, you remember all that hoo-ha earlier in the year with those foxes being shot? I rescued one of the cubs.'

'Yes… Yes…' I was now expressing as much interest as I had in expressing those glands.

Mrs Dixon leaned over the consulting table and whispered, 'Well, I've seen another fox since. Just in the last few weeks. Cheeky little thing. Seems very tame. Comes into my garden and pinches the food I put out for the badgers.'

Mrs Dixon had been told about what had happened to Fergie when she's phoned Beryl to ask after the cub's welfare a month or so back. Hence, she now added, 'Do you think it could be your Fergie?'

'It would be nice if it was. But I daresay there are quite a few youngsters around this time of year.'

Still it left me thinking. *What if?*

'Rather you than me,' said Lucy that evening as she settled down to watch TV while I donned wellies and a warm anorak. 'What if you do spot that fox? You couldn't be certain it was Fergie.'

She had a point of course. But then I felt it was worth a try. Just on the off chance.

It was a typical September evening. A hint of autumn's mellowness hung in the air. Ripening fruit. Leaves touched with gold. A white blanket of mist rolled through the copse behind Mrs Dixon's cottage. I scrambled down a moss-covered bank to where the gnarled roots of an oak jutted out to curve and sink into a deep bed of leaf mould. The bed topped by an early fall of leaves – a brittle, dry counterpane that crackled and crunched beneath me as I settled down in it to wait.

A few yards away, I could just make out the gap in Mrs Dixon's hedge that she'd mentioned. The way in to her garden for her badgers and fox.

I had positioned myself downwind of the gap to ensure my scent wouldn't frighten off any possible visitors. But would I be lucky in spotting one?

As the sky darkened, two wood pigeons crashed in to roost in the branches above me. Likewise, a blackbird. But his sharp eyes spotted me and he whirled away with a flap of wings and a shrill cluck of alarm.

The glossy-brown shape of a wood mouse appeared at eye-level, just inches away, darting over the roots to disappear into a tunnel of moss.

The darkness lightened as the orb of a huge harvest moon gradually floated up through the branches, showering the copse with silver-white shafts.

I continued to sit there, cocooned in my nest, the scent of dank earth filling my nostrils. Then, on an eddy of breeze, another scent drifted across. Distinct. Pungent. No mistaking it. Fox.

I focussed on the line of hedge, straining to see. From the depth of its shadow, a fox briefly appeared, bathed in moonlight, to slip through the gap and into Mrs Dixon's garden. It was a juvenile. Petite. With a fine brush. Fergie? Possibly.

I waited. It reappeared about ten minutes later, no doubt having polished off the food Mrs Dixon had left out. Now it was slinking towards me, getting close and closer. Only now the breeze had turned on itself. Now *my* scent was blowing towards the fox. Not away from it. It stopped in its tracks. Raised its head and sniffed the air. My scent had been picked up. It looked directly in my direction and sniffed the air again, nostrils quivering. But didn't move; didn't somersault away in fear, remained stationary and silver-coated. Haloed by the moon. A wild fox would have turned and fled in similar circumstance. So, was this Fergie? I had a feeling it was.

Our eyes locked. I had been spotted. But still no fear registered. My mind spun back through the months: the bundle of grey with milky-blue eyes, the ball of fur curled between Emily and Bertie, the sleepy head framed in the cubby-hole, the bounce, the play, the leaps through the grass. Fergie. Dear Fergie.

The fox started to move. Small, tentative steps towards me. Nearer. Nearer. I slowly stretched out my arm, palm up, as she approached. *Would she, could she, let me touch her?* So close.

She stopped again. Tested the air again. I could see the moonlight dance in her eyes. Eyes still filled with uncertainty. Wariness.

I ran my tongue over my lips and spoke softly in a hushed tone.

'Hello, Fergie.'

Barely had those two words been uttered when the yowl of a dog fox rang out from the far side of the wood.

Fergie, for I was certain it was she, sprang back, turned and sped away in its direction. A silver arrow winging through the trees. Gone.

She'd made her choice.

I wasn't wild about it.

But she clearly was.

8
Scenes from the Green

'Have you always wanted to be a vet?' It was a question that had been posed by several clients in the 18 months since I'd started as a new graduate at Prospect House. Only on this occasion, it was asked by Beryl as we sat on a bench over on the Green from the animal hospital. We were having our lunch break together, enjoying baguettes from Bert's Bakery and making the most of a glorious June day. Likewise, many office workers and local residents were also taking advantage of the sunshine. They were sprawled out on the scorched brown grass that separated some rather sorry-looking borders of wilting bedding plants: scarlet splashes of salvias jarred with stunted orange marigolds thinly spaced out in paltry rows. Westcott-on-Sea was obviously not intent on competing for the best floral town in West Sussex that summer.

I finished chewing on a mouthful of tuna and mayonnaise before answering. 'Ever since I was eight.'

'That's very specific,' said Beryl, picking a crumb of baguette from her teeth with one of her red claw-like nails. 'How come?'

I explained. My parents were living in Nigeria at the time. And we had a menagerie of animals: an African Grey parrot, a monkey, several tortoises, guinea fowl, a black cat called Sooty and most precious of all, a black and white African bush dog called Poucher.

'She sounds a real sweetie,' commented Beryl as I described the dog, Labrador-sized, black save for a white blaze on her chest and white socks.

'She was,' I said. 'Adorable. With such a gentle nature.' I took another bite of my baguette just as a group of students from the local Sixth Form College chose to descend on the grass in front of us, T-shirts being pulled off, limbs displayed, suntan lotion applied to exposed skin. I saw Beryl scrutinise the group from behind her vast Lolita-style dark glasses and thought I heard a sharp intake of breath from her when one particularly beefy lad stripped down to latex shorts that moulded a neat posterior.

I continued. Poucher went missing for three days. We feared the worse: that she'd been savaged by some wild animal, killed and eaten. But she returned on the third day, dragging her right hind leg in which there was a tremendous gash.

'Guess she needed stitching up,' said Beryl, still eyeing the group.

I nodded. 'It was the army doctor who operated on her and I watched as a goggled-eyed eight-year old. He saved her life. From that moment, I vowed to become a vet.'

'And you made it,' exclaimed Beryl, spreading her arms out. 'A vet here in Westcott-on-Sea. Which reminds me,' Beryl paused to glance at her watch, 'time to get back. You've a fair number of appointments this afternoon.'

Having crossed the main road which took visitors to Westcott down to the coast and the resort's pebbly beach, Beryl and I walked back up through the tunnel of rhododendrons in the grounds of Prospect House. The gloom in that tunnel was in sharp contrast to the dazzling sunshine in which we'd just been sitting. I shivered a little despite the heat. Was it a premonition of what was to come? For in the afternoon's list of appointments, there turned out to be a real challenge to my veterinary skills.

Those weekday afternoon appointments at Prospect House took place between 3.30 and 6.00 pm with a 15-minute break for a mug of tea. Though very often, the ten minutes allocation time for each appointment overran and I'd found myself staggering out of my consulting room way past six thirty, having been seeing people non-stop for three hours. Exhausting and often stressful.

'You should pace yourself a bit more,' Beryl advised. 'Don't let clients natter on, telling you all their problems.' Even so, I still found it difficult to keep to the ten minutes per client especially when a serious problem was encountered.

That afternoon after lunch on the Green proved no exception. I was running late with the appointments when Beryl warned me about my next consultation. 'It's going to be a tricky one,' she said as I showed out my previous client and hurried back into the consulting room to read the notes on the computer which Beryl had just sent through.

Seems I was going to see Mr Jarrett with his miniature dachshund called Strudel. I already knew her. She had a short, dark coat that always gleamed, matched by large brown eyes that always shone. And she lived up to her name by being a very nice-natured dog. A real sweetie.

I often met her over on the Green when Bob Jarrett was playing cricket. She would meet me with a knowing yap and briskly trot up to me, her tail wagging furiously. Her eyes would constantly flicker across to the cricket pitch if Bob was out in the field but would wait patiently by the cricket pavilion until he returned. Bob was an enthusiastic cricketer and never missed a match if he could help it. So, I was surprised he was coming in this afternoon as there was a match on that evening. It had to be something serious. And it was.

'Strudel's lost the use of her back legs,' he exclaimed, his voice thick with emotion, as he gently eased his dachshund on to my consulting table. She scrabbled up on to her front legs, her tongue lolling out, her chest heaving. 'I was just getting ready to leave for the match when I heard this yelp from downstairs. Don't know how it happened. Maybe she jumped off her favourite chair awkwardly.'

'Now, sweetie-pie, what have you been up to?' I asked, tickling her under the chin. Strudel gave me a lick but her eyes were full of pain. I gently manipulated her spine, pressing on each vertebra with my thumbs. Three quarters of a way down, she gave a sharp yelp and swung her head around. But didn't attempt to bite me as many dogs might have done.

'Slipped disc?' queried Bob, looking glum.

I nodded. ''Fraid so.'

'And the prognosis?'

I grimaced. 'Rather depends on how much pressure there is on the spinal cord where the disc has ruptured. If not too severe, then she'll gradually regain the use of her back legs and tail as the pressure subsides.' I gave the dachshund a gentle pat on her head. 'The biggest problem will be you, my pet. Rest is going to be absolutely essential.' I looked up at Bob. 'I'll put Strudel on a course of anti-inflammatory pills. But you're going to have to stop her from dragging herself around too much.'

'Can she still go to cricket matches?'

'I don't see why not. Providing you restrict her movements.'

The following weekend, I spotted Strudel outside the cricket pavilion confined to a playpen. She gave me a muted bark and pushed her nose through the rails. But there was no wag of the tail. No movement of her back legs. But then it was early days. Any improvement was likely to take weeks.

Bob stomped off the pitch having been run out and threw himself down in a deckchair. 'As you can see, Strudel's not better yet,' he said, leaning over to unstrap one of his cricket pads.

'No,' I murmured. 'You know, it might help we could immobilise her back. Give things a chance to settle down.' I suddenly clicked my fingers. 'Here's an idea. But it will mean sacrificing one of your pads.' I elaborated on my plan.

Bob was full of enthusiasm, willing to try anything if it was going to help his precious dachshund. So, between us we cut down one of his cricket pads and made Strudel an orthopaedic corset, strapping it along her back to keep her spine rigid.

'Howzat!' exclaimed a delighted Bob when, a month later, Strudel trotted into my consulting room, tail wagging six to the dozen.

I was truly bowled over.

For some people, their lives revolve around their pets, their daily routine dependent on their pets' needs. Bob Braithwaite was one such person. He was a bachelor, living in a first floor flat – part of a conversion of a Victorian mansion that overlooked the Green, Westcott's answer to Hyde Park. Only its Serpentine equivalent was a small algae-smothered pond and three stunted sycamores – a sorry substitute for the London park's avenues of plane trees. Though the traffic that piled down the side of the Green heading for the delights of Westcott's seafront and pebbly beach more than matched the roar and fumes of Pall Mall.

'My garden,' Bob would say, as he sat by the open bay window in his lounge, gazing out across the ill-named Green, threadbare and yellowed every summer by lack of water and constant wear from local residents' feet.

'Bob's a retired gardener,' Beryl explained to me. 'He likes fresh air, hence he keeps his window wide open. Weather permitting.'

It was the open window that led to his downfall. Or rather that of his cat.

'Gloria's had a tumble,' said Beryl. 'Bob's requesting a visit. As he lives just over the Green, perhaps you could pop across before afternoon surgery starts. You'll find him a little strange. His sister died a year or so back and he hasn't quite got over it. But just humour him.' She gave me an enigmatic smile. I was to realise its meaning when I turned up at Bob's flat. Having been buzzed in, I found him at the top of the stairs, waiting to greet me. He was a little humpty-dumpty of a man, with stooped shoulders from which hung a shapeless brown cardigan, that matched baggy faded jogging bottoms which had long since lost their raison d'être for running. Silver-framed spectacles framed a marsh-mellow face on top of which was a dusting of white hair.

'Come in… come in…' he said, ushering me through a small hallway and into a large room with a bay overlooking the Green.

I spotted a black and white cat, curled up in a low-sided cardboard box padded with towels, next to an armchair, on the arm of which was an open gardening magazine. Alongside was an occasional table with two mugs on it. Bob addressed the chair. 'The vet's here to see Gloria.'

A little puzzled, I approached the cardboard box, placed my black bag on the carpet and knelt down. 'So, what actually happened?' I asked as I carefully began to examine the cat.

'Well, the window was open and for some reason, Gloria got spooked and fell off the sill. There's a tarmac parking space directly below. A couple spotted her crawling across it. They were the ones who brought her up for us. Bless 'em.' Bob shuffled across to the armchair and patted its back. 'My sister thinks Gloria may have broken a bone or two.'

In the absence of any physical form that could represent Bob's sister, I recalled Beryl's advice and decided tact was the order of the day. 'Well, your sister's absolutely right. Gloria's broken both her front legs. I'm going to admit her to the hospital and get them pinned or plastered depending on the extent of the damage.'

The X-rays I took clearly showed that both ulnas had hairline fractures. Fortunately, there hadn't been any displacement of the bones. A fact pointed out by Mandy once she'd processed the radiographs and had pinned them up on the screen for viewing. 'So, you'll be plastering rather than pinning,' she said, with a bossy swish of her hair. Before I could answer, she'd already marched down to the prep room and was assembling the necessary stocking and rolls of plaster.

Gloria's front legs were each encased for three weeks. But despite the weight of the plaster casts, she adapted her gait to them; and was soon able to manoeuvre herself round.

'No jumping out of windows now,' said Bob, once I'd gently eased her out of a cat carrier on her first day home after the casts had been removed. 'If you know what's good for you.'

There was no reference to his sister.

It was only then I noticed the gardening magazine on the arm of the chair, as before. But this time, just the one mug on the table alongside. While a photograph of his sister on the mantelpiece had been replaced by one of Gloria.

'Sis never really took to Gloria,' said Bob, crossing to the open bay window and gazing out pensively as the cat jumped up alongside him. 'Always shooing her away. Scaring her. But she's gone for good now, so Gloria will feel much safer. Isn't that right, puss?'

Gloria meowed her agreement from the windowsill.

Unnerved, I left in haste. But not through the open window.

Eric enjoyed his pint. So did I. Often after we'd both had a busy day at the hospital, he'd suggest we popped down to our local, The Woolpack, the other side of the Green.

'Just for a quickie,' he'd say. 'Help us unwind a bit.'

The Woolpack was run by Brenda and Bernie Adams who owned a yellow Labrador called Peggy. The pub sign depicted a shepherd with a lamb slung over his back, harking back to the time sheep still grazed the Green. The only "shepherds" that cropped up now were on the pub's menu board alongside pies; and "fleece" only referred to the exorbitant bar prices. Still Brenda and Bernie were genial mien hosts and Peggy was popular amongst the clientele. Her lopsided grin and the frenzied wag of her tail ensured countless cadged titbits from them. That led to a rapidly expanding waistline. Mind you, Brenda and Bernie weren't much better. Barrels, both of them.

That had been a year back. Since then, with some strict dieting, Peggy, if not Brenda and Bernie, had lost a considerable number of pounds.

But now, things seemed to have gone too far the other way.

Eric and I were in The Woolpack's beer garden downing a couple of end-of-day pints. Peggy was stretched out between us, snoring quietly, enjoying the heat of the patio stones, still warm from the afternoon's sun. Not even the rustle of the packet of pork scratchings I opened made her stir.

I remarked on her quietness to Brenda when I went through to the bar to refill our glasses.

'I was meaning to have a word with you about that,' she replied. 'Peggy does seem to have lost rather too much weight. Yet her appetite...' Brenda raised her thickly arched eyebrows. 'She's always on the scavenge. Ravenous.'

'And there's her drinking,' this was Bernie, an elbow leant on the bar. 'We're forever filling up her bowl.'

When I returned with our second pints, I told Eric about Peggy's symptoms. 'What do you reckon, girl, eh?' He reached down and patted Peggy's head. 'Diabetes?'

Before leaving, I instructed Brenda to pop a urine sample up to the hospital the next day. 'Just make sure it's in a clean container. Anything will do.'

'Shouldn't be a problem,' said Brenda. 'Peggy's been doing plenty of pees.'

The evidence of that appeared in reception the following morning. Beryl told me what happened next.

'What's this?' Eric had asked, picking up a wine bottle labelled Sauvignon blanc.

'Bernie Adams from The Woolpack just brought it in,' she told him.

'Two thousand and twelve... A good year,' said Eric, reading the label. 'Kind of him. But to what do we owe the honour?'

'It's Peggy's pee, 2019 vintage,' replied Beryl, a smirk on her face.

There was sugar in it when tested. But to make certain, I wanted a fasting blood sugar level. A blood sample taken after being starved overnight.

Peggy didn't seem to mind going hungry and sat still to have the blood sample taken. It proved positive, confirming she was diabetic.

There followed a short stay in the hospital to set up her insulin regime, daily injections and blood samples taken for sugar estimation each afternoon. Within four days, her diabetes was under control and she was able to go home. Bernie and Brenda were shown how to give the insulin injections in the scruff of the Labrador's neck and what times she had to be fed.

I warned them to look out for signs of low sugar levels. 'She might become sleepy or a bit staggery early in the afternoon.'

'If that's after the pub's closed, she won't be the only one,' quipped Bernie.

A routine was soon established whereby I picked up a urine sample from The Woolpack every two weeks to check if Peggy remained stabilised and that her thirst remained quenched.

At which times I was asked if I'd like to quench my own thirst on the house.

'I'll drink to that,' I'd say, smiling broadly and with no need to pee in a pot.

On the western boundary of the Green was Westcott's Primary school.

I'd had a bevy of pupils in the previous Christmas when I was presented with a gerbil that had a damaged tail which required amputation. It had been a lively consultation since the group of eight children that turned up were all dressed in Nativity costumes. Homemade outfits to which varying degrees of imagination had been used in adapting items to suit. Five lads had turned up in dressing gowns, their heads encircled with red-checked tea towels. White cardboard wings were pinned to the backs of two girls. While the remaining lad was engulfed by a large sheepskin coat, draped inside out on his tiny frame, leaving it to the onlooker to guess what he was supposed to represent. All very seasonal.

Now it was Easter, and I did wonder if there'd be a similar appearance in appropriate seasonal attire. A flock of chickens maybe. Possibly an Easter bunny. Even an egg.

So, I was a tad disappointed when I entered the waiting room to find that the cluster of children – three boys, two girls – didn't have a feather or egg between them. All respectably dressed in school uniform. Grey flannels. Grey skirts. Matching grey blazers with the school badge on the lapels. A boy with glasses turned to one of the girls who was holding a wicker cat basket, both hands firmly clenched over the handle.

My heart sank as I recognised the lad. Gavin. A pushy little boy who wasn't afraid to speak his mind. A right little handful, I shouldn't wonder.

I'd been reading a feature in last Sunday's newspapers about some professor of paediatrics and psychiatry at the University of California over in San Francisco. He'd divided children into dandelions and orchids. Most he considered were dandelions; hardy, resilient, able to thrive in most types of family and school. Just like dandelions: would prosper and thrive almost anywhere they were planted. Whereas one in five were orchids: more sensitive, more vulnerable and reactive to their environment and needed empathetic parenting and teaching.

There was no question what Gavin was.

'Go on, Emma,' he said, shoving her forward, 'Let the vet have a look at Felix.' His tufty yellow hair just reinforced the dandelion nature of his actions.

I wasn't so sure of the girl. I had thought she was possibly an orchid but her 'Shove off, Gavin' retort, pushing him back a sharp elbow in a very unladylike fashion, made me wonder if she was more of a hybrid.

Their teacher, Mrs Jennings, who had been with them last time, hastily intervened. 'Now… Now… Behave yourselves, you two.'

'Er... let's go through to the consulting room, shall we?' I said.

'Are we all allowed?' said one of the other boys.

'Only if everyone's on their best behaviour. Understand?' said Mrs Jennings.

Mmm... chance would be a fine thing, I thought. *What with the likes of dandelion-boy present?*

As their teacher ushered them through, Gavin elbowed Emma to the front, her hands still firmly grasping the cat basket.

She swung it on to the consulting table and five anxious faces bunched around me as I cautiously slid the cane fastener out and lifted the lid.

Inside, hunched up on a towel, was a smoky-grey shorthaired cat.

Gavin stood on tiptoe and peered into the box, his pebble spectacles, sliding down his nose as he exclaimed, 'His name's Felix.'

'He's very poorly,' said Emma.

'That's why we've brought him in,' said Gavin. 'See if you can make him better.' He gave me a hard stare. 'You can make him better, can't you?' he added. 'Otherwise, he'll snuff it.'

'Don't say that, Gavin,' said Emma, tears glistening in her eyes – her orchid nature beginning to exert itself. She pulled out a tissue and blew her nose.

'What a wimp,' I heard Gavin mutter as he pushed his spectacles back up.

'Now, now, children,' said Mrs Jennings. 'Let Mr Mitchell take a look and see what's wrong.'

'I know what's wrong,' said Gavin. 'Felix can't pee.'

Mrs Jennings explained that the children had noticed Felix crouched in his litter tray, straining.

'Either that or he's bunged up with poo,' said Gavin. 'But he did have his willie sticking out,' he added, matter-of-factly.

The group tittered.

'Can you do anything for him?' sobbed Emma, sniffing back another tear.

'Should do, he's a vet,' said Gavin gruffly, giving the cat basket a poke as I gently lifted Felix out and lowered him on to the consulting table.

The cat sat there, hunched up, looking thoroughly miserable. I eased my hands over his flanks, noticing the distension of his abdomen. No surprise when I cautiously palpated it to discover an overextended bladder. 'I think Felix has got a blockage, stopping him from peeing,' I said.

'Is something stuck in his willie then?' asked Gavin, his eyes widening behind his goggle-spectacles.

'Well, actually, yes, that's the most likely explanation,' I said, somewhat taken aback by Gavin's perceptiveness.

I turned to Mrs Jennings. 'I'll have to admit Felix as a matter of urgency and get his bladder unblocked.'

'He'll stick something up his willie,' said Gavin, turning to Emma. 'My dad once got kidney stones. They stuck a tube up his.'

'Gross,' exclaimed Emma with a shudder.

'Yes... well... okay, children,' said Mrs Jennings, 'I suggest we all go home now and let Mr Mitchell do what's best for Felix.'

'My dad had a tube up his willie for weeks,' said Gavin as he was bundled out.

Once the children had trooped out, I took Felix down to the prep room. Mandy was the duty nurse that afternoon and she bustled in, her starched green uniform crackling. 'Urinary obstruction,' I explained. With her customary efficiency, Mandy drew up a shot of ketamine for me to sedate Felix; and as he slipped into unconsciousness, she sorted out a cat catheter ready for me to flush Felix's urethra. Least I hoped that would be the case. If there was a stone lodged there, it might mean it got forced back into the bladder which might then require me to perform a cystotomy, opening the bladder to remove the calculus and any other stones that could be present.

'Fingers crossed,' I muttered as I gently extruded the cat's penis and slid the tip of the catheter in. There was a little resistance as I gradually eased the tube further and further up

Felix's urethra. But then the catheter suddenly jammed. No further movement. *Had I hit a lodged stone?* I cautiously rolled the catheter between the fingers of my left hand while continuing to anchor the cat's penis with my right hand. Still no movement. I eased the catheter back a little, then pushed it forward again, muttering under my breath, 'Come on, Felix. Give way.'

'Seems your prayers have been answered,' said Mandy, peering over the cat's back as he lay stretched out between us. Yellow cloudy urine, flecked with blood, had begun seeping out of the end of the catheter. More spurted out as the tube began to slid in easier until the length of it disappeared, meaning it had reached the bladder. Holding the end of the tube in place, I cupped my hand around Felix's abdomen and felt his bladder contracting rapidly, accompanied by a stream of urine now pouring out of the catheter.

'Phew, what a relief,' I said.

'Especially for Felix,' said Mandy, a grin on her face.

I now had to make sure there were no stones in his bladder which might cause another blockage. An X-ray revealed there were none. The obstruction had just been due to build-up of sediment. Nevertheless, Felix was kept in the hospital for three days with the urinary catheter in place to ensure any urethral swelling had subsided and that he was able to urinate freely.

Felix was collected by a delighted delegation. Instructions were given to Mrs Jennings on dietary changes for Felix and the use of vitamin C to keep his urine acidic and so help prevent any possible stone formation.

'You unblocked his willie okay, then?' observed Gavin, pushing his spectacles up his nose, as he peered into the cat's basket.

A week later, just before Easter, Beryl flapped a large brown envelope in my face as I walked into reception. 'Guess what?' she said.

I was about to reply with a 'What?' but she got in with a 'You'll never guess' before I had a chance to.

'From the school, addressed to you,' she added. 'Probably an Easter card from the kids. Like that Christmas one they did. Remember?'

I did remember. Inside that envelope had been 18 handmade Christmas cards from all the pupils in Mrs Jennings' class. Lumpy smudged-red misshapen Father Christmases. Bendy-stick-legged reindeer. A forest of Christmas trees. Plenty of silver stars. And a couple of rather rotund robins.

This time there was a plethora of yellow-crayoned chicks interspersed with several rabbits – or at least what I assumed were rabbits if I'd correctly interpreted the jumbles of whorls and lines to be lagomorph ears, coats and whiskers.

One card stood out from the rest. It was a crayon drawing of a grey cat which I guessed was meant to be Felix. It had a leg cocked against a lamppost with an arc of yellow crayon linking the two. Below was written:

"Dear Mr Vet,
Thank you for saving Felix. He's using his willie well.
Happy Easter from Gavin."

The Green was an obvious place for local residents to exercise their dogs. And the council did provide a good number of poo bins for the deposit of what was produced from that exercise. Plus, it did provide a chance for dog owners to exchange pleasantries – not of an alimentary nature when dumping dogs' dos – but more of the small talk associated with trotting their pooches around the Green while the pooches in question conducted their own interactions by sniffing each other's bums.

Often, I'd indulge in a spot of people watching while having a baguette-lunch with Beryl on one of the Green's benches. Inevitably, some of the people observed turned out to be clients of the practice. One lady in particular springs to mind. My attention was first drawn to her by way of the child's buggy she was pushing. Nothing unusual about the actual pushchair. Navy blue. Hooded. Straps to keep a toddler from falling out. Only the straps on this buggy were for keeping two pekes in. Cream-coated pooches with dark brown ears and dark brown staining of undershot jaws from which protruded crooked rows of lower incisors.

I commented on her to Beryl as the lady plodded along the far side of the Green stopping at a lamppost to unstrap the pekes to allow them to jump out and relieve themselves before scrabbling back into the buggy.

'Ah, yes, that's Mrs Potter,' Beryl informed me. 'A widow. Lives in the third house off the top end of the Green. One of those large Edwardian mansions that hasn't as yet been converted into flats. She is a bit of an odd bod, I have to admit.'

'What's with the buggy?' I questioned.

Beryl shrugged. 'Just one of her eccentricities, I guess. Though rumour has it that she lost two babies. So maybe the pekes are her child substitutes.' She bit into her baguette and chewed purposely for a few minutes before adding, 'If you do see her as a client, be warned. She is a rather cantankerous old biddy. Liable to bite your head off.' As if to emphasise the point, Beryl took another large bite of her baguette, leaving me to chew over what she'd said while munching mine.

A month later, I came face to face with the lady. 'I'm afraid I've had to book in Mrs Potter with you,' Beryl informed me. 'You know, that lady with the two pekes in the buggy. The one that always tends to be rather grumpy.' She paused to look up from her computer at me.

'What's this... what's this...?' exclaimed Eric, bouncing into reception. 'We can't be having with grumpy clients.' He swirled to a halt, his white coat – two sizes too big for his portly frame – was, as usual, flapping around his ankles, collar loose, tie at an angle. 'Who are we talking about?'

Beryl twisted around on her stool and gave him one of her customary one-eyed laser stares. 'Mrs Potter.'

'Oh, *her*. Potty Potter.' Eric puffed his cheeks and let out a high-pitched whistle. 'Nothing's ever right with that lady.' He turned to me and with a sympathetic pat on my arm, added,

'Mark my words, you'll have your work cut out with our Mrs Potter,' before breezing out

Thanks, Eric. That makes me feel heaps better.

I grimaced at Beryl. *Oh, dear. Just what was I letting myself in for with this lady?*

I was soon to find out. A raised voice, peppered with exclamations, announced the arrival of Mrs Potter in reception. 'I really don't see why I had to make an appointment. Extremely inconvenient. Besides which, Zhang Yong and Wang Li will get so distressed. You can't imagine.' All spoken with a hiss of exasperation as if air was being released from a deflating tyre.

Ah, I thought. Beryl had obviously insisted the lady make an appointment as was practice policy these days rather than have a house visit. Even if it was just across to the other side of the Green. And when Mrs Potter made her entrance into my consulting room, I feared her face would say it all. I was anticipating a brazier full of glowing coals. But when she did bundle in with her buggy, there was no face to be seen. Well, precious little. On account of a bush of straight brown hair through which only a nose poked. In addition, I felt I was being confronted with a ragged pile of Oxfam cast-offs due to the shapeless bundle of brown scarves and shawls that covered any contours she might have had. The effect heightened by innumerable different-coloured bulging plastic bags tied to each of the buggy's handles. All very disconcerting.

Nevertheless, I pulled myself together, reminded myself of my duty of care, ensured my lips were curved in a smile and said in the best bedside manner I could muster, 'Good morning, Mrs Potter.'

'Nothing good about it,' replied a voice behind the hair as she shuffled to a halt, the bags rustling, her two pekes just visible, peering over them, snuffling.

'Ah, well, yes. We have had a shower or two.'

'Still more to come.'

'Oh, dear. Really?'

'A deep depression heading our way.'

The way this conversation was heading, I felt the depression had already arrived and was sitting fair and square over my consulting room. A change of tact was definitely required. Hence my 'So, what can we do for you?' delivered as brightly and breezily as possible.

'You can't *do* anything for me. It's Zhang Yong and Wang Li that need attention,' replied the mop of hair.

I felt the tic in my forehead start to throb. My usual warning of an upsurge in my blood pressure. *Calm down, Paul. Calm down.* 'Yes, right. Let's see what the problem is with er… your two pekes then, shall we?'

'Won't be able to treat them if you don't,' said the hair.

I felt my lips lowering, my smile fading. 'Yes, of course. So, let's take a look then,' I said, a little short.

'You want them on the table?'

'That would be the easiest option.' *(shorter)*

'Can't you look at them in the buggy?'

'On the table, please.' *(shorter still)*

'If you insist.'

'I do.' *(very short)*

The hair bent down, parted the bulging white plastic bags bunched around the front of the buggy and levered out one of the two pekes that had been straining to look over them. 'Zhang Yong,' I was told as the dog was eased onto the consulting table. 'You don't need to be a vet to see what's wrong,' added the hair.

She was right. It was obvious. There were patches of hair loss down Zhang Yong's back and where the skin was exposed, several raw spots.

'She's been under my yew hedge,' the hair said. 'That's what's done it.'

I was momentarily puzzled, long enough for Mrs Potter to spot my uncertainty. She gave an exasperated sigh. 'It's her itchiness. Making her rub her back on the lower branches.'

'Oh, I see what you mean.'

Just to verify the fact, I tickled Zhang Yong's flank and immediately her back leg swung up in a vigorous scratch reflex.

'Yes, she certainly is itchy. And your other peke?'

'Wang Li. He's the same.' Mrs Potter told me to hang on to Zhang Yong while she extricated the other peke from the buggy and placed him alongside her. He had similar skin lesions and just as strong a scratch reflex.

Okay. Now I needed to find out why they were so itchy. I had one obvious cause in mind. It was the commonest one that resulted in this type of dermatitis. As if reading my mind, the hair huffed, 'It's not fleas if that's what you're thinking. I brush them both regularly and haven't seen any. Not that I'd expect to. I pride myself on keeping them up to scratch.'

Uhm. An unfortunate turn of phrase to use under the circumstances. But it was precisely what I *was* thinking. If the itchiness was due to fleas, I just needed to confirm the diagnosis. So, I started to carefully examine Zhang Yong's back, parting the fine hair at the edges of the lesions. I was looking for black flecks. The idea was for me to then transferred a few of the flecks on to the consulting table, squeeze some water from a wet lump of cotton wool over them and wait for tiny red streaks to appear. This would be digested blood from flea dirt. Proof that pekes' problem was due to fleas. But to my dismay, I couldn't find any. Same went for Wang Li. Nothing.

The hair's antennae were quickly at work again, fine-tuned to my uncertainty. 'You don't know what's causing it, do you?' it queried.

Come on, Paul, show you have some grasp of the problem. So, in as an authoritative voice as possible, I explained that the itchiness and consequent dermatitis was allergic in origin. Even one fleabite could set it off. So, an anti-inflammatory injection and some follow-up steroid pills for each dog should help to ease the itchiness and calm their skins down. I didn't add that I hadn't any real idea as to the cause.

'I suppose I'd better give it a go,' said the hair. 'But I'll be back if they're no better.'

Short of a miracle, I could see that was very likely.

But it seemed to do the trick. Least according to what Beryl told me a few weeks later.

'Mrs Potter phoned through to say both her pekes are fine now. No scratching. And their hair's re-growing.'

'Really?' I was unable to keep the surprise out of my voice.

Beryl nodded, a mischievous glint in her good eye. 'But then, before she left, I did persuade her to try out one of our new dietary ranges. Well, it was on special offer. I suggested the low protein one. You know, the one that's good for allergic skin conditions due to diet.'

Uhm… Okay. Point made, Beryl.

Time for me to eat humble pie. Just hope I wasn't allergic to it.

9
Creeping with Crawlies

I'd met Mr Hargreaves in my early days at the hospital.

His hobby was herpetology and he was proud of his collection of reptiles and amphibians. He was tall, bony-bodied with nipped in shoulders and stick-like arms, his hair a thin web of grey filaments on a domed head. A praying mantis sprang to mind. Or a *Carausius morusus* as he would like to call it, since Mr Hargreaves had a propensity to call everything by their Latin names. Including his *Canis familiaris*, a Welsh springer spaniel. Eric and I had operated on one of Mr Hargreaves many reptiles, a *Trachysaurus rugosus*. A stump-tailed skink. It had suffered a prolapsed rectum which we managed to correct with the use of a thermometer.

I swear his filamented hair shot up a few centimetres on being told about Beryl's experience with the frog. One she embellished with great delight.

'The size of a tennis ball, you say?' His bulbous grey eyes grew even more bulbous. Almost bulged out on organ stops.

Really, Beryl? I thought. Next thing we'd hear, it would be the size of a football with the way she was expanding her story. As to its colour. I couldn't recollect it having quite so many red and black stripes that, as she put it, gave it a savage, threatening appearance. In fact, I thought it looked rather cute nestling in her raven's wings. Apart from the fact it could have potentially squirted us with deadly poison. Well, not so cute then. As Beryl was quick to point out to Mr Hargreaves.

'To think, one tiny droplet on my scalp and I'd have been a goner.' She drew a hand dramatically across her scrawny neck. 'Dead, here on this very spot. Within minutes.' She peered down at the reception floor. A floor which had been thoroughly scrubbed with disinfectant following the creature's demise under Major Fitzherbert's shoe.

Mr Hargreaves scratched his chin thoughtfully. 'How big did you say it was?'

Beryl stretched the forefinger and thumb out of each hand to form an elliptical shape the size of a football.

'Really, that big?' exclaimed Mr Hargreaves.

'Well, maybe a bit smaller.' Beryl's fingers closed in a fraction.

'Still very large for the type of frog you've described.'

The fingers shrank in more.

I was reminded of the fisherman's story about the one that got away.

Eventually after a bit more probing by Mr Hargreaves, Beryl's fingers gave a better approximation of the frog's size. Two thumbnails.

'I reckon it was a *Hyperolius viridiflavus.* They're very attractive *little* amphibians. If you've still got him, he'd be a very welcome addition to my collection.'

'But surely not if it's poisonous,' said Beryl, pulling her cardigan tightly around her shoulders.

'Who said anything about him being poisonous? No, no, not this species. Rest assured you'd have been dead by now, had it been. So, you can keep your hair on.'

Beryl patted hers, no doubt reminding herself of where the tree frog had recently been. *Would she tell Ernie later?* I wondered. Whatever, it had been a hair-raising experience for her; and no doubt one she would continue to milk for all it was worth.

Mr Hargreaves was disappointed to learn of the frog's fate. He looked as down-trodden as the frog must have been. 'Poor soul,' he murmured. *A rather apt way of describing its departure under Major Fitzherbert's foot,* I thought.

But my mind soon focussed on the real reason Mr Hargreaves had come in that afternoon.

He slid a small but tall vivarium onto my consulting table and stood back, waiting for me to comment. I peered through one panel at the tangle of luxuriant greenery within. A miniature tropical paradise criss-crossed with small branches and twigs. Last time I'd been confronted with such a scene had been when Mr Hargreaves had brought in a *Hyla cinerea* – a tree frog to you and me. Its bright green colour blending in with the foliage made it impossible to detect. Mr Hargreaves had chuckled at my discomfort at not spotting the inmate, slid open the vivarium and allowed what I thought had been a leaf to leap out onto the consulting table and hop across it. Well, to be exact, to hop around in circles on it, trailing its right hind leg. An X-ray picked up a fractured fibula in that leg which was allowed to mend of its own accord.

So, here we were again. Similar scene. A vivarium stuffed with vegetation. Inside, some living creature. Some living creature I couldn't see. Outside, some living creature becoming vexed at not spotting it. Me.

'Difficult to pick it out, isn't it?' said Mr Hargreaves, a note of amusement in his voice. 'But that's all part and parcel of his camouflage. Nature's way of keeping him free of predators.'

For a moment, I felt like some sort of hawk waiting to swoop down on the beast – whatever it was – and snatch it out. I felt my talons *(fingers)* tighten in a ball. My beak *(nose)* hovered in the air above the vivarium's lid.

'Shall I do the honours?' asked Mr Hargreaves, sliding the lid back and sliding his hand in.

I felt like saying 'Prey do' in response but felt the pun would have been lost on him so I merely nodded.

'I'm sure you'll find him a fascinating specimen of his kind.'

I wasn't so sure. It kind of depended on what kind it was.

'It's a chameleon.'

Ah, that sounded simple enough. But Mr Hargreaves was not one for simplicity. As he rooted around in the dense foliage, attempting to find said chameleon, he explained: 'There are two subfamilies in the family *Chamaeleonidae*. *(Right. That seemed easy enough. But he'd only just started.)* Typical and dwarf chameleons belong to the subfamily *Chamaeleoninae*. Okay? *(Er... yes. I think so.)* Whereas the atypical stumptailed chameleons are members of the subfamily *Brookesinae*. Still following? *(Just about.)* Now each of these groups is divided into genera, each with its own characteristics. *(Oh dear. I was beginning to lose it.)* The genera in the subfamily *Chamaeleoninae* are the African chameleons *Chamaeleo* and *Bradypodion*... *(Now lost. Let's hope he'd finished. He hadn't.)* Also in that group, the Madagascar chameleons *Calumma* and *Furcifer* mustn't be forgotten *(I already had)*. Finally, the subfamily *Brookeslinae* contains the genera *Brookesia* and *Rhampholeon*. Is that clear?' *(As mud)*

'So, here we have him,' declared Mr Hargreaves, extracting a small branch to which clung a chameleon. Typical, atypical, dwarf, whatever, it was definitely a chameleon. No mistaking the independently rotating eyes with eyelids that reduced the pupils to pinpricks. The tail coiled up like a spring. And the feet with their fused toes forming pincers with which this chameleon was gripping the branch. And if I'd had a fly on the end of my nose, the chameleon might have been tempted to open its mouth and unfurl a surprisingly long tongue to make a tasty snack of it *(fly not nose)*.

'Splendid fellow, isn't he?' said Mr Hargreaves, holding the branch up to display the mottled dark and light green creature to better effect. And which enabled me to spot the small horny protuberances on its head. So making it a male. I didn't enquire what sort of chameleon he was, for fear of it being a species with a long Latin name which I wouldn't be able to spell on his case sheet. I was given it all the same.

'He's a *Chamaeleo jacksonii.*'

Uhm. Why wasn't I surprised? 'And what do you call him?' The obvious one would have been "Jack" but I had a feeling Mr Hargreaves didn't do "obvious". More likely to be a Sophocles. Maybe a Tiberius. Or even a Plutarch. There again, perhaps a name with an African association: Adebowale, Abimbola or Olamilekan. Names that didn't exactly trip off the tongue but nevertheless had resonance. Some power behind them. I duly enquired.

'Dave.'

'Dave?'

Mr Hargreaves nodded. And looked down at the chameleon. 'Dave,' he repeated with obvious affection in his voice.

Dave then. Not quite the name with exotic connotations. No conjuring up some inspiring philosopher from ancient times. Or an imposing Masai warrior with spear in hand, gazing across the Kenyan grasslands. More of a Dave associated with staring down at the broken ballcock of one's toilet cistern.

Okay, with the name out of the way and the patient on display, it was time to find out why Dave had been brought in. What, if anything, was wrong with him? Hence my first question. 'So, you've a problem with er... Dave, then?'

'He's rather out of sorts.'

Uhm... none too helpful. I gave an encouraging nod.

'A bit under the weather,' Mr Hargreaves added.

Obviously my first nod hadn't been encouraging enough so I kept on nodding, feeling like one of those mechanical dogs you see rocking their heads in the rear windows of cars.

'Not himself.'

I abruptly stopped nodding as my nodding was getting me nowhere. Besides which I suddenly recalled having read somewhere that male chameleons begin their courtship rituals with rhythmic head bobs – as many as eight at any one time. I didn't want Dave to think I was challenging him – a rival male that he should attack.

'One minute, he's bright green. Eating. Cheerful enough. Next, he's changed colour: grey, grumpy and miserable.' Mr Hargreaves held Dave up on his branch. 'This is one of his better days as you can see.'

I was about to nod again. But that would have been a false move as I couldn't see, so I didn't. Okay, he was in full emerald-green display mode, so presumably not too down in the dumps if I were to go by what Mr Hargreaves had just said. Other than that, I hadn't a clue as to how Dave was feeling and the cause of the apparent downturn in his behaviour. So instead of nodding, I shrugged.

Mr Hargreaves picked up on that in an instance. No need for me to turn grey – miserable at the thought of trying to work out what was wrong with Dave, if indeed anything was wrong. My shrug said it all. I hadn't a clue.

'Forgive me for asking,' said Mr Hargreaves, 'but do you know much about chameleons?'

'Well, not a great deal, no. But I used to have one as a pet when I was a lad. Brought it back from Nigeria. Though it was a long time ago now.'

'Ah, that would probably have been a *Chamaeleo senegalensis*,' said Mr Hargreaves. 'They were very popular in the pet trade in those days. Being hardy and used to the rigorous weather of West Africa, they were more likely to survive over here.'

My chameleon, whatever its species, had simply been called Chloe. I'd first spotted her lurking in a bower of purple bougainvillea outside my bedroom window during one of my UK school-holiday trips out to Ibadan, Nigeria, where my father was stationed in a two-year army secondment. Fascinated by her and not wishing to part company, I brought her back to the UK, smuggled in a large Oxo tin, the lid perforated with holes; flying home with her encased in that tin, tucked inside a BOAC flight bag, crammed under my seat.

My auntie, with whom I was living at the time while attending the local grammar school in Bournemouth, was delighted when I arrived at her house and unzipped my flight bag to give her a present of a bird carved from a cow horn. A dark-grey and cream, curved, hollowed out object; the tip of the horn being the tip of the bird's beak, the base its feet. A crane at a push – providing you were able to stretch your imagination sufficiently.

'How kind,' she said hesitantly, rolling the crudely carved crane in her hand. 'Oh, and something else?' she added as I slid the Oxo cube tin onto her kitchen table.

'Chloe,' I said as I carefully levered the lid up. My auntie's face – not generally the most expressive of physiognomies – took on a pallor a ghost would have been proud of with features worthy of a frozen mammoth. From that, one could safely assume the contents of the Oxo tin was not the "stock" she'd been expecting.

I was diligent in ensuring I set up the right quarters for Chloe. A terrarium with all the trimmings befitting a lizard that had travelled three thousand miles from the comforts of a bower of bougainvillea. Albeit it had to land up, unfortunately, in the dingy, drafty stairwell of my auntie's house – for that's where she decided Chloe had to reside. Illumination was via by a small fluorescent light. Heat via an infrared lamp. And humidity via a dish of water. Branches from my auntie's apple tree provided the perching places. Vegetation from her garden, the hiding places: a clump of primulas, some pansies, strands of ivy pulled off the garage wall. Not quite a tropical paradise. But the best I could do under the circumstances.

Nutrition was to be an important factor of course. I made sure I did my research to ensure Chloe's dietary requirements would be met. Herein did lie a problem. Chameleons like live food. Chloe was no exception. We were talking live locusts and grasshoppers. Flies. Mealworms. Each with the potential to hop, fly or wriggle into my auntie's living room. And many did. Hence, the occasional mealworm discovered in a slipper, a grasshopper on the back of the chair and up to three or four bluebottles – having hatched from the grubs I'd bought from the pet shop – forlornly droning around the room or alighting on the television screen to parade up and down over Coronation Street. And once I had one stuck, upturned, in a sticky sea of strawberry jam spread on a sandwich, its legs waving at me as I was about to take a bite.

Looking back, I'm not sure Chloe had much of a life. From her quarters, on the edge of our bungalow's veranda, she would have looked down the slopes of a garden ablaze with the orbs of orange marigolds, the clustered striped heads of pink zinnias, the crimson blades of canna lilies offsetting their dark purple leaves. Each shimmering in the intense tropical heat. Each alive with bevies of butterflies flitting from bloom to bloom. Yellow and black Swallowtails. Scarlet Tips. Tiny orange Skippers. Whereas auntie's hallway had little to offer in comparison. A row of hooks on which were mounted a monochromatic array of winter wear – which screamed dullness as soon as you saw it. An umbrella-stand with two black brollies in it. And a hall chair covered in dark-brown baize. The only potential to lighten the scene, give the hallway some colour and lift the spirits was the space on the wall opposite the coats. A space to position a painting. Something cheerful. Van Gogh's *Sunflowers* perhaps. Or a seaside scene, filling the canvas with vibrant strokes of turquoise water, waves tipped white, offset by sunlit sand on which laughing, rosy-cheeked children made castles. Even the *Laughing Cavalier* might have jollied things up a bit though he might have had a hard job doing so.

And Auntie did indeed have a picture there. A crucifixion scene. Christ writhing on a cross. His face creased in agony. At his feet, followers, their faces full of woe. Full of anguish. Full of despair. It made the hall intimidating. Made you thankful for small mercies in your journey across it. To genuflect or cross yourself whenever you passed the picture if you were that way inclined.

Chloe's life passed peacefully enough at the foot of the stairs. It was always fascinating to watch as she fixed her eyes independently on a fly ahead of her on a branch. The way she'd creep forward, claw in front of claw. Then stop. Poised ready to strike. Mouth suddenly opening. Tongue suddenly whipping out, uncoiling from the front of her mouth to stretch and strike the fly. Recoiling swiftly with fly pinned at the tip of it.

She did have her grey days. Maybe her surroundings didn't suit her sufficiently. Put her in a bad mood. Or maybe it was just the sight of Auntie coming down the stairs each morning, hair in curlers, face pack on, housecoat tucked tightly around her as she edged around Chloe's terrarium on her way out to the kitchen for the first cup of tea of the day and first cigarette. One early October morning, I discovered Chloe had turned from grey to black and was lying in the sand on the bottom of the terrarium, drained of colour, drained of life.

Naturally, I didn't want Dave to go the same way and so put on a brave face to meet the challenge ahead.

'He's not dehydrated,' Mr Hargreaves was saying. 'See?' He'd pinched the skin on the lower edge of Dave's abdomen. The flap of skin slipped back to normal when he released it. Which wouldn't have happened if he'd been dehydrated. Even I knew that.

'And he's gripping all right. No loss of balance.' Mr Hargreaves pushed the branch gently from side to side. Dave rode with it.

'How's his appetite?' I asked.

'Seems okay. He's still able to catch flies as far as I can tell. Bit difficult as he's so fast at doing it. But the interest is certainly there.' Mr Hargreaves paused. 'Mind you, might be a good idea to check his mouth out. Make sure we've no mouth rot brewing. I have had a look but couldn't see anything. But then I'm not a vet.'

I felt myself redden slightly. Would that make any difference? But actually, I did know all about mouth rot. I'd seen it in several reptiles. A fungal infection that gets into the lining of the cheeks and tongue, eroding the tissues, making it difficult to eat. Only problem was that I hadn't seen it in a chameleon and was unsure of the best way to open Dave's mouth and take a look.

I needn't have worried. Mr Hargreaves was doing it for me. He'd transferred the branch carrying Dave to his left hand; and with the forefinger and thumb of his right hand, he'd squeezed each side of Dave's head just behind his jaws. Those jaws dropped open without a struggle and remained open while Mr Hargreaves maintained the pressure on them; plenty of time for me to have a good look inside, which I did with the aid of the light and magnifying attachment of my auriscope. Tongue, though coiled up like a tight spring, appeared pink and healthy. No white cheese-like patches indictive of diseased tissue. So, no tissue affected by stomatitis bacteria. Likewise, the inside lining of the cheeks and that of the back of the throat: all fine.

'Well, that's a relief,' said Mr Hargreaves when told and released Dave's head from his grip. 'Infectious stomatitis can be a bugger to treat, as I'm sure you know. Those 50 mg per ml per kilo injections over seven days.'

'Er... Yes...' I said feebly. I was beginning to feel a little uncomfortable. A little surplus to requirements. Who needed a vet with the encyclopaedic knowledge this chap seemed to have?

However, it was still my duty to reach some sort of conclusion. Some sort of diagnosis. But what?

'I've been scratching my head as well,' said Mr Hargreaves as if reading my mind. 'Just wondering if it might be due to one of the nemathelminths.'

The thought might have crossed my mind if I knew what they were.

'Roundworms to you and me,' added Mr Hargreaves, seeing my thinly disguised puzzlement. Though my puzzlement became less disguised, my face a full-blown picture of puzzlement, when he went on to explain that it rather depended on the transmission of the migrating worms as to how it affected particular species of chameleon.

'Take *Rhabdias gemellipara* for example.'

I'd rather I didn't. Such a mouthful.

'That chameleon gets affected in its lungs. Not like Dave here.

Well, that's a relief, I thought.

'No. Dave's more like *Physalopteroides chamaeleonia.*'

'Oh, really?' I squeaked.

'Stomach.'

Mine was feeling queasy.

'Though one can't rule out those that affect the likes of *Hexametra angustaecoides.* Their intestines.'

Mine were loosening by the minute.

'So, you need to know what's going on.'

I did know. 'Do excuse me a moment,' I said to Mr Hargreaves. 'I need to use the loo. Be back in a jiff.'

When I returned, Dave had been returned to his vivarium; and Mr Hargreaves was holding a specimen jar which he waved at me. 'A stool sample from Dave for you to check out. See what worms you come up with.'

'Just the job,' I replied, the pun unintentional.

And indeed, it did the job. Laboratory examination of the sample showed Dave was suffering from a low-grade level of roundworms. Not a parasite liable to affect internal organs. And not a serious infestation. Just enough to put him out of sorts. Under the weather. Not himself. As Mr Hargreaves had put it. And fortunately, easily treatable with a subcutaneous injection of a drug called Ivermectin.

Dave's grey days were to become a thing of the past even if I'd made heavy weather of diagnosing his problem.

Mr Hargreaves was to be our saviour some months later. Riding in like St George, banner waving, sword flashing. Ready to do battle with a rather unusual patient that I'd been presented with.

It was a Tuesday in early May. Beryl perched on her stool over the reception computer, raven-hair in tidy wings each side of her head. Her jaws rotating in methodical rhythm over a toffee she was attempting to chew. Other than that cow-like cud movement, her composure was completely unflappable. With the merest flicker of her hooded eyelids, she looked up at me as I walked into reception and said between chews, 'I've got an interesting case coming in for you this afternoon.'

I waited as another chew came and went. 'I've booked you in to see a dragon.'

'What on earth do you mean?' I exclaimed, immediately conjuring up an image of some fire-belching monster storming into my consulting room.

'You'll find out soon enough.' Oh, dear. Beryl was in one of her enigmatic moods. A time when she would choose her words for maximum obscure impact. Perhaps today, that should have been "chews", bearing in mind the said sweet gliding around her gums at that moment. In my two years at Prospect House, I'd learnt to play along with her moods whenever they arose. Never do battle as you'd never win. Not so Eric.

'Dragon? What's this about a dragon?' he queried, popping his head around the reception door, his bald pate glowing, his eyes twinkling behind his glasses.

'It's an appointment I've booked for Paul,' said Beryl, glowering at him with her good eye.

'My... My... Sounds fun. Who's bringing it in? St George?'

Beryl began to smoulder.

'What's wrong with it? Burnt itself out?' Eric caught my eye and winked. *Careful, Eric. Forget about dragons, you're playing with fire here.*

'Very funny, I don't think,' snapped Beryl.

'Well, whatever, Paul,' said Eric, ignoring her. 'Have a box of matches to hand just in case.' With that, he smartly backed out of reception and retreated down the corridor whistling the tune from *Light My Fire*.

'Some people never grow up,' seethed Beryl, turning to furiously stab her red-painted talons at the tabs on her keyboard.

So, none the wiser, I awaited with baited – if not fiery – breath the arrival of said dragon.

I would like to say it landed with a thump on my consulting table in a cloud of smoke. In reality, it slid onto my table in a small oblong wooden box with a mesh-gridded door panel at one end, secured in place with a catch. So, for a start, I knew it wasn't going to be a very large dragon. *Ha... Ha... Very funny, Paul.*

Two lads around 12 years of age brought it in. Both wore Harry Potter T-shirts patterned with Hogwarts' characters – though I couldn't spot a dragon amongst them. I wondered from where they had conjured up this creature and asked them.

'It was on a bus,' said one freckle-faced boy, half his face dwarfed by black-framed spectacles.

'A bus?'

'Yes, a bus. You know. One you wait for at a bus stop.'

Was the lad winding me up here? He looked a picture of innocence. But I suspected he was streetwise. Especially if it involved a bus passing down it.

'The number ten,' said the other lad, shoving a lock of lank fair hair back from his forehead.

My puzzled look prompted him to add, 'The one that goes down to Westcott Pier,' as if that would make it clearer. It didn't.

Further probing revealed that the creature had been left on the bus in this carrying crate. The two lads had discovered it. They told the driver they'd bring it here so that the owner, once realising it had been left on board, could phone us to come and collect it. I did wonder whether that would happen, rather suspecting the creature had more likely been abandoned.

I peered in through the mesh door and could just make out a lizard-like reptile, sandy coloured, with a flat body and broad triangular head, at the back of which was a row of spiny scales.

'It's a bearded dragon,' piped up the bespectacled lad.

'Really?' I remarked, impressed by his knowledge. *What a clever lad.*

'Yes,' added his mate. 'Says so on the back here.' He spun the crate around and pointed to the label stuck on the other end. It stated, "Dino. I'm a bearded dragon."

Ah, not that clever, then.

'In case you're going to ask, we can't,' said bespectacled lad.

'What?'

'Keep it.'

Ah, I was going to ask. 'Neither of you?'

Two heads shook.

'We've got a cat,' said one head. 'Always bringing in birds, mice. Soon make a meal of him if he escaped.'

'And my mum hates things like 'em,' said the other head. 'Bad enough seeing 'em on the telly, like. For real… well…'

'It would do her head in,' said his mate.

'Go stark raving nuts.'

'Freak 'er out.'

'Okay… Okay…' I interrupted. I'd got the picture fair and square.

The boys wouldn't be allowed to keep it.

Hence, that lunchtime, I found myself down in the office, Dino on my shoulder, nibbling a piece of watercress I'd extracted from my baguette. Beryl had been about to join me but shuddered to a halt at the doorway, a thunderous black look on her face. Clearly, she had no desire to share her lunch with a dragon. The feeling seemed to be mutual as Dino bobbed his head up and down and the skin on his throat turned black. Something that occurs when stressed or when these lizards see a potential rival.

'Dragon meets dragon, eh?' said Eric, breezing into the office just as Beryl disappeared down the corridor to no doubt have her customary lunchtime fag out in the back garden. 'You keeping him?'

'No way,' I replied, shaking my head vigorously. 'Willow Wren is already bulging at the seams with rescue animals. Besides which, Lucy's cat would just see Dino as a tasty snack.' Echoes of bespectacled lad there.

'Mr Hargreaves then?'

'You know, I think you may be right.'

It seemed the obvious choice. So, Mr Hargreaves it was who came to collect him.

'Splendid specimen of a *Pogona vitticeps*,' he declared, waving a spindly arm at the lizard.

Dino responded by waving a spindly front leg at him – another mannerism of bearded dragons. Clearly, these two were going to be brothers-in-arms. Spindly ones or otherwise.

If I thought my association with creepy crawlies was over, I was sadly mistaken. Beryl made sure of that. A good example was Mr Spencer – the proud owner of a tarantula called Tammy. Trouble was I could never consider myself as the vet proud to be tending to the ailments of such a creature – a *Brachypelma,* as Mr Hargreaves would have it. I didn't mind administering to the needs of familiar pets. Doing my St Francis of Assisi bit for them. Exhibit my caring nature. Show my compassion for God's creatures by soothing the brow of a febrile dog before ramming a thermometer up its backside; or stroking the wings of a poorly pigeon. But a spider? Especially one as big as Mr Spencer's tarantula? What was I supposed to do there? Show empathy for it with a quick tickle under its fangs? Shake-a-paw one of its eight legs? The mere thought made me bristle. Much like the tarantula had done when I had first met it. During that meeting, I managed to determine Tammy was under the weather as a result of ecdysis. Once he had shed his outer skeleton, he felt much better. Bigger. Better. More beastly.

When a second appointment was later required, Mr Spencer had insisted on seeing me. I was the guy who related to Tammy. Felt for him. *Really? What a show I must have put on. Enough to make your skin crawl if not the spider's.* This time it was a different story. But same spider. Just as beastly. It nestled in Mr Spencer's huge hand, its legs dangling over his fingers before it decided to crawl down onto the table.

'I'm concerned about the white spots Tammy's developed on his undercarriage,' said Mr Spencer.

When he flipped the spider over to show me, my stomach flipped as well. Between us and the info Mr Spencer had printed off the internet, we decided the spots were due to a fungal infection. Treatment being Gentian Violet dabbed on them. Environment to be dried up a bit to lessen the damp conditions that had allowed the fungus to grow. *Good old Google!*

During that consultation, I did learn a bit more about spiders.

Not that it really helped when I spotted one weaving across our carpet that evening while Lucy and I were watching a dancing contest on the TV. The spider shot out from under the settee and did a Paso Doble across the carpet.

'Hey, look at that!' cried Lucy, pointing.

'A well-executed high kick,' I declared as the spider stopped to wave two of his eight legs before disappearing under the TV.

'No, I meant the spider, not the dancer,' muttered Lucy, curling her legs back up on the settee. Meanwhile, Emily and Bertie had scooted across to sniff eagerly under the screen, rear ends up, tails wagging.

I told Lucy about the tarantula I'd seen earlier in the day, imparting some of the information Mr Spencer had given me.

'Did you know that when they walk, there are always four legs on the ground and four off it at any one time?' I said.

The grunt she gave, her eyes remaining glued to the dancing, indicated her lack of interest.

I still prattled on. 'Luckily, the one I saw today didn't stop to lean back on his haunches, and raise his head and legs. That would have been his attack mode.'

Still little response from Lucy, other than to comment favourably on the next dancer who was executing a tango in much the same way as an attacking tarantula – rearing his back, raising his head, kicking out his legs smartly. Though I doubted he'd turn his back on his partner and squirt a nasty liquid in her face as a tarantula might have done. Perish the thought.

Coincidently, there'd been an article in the newspaper that morning about the large influx of spiders we were currently having. Males were coming indoors in search of mates. Hence, the spider that had just disappeared under our TV. A giant house spider – *Eratigena atrica* – to give it its Latin name. Twelve centimetres in size, dark orange-brown in colour. The most common critter to invade our homes. Seems it's the urge to seek out a mate that brings them in. And suddenly, they're everywhere.

I could also have told Lucy that it's because the females rarely leave their nests that the males have to scurry around looking for them. Webs are spun in corners, between boxes in cellars, behind cupboards, in attics and near window openings. We've a big one in the cables behind our TV. No doubt that's where our spider was heading to have a passionate knees-up with a mate – and as they have 48 kneecaps, that could be very passionate.

'Well, I wish he'd bugger off elsewhere,' said Lucy when I told her of our spider's intentions.

As to stopping them from waltzing into our homes in the first place, that was tricky. The newspaper article informed me that spiders are able to squeeze themselves through tiny gaps and holes, so it's impossible to completely proof your house against them.

The article also mentioned the false widow spider – *Steatoda nobilis*. These are only two centimetres wide, dark brown with a bulbous abdomen, but are Britain's most venomous spider. Though not deadly like the black widows of Australian notoriety, their bite is not pleasant. Symptoms range from a numb sensation to severe swelling and discomfort. In serious cases, there can be various levels of burning or chest pains which will depend on the amount of venom injected.

Seemed one such arachnid had been spotted locally here in Westcott. A fact that had Lucy scooting quickly out to make sure the back door was firmly closed and all windows fastened.

The next day, I was instructed to do an exhaustive vacuuming of the entire cottage, with the extension nozzle fitted to target sheltered spots and corners of the ceilings.

'Well, we can't be too careful, can we?' said Lucy. 'Who wants to get bitten when we can avoid it if we do a bit of extra cleaning?'

I noted the "we" as *I* continued that extra cleaning.

But at least I was ensuring no webs were being spun and that there were no dead flies or other small crawling insects around for any spiders to feed on.

Lucy went on the internet to see if there were any other things "we" could be doing to lessen the risk of "her" being ravished by a rampaging false widow.

Hence, "I" found myself purchasing several tubes of ready-mixed filler, and "me" squirting it into gaps around pipework and skirting boards throughout Willow Wren.

Lucy learnt of another way to limit spider influxes. Reduce lighting. Insects are drawn to light, and flies and moths are perfect spider fodder. So, reducing outside lighting would, in theory, reduce the number of spiders around.

'Seems sensible,' I said. 'And will save on electricity.'

So, I did attempt that with the light that illuminated the gate as you came around the side of the cottage. It was a dark corner and did need to be lit up in order to see your way across to the front door.

'What the hell do you think you're doing?' yelled Lucy one evening later in the week. She'd been suddenly plunged into darkness while coming through the gate having just put the recycling bins out. I'd switched off the lights thinking she was already indoors. As a consequence, she stepped into an unseen Emily poo (one missed for eating by the spaniel) and stomped in leaving a trail of faeces across the floor. The result? A foul tempered, foul-smelling fiancée. That sort of smell wouldn't deter spiders.

But it seems the smell of citrus fruits like lemon, or eucalyptus, tea tree and peppermint oils would. So said the internet, Lucy discovered.

'We could give it a go,' she said.

"I" found myself rubbing lemon peel around all of the cottage's window and doorframes. Didn't make the slightest bit of difference.

When our giant house spider reappeared a couple of evenings later, Lucy demanded its instant capture. She noted my doubtful look.

'Not scared, are you?'

'No, no. Of course not.' But I was. Just a little uneasy.

I resorted to using the standard "tumbler and a stiff piece of card" technique. But house spiders can move at a rate of knots and our current visitor was the Usain Bolt of the arachnid world and sped away before I'd barely dropped to my knees. So, I missed him. Likewise, on several more attempts over the ensuing days.

It was Lucy who provided the solution. No, she didn't do the trapping herself – surprise, surprise – but purchased a more effective device for "me" to do so. It was called My Pink Pals Bug Buster, conjuring up the image of some sort of sex toy.

'What on earth...?' I faltered when she first flashed the long vacuum tube at me with a flourish worthy of Darth Vader in *Star Wars.*

'It will suck it up,' she explained, switching the gadget on before prodding me with it. 'The spider, Paul,' she added, seeing the worried look I was giving her.

The device consisted of a 64 cm long tube, handheld and battery-powered, enabling me to vacuum up spiders safely at arm's length. Then a quick release outside without the need to touch them.

'Now, matey, let's be having you,' I muttered, poking my buster around the back of the TV as I danced around it.

It did indeed prove a quick step to success.

10
Parrot Patter

I'm not too sure how I came to be the parrot man at Prospect House. Perhaps it has something to do with the fact that as a lad, we had an African Grey parrot called Polly – yes, I know, a *very* original name. And when first qualified as a vet, I had to operate on my dear friend – 23 years shared by then. She'd developed a growth on her neck. The local vet in Bournemouth where my parents lived at the time said it was inoperable. Nothing he could do. Well, I couldn't let those 23 years of companionship just slip away, could I? So, I decided to have a go myself and actually operated on Polly to remove the growth on my parents' kitchen table. And yes, Polly did survive. And yes, it did give me confidence in my attempts to treat other parrots that were to fly into my surgery at Prospect House.

And many did; Mr Drummond's Aggie being a good example. Though the first confrontation I had with him and his parrot was far from good.

It was in reception I first set eyes on David Drummond, when he had come in to enquire whether there was a parrot expert in the hospital. There was a rather huffy-puffy nature about him. He reminded me of one of those vintage traction engines you see at steam rallies. Once cranked up, all rattle, shudder and puffs of steam. The image was reinforced by a ruddy complexion that positively glowed coals and wisps of white hair that curled from each of his nostrils.

'So, you deal with the parrots then?' he barked when Beryl pointed at me, his brow creasing like a winter's furrowed field. And before I could reply, he'd already quizzed me further.

I eventually managed to say something but it was not to his liking. 'I have treated the odd parrot or two,' was my comment.

'There's nothing odd about my scarlet macaw, I can tell you,' was his reply.

Huh... Huh... I could see where this was heading and I didn't like what I was seeing.

Mr Drummond's three chins quivered; saliva glistened on his lips. Then momentarily, his mask slipped, his shoulders drooped, his voice softened. 'Though Aggie is proving to be a bit of a handful.' He raised his right hand. Two fingers had plasters on them. 'I know, I know,' he growled. 'You don't have to tell me.'

No, I didn't, I thought. *You're going to tell me yourself.* And he did.

'Scarlet macaws are known to be nippy. But then, I didn't want a cuddly cockatoo. And I understand Amazon parrots are hormonal. But I expect you know that being a parrot man.'

Hormonal eh? I wondered. What on earth did he mean? But I didn't dare ask for fear of exposing my rather patchy knowledge of parrots and risk being shot down in a blaze of facts.

'So, what do you suggest I do?' he queried.

'Sorry?'

'About Aggie.'

It was Beryl who intervened.

'I think it best if a visit were booked so that Mr Mitchell can assess Aggie's behavioural problems in her home environment,' she said, giving Mr Drummond a fixed 'I hate your guts but you are a client' smile.

Strewth. Where did Beryl suddenly dig that up from? Had I missed something?

'Am I right, Paul?'

'Er... Well... Yes...'

'I'm sure you'd agree, Mr Drummond?' said Beryl, the smile still rigid on her face.

'Of course, my dear,' replied Mr Drummond. 'You're the experts. I can only go by your advice.'

Hey. Hang on a minute. Where was I in all of this?

Turned out I was to be up a wet, slippery pathway to Mr Drummond's terraced house one gloomy March morning. I rang his front door bell and heard a raucous screech from within followed by a snarled 'Shut up.'

On opening the door, Mr Drummond, his cheeks reddened, ushered me into a front room dominated by a large, metallic cage in one corner and a T-perch in the other. On the latter sat a scarlet macaw: a fine specimen with her vivid plumage and white facemask which, at this particular moment in time, seemed rather flushed. But I didn't need to be much of a parrot man to realise she was angry. Her head was dropped. Her beak open. The feathers on her shoulders and upper part of her back fluffed up. Wings slightly away from her body, tail fanned. Boy, was she pumped up. Everything about her screamed "I'm in a paddy." And just in case I hadn't cottoned on to this fact, she emitted a long, deep growl as I approached her. Enough to stop me in my tracks. I screeched to a halt. She just screeched.

'Not afraid of her, are you?' barked Mr Drummond, waving his hand at me. I noticed three fingers were now plastered.

'Er... well... she does seem a little agitated,' I ventured to say.

Mr Drummond suddenly sat down at a table and rammed his fist on it. 'Well, if you're not, I certainly am,' he confessed. 'It's all getting out of hand.' He stroked his three bandaged fingers. 'I have tried showing her who's boss.'

Ouch. That was something I didn't want to hear. But hear it I did when Mr Drummond went on to explain he'd tried yelling at Aggie. Tried saying, 'No bite.' Tried shaking a finger at her – only to have it bitten. He hadn't tried beak grabbing and shaking. For obvious reasons.

'I've even dropped her on the floor,' he confessed. 'In the hope that she'd be thankful I was around for her to climb back up again. But not a bit of it. Or should that be bite.' He gave a rueful smile. 'Oh, and before you ask, I have tried putting her back in her cage. But of course, what does she do?' He held up the recently plastered finger.

There was no need to tell Mr Drummond that punishment was not going to modify Aggie's behaviour. His finger count was proof of that.

So, what was to be done? I had to be careful. As tactful as possible. I had combed the internet before this visit. Took some printouts. Now I sat down opposite Mr Drummond, took a deep breath, and started to spout.

'It's all to do with positive reinforcement,' I said. 'You need to avoid circumstances that elicit aggression from Aggie.' That was according to one of my printouts. Another had given me a list of such circumstances to go through. On questioning Mr Drummond, one in particular stood out.

'It's when Aggie doesn't want to go back in her cage,' he explained.

Ah, right. There we had it. Now, according to my internet info, a number of options were at hand. Not that I mentioned "hand" to Mr Drummond. It was a sore point – or rather finger – with him at that moment.

'You could just let Aggie stay out of the cage,' I said.

Mr Drummond shook his head. 'Not safe when I have visitors.'

Aggie emitted a vicious growl to emphasise the point.

'Maybe move the T-perch over to the cage and let her crawl in?'

'Tried it. She refused.'

'Well, then you must go for positive reinforcement that I mentioned.' *(so said the internet)*

Mr Drummond sighed.

I persevered. 'You must reinforce good behaviour and ignore bad behaviour.' *(internet again)* I went on to explain that Mr Drummond should feed Aggie a titbit such as a peanut whenever his hand was near her and she didn't bite. Also, this could be used to lure her onto his hand. I also explained how to teach Aggie cooperation, to be done in small steps. *(guess where that came from)* I saw his doubtful look. Fortunately, he didn't see mine as I slithered back down the path afterwards, Aggie's screeches ringing in my ears.

I was in the local charity shop a week later, rummaging through the half-price Christmas cards, wondering whether I really wanted a robin with a woolly hat on, when I spotted Mr Drummond browsing through the bookshelf. I saw him fumble with a book due to a heavily bandaged hand. He turned and saw me standing there.

'Aggie?' I said, staring at his hand in dismay. They must still be at loggerheads.

He shook his head and held up his plastered fingers. 'This was due to a chisel. But Aggie's a bit better. Least I haven't been bitten again. As yet. Fingers crossed.' He held up two unbandaged ones.

I was definitely feeling down in the dumps one morning.

'What's new?' I could hear Lucy saying. Grumpy old man syndrome, eh? And I'm only 25 years old. God knows what I'll be like in 50 years' time. I suspect a right old grouch. Anyway, like I said, I was down in the dumps. No particular reason. Just one of those days. A touch of the January blues even though it was April. Beryl noticed my mood and was quick to comment on it. But that was typical of her. Never slow in coming forward.

'If you don't mind me saying,' she said, giving me one of her customary laser-looks, 'I think you need bucking up.'

Ah, here we go, I thought. *In need of a holiday. Should get away. Things are getting on top of me. Blah. Blah. Blah.*

'This might help.' Beryl had a leaflet in her vermilion-clawed hand which she now waved at me. 'It's a bird-taming workshop. It's an American expert. He's some sort of bird whisperer.'

It ignited a spark of interest. American eh? Here could be an excuse to fly off to Florida for a week to attend a parrot convention. Yes. That could be just what I needed.

'Where's it being held?' I asked, thinking Florida in April could be pleasant.

'Clapham,' replied Beryl. Ah. Not quite the sunny resort I had in mind. 'This chap's rather famous apparently,' she went on. 'Cornelius Bergman. Heard of him?' Beryl gave me another of her penetrating stares – one of those which could wheedle out your innermost thoughts.

No use pretending I'd heard of this chap then. So, I shook my head. Beryl proceeded to enlighten me, reading from the leaflet. 'It says, "People call him a miracle worker and compare his demonstrations to magic. They come from all over America to bring their parrots to him. It's like a modern-day pilgrimage hoping this new holy man of bird taming can lay his hands on their pets and make them loveable again".'

'Pah,' I said. 'All that sounds a bit over the top.' I felt an instant and unreasonable dislike for the man. Holy man of bird taming indeed. I muttered, 'I'll think about it,' then promptly forgot about him in the rush of afternoon surgery. Only for him to resurface when David Drummond, the owner of that scarlet macaw, Aggie, strode briskly into reception. My heart sank. Why, I'd only just seen him the previous month and hoped I'd sorted out the aggression that Aggie had been exhibiting. But when Mr Drummond held up his freshly bandaged finger, I knew that I hadn't succeeded.

'I'm none too happy,' growled Mr Drummond, wagging his Elastoplastered appendage at me. 'Aggie's reverted to her old ways. Can't lay a finger on her. As you can see.' His plastered one was shoved in my face. Seemed there was no getting away from it. Neither the finger nor Aggie's aggression. 'So, what are you going to do about it?' A glob of spittle sprayed in my face. 'I need answers.' *(Help! Internet, where are you?)*

I felt a tic throb in my forehead. My heart thumped against my ribs. I had no answers other than telling him to stuff his parrot. Another of Beryl's stares made any such words wither on my tongue.

It was she who said, 'Mr Mitchell's just been telling me about this American Bird Whisper who's over here to do a workshop. He immediately thought of you and your Aggie.'

I did? She saw my quizzical look. 'You did, didn't you, Mr Mitchell?' Another look torpedoed in my direction.

'Well, yes, it did cross my mind,' I spluttered. *(it hadn't)*

'And you were going to ask Mr Drummond whether he'd like to accompany you with his Aggie up to Clapham.' *(I wasn't)*

Another torpedo-look defied me to disagree. *(I didn't)*

And thus, two weeks later, I found myself perched on an uncomfortable seat at the back of a function room in a hotel just off Clapham Common with a flock of fellow onlookers, chirruping and shuffling as if settling to roost for the night. The chatter was very animated. Cornelius Bergman was a marvel. Cornelius Bergman was a master. Though an unwilling listener, I was forced to learn that he gave his training techniques catchy titles such as "bubble of fear", "the swipe" and "crystal ball". My own crystal ball predicted it would take a lot to convince me of his abilities to be the Pied Piper for psittacines.

As for Aggie. Well, there she was. Glowering at the front. Perched next to Mr Drummond. Alongside were two other parrots awaiting their baptisms of fire. A spotlight suddenly played on the stage and onto it bounded the man who was to make it all happen. Cornelius Bergman. He didn't have the horns and forked tail that I half-expected. Instead, we were presented with a mild-mannered man in spectacles, wearing jeans and black T-shirt.

Aggie was the first parrot to be manhandled. Cornelius put on a pair of gloves and then to a few gasps, opened the bird's cage, grasped the parrot by a leg and hauled her out amid a torrent of abuse. Once perched on his hand, Aggie tried to jump off several times. Each time, Cornelius held onto a leg and let his hand fall with the leg and then swung the bird back onto his hand. This happened over and over again; Aggie swinging in a circle each time. She eventually ran out of oomph and panting, remained perched on his hand. But not for long. She suddenly decided to make a break for it by scuttling up Cornelius's arm.

'Oh, no you don't, my pretty,' he drawled as he nonchalantly blocked her route with a flicker of his other gloved hand. She lunged out to bite him. He lunged back with a poke at her feet until she stopped. Wow. What feisty stuff. All so different to my softly-softly approach. Eventually, Aggie gave in and sat obediently on Cornelius's hand. Begrudgingly, I was impressed. David Drummond, meanwhile, seemed transfixed. Rooted to his seat as his beloved Aggie was subdued into submission. 'That's just amazing,' he gasped.

But that wasn't the end of it. A real showmanship piece followed. Cornelius removed a glove and tried to stroke Aggie on her back. She of course was having none of it. She whipped from side to side, eyeing the approaching hand. Then to my astonishment, Cornelius offered his bare forefinger. I thought of Mr Drummond's bandaged ones. But somehow, Cornelius managed to fold his thumb over Aggie's beak and push the lower mandible away to lessen the impact of the bite.

'See,' he said, walking down to the front row. 'She thinks she's got stuck.' His forefinger and her beak seemed glued together. After several minutes, he released her beak. He then offered his finger again.

Fool, I thought. *She'll lash out.* But she didn't. On the contrary, she just pushed it away, seemingly uninterested. The finale had Aggie perched on a stand while Cornelius placed his hands, palms out, against an imaginary ball around the bird. 'Her bubble of fear,' he called it. Intoning to himself and intensely watching the parrot, he gradually shrank his hands in. Within a couple of minutes, Cornelius was able to scratch the base of Aggie's tail. He then moved his palm close up to her face. She didn't flinch. Completely mesmerised. He touched her beak. No hiss. No bite. With his palm resting on her beak, he moved his other hand around and started to scratch the top of her head.

A spontaneous ripple of applause broke out from the audience, especially from David Drummond, his bandaged hands furiously flapping together. I, too, found myself clapping. Spellbound, my spirits lifted. And it was a spell that wasn't broken even when the next day, Beryl subjected me to one of her "I told you so" looks.

'Hey, Paul,' exclaimed Beryl one early summer's day, 'I've got Mr Hargreaves coming in to see you this afternoon. And guess what he's bringing in?'

Oh, dear. Surely not charades time again? Please, please, no. I couldn't stomach the thought of Beryl playing party games at tea break, bunny-hopping or bat-flapping around the office, trying to make me guess what was I was going to see. Besides which, if it was Mr Hargreaves, it was most likely to be some sort of reptile or amphibian. Possibly Dave, his chameleon. The thought of Beryl trying to depict him, eyes rolling independently, tongue darting out to catch an imaginary fly was enough to make me turn grey on the spot, even if Dave didn't. In the event, it was an animal that was more of a mouthful than an eyeful to describe.

'Here's my *Melopsittacus undulatus* to have her beak trimmed,' quipped Mr Hargreaves as he slid a cage containing a green and yellow budgerigar onto my consulting table. Even then, it wasn't typical as Mr Hargreaves was quick to inform me.

'It's a spangle light green,' he said. 'As you can see, this mutation primarily affects the markings rather than the body colouration.'

Yes, well, it just looked like a pretty budgie to me. Of course, I didn't say that. Just merely nodded as Mr Hargreaves continued to expound on the barring and throat spots this bird had. And how this mutation had first appeared in Victoria, Australia, in 1972.

And now appeared here in my surgery in 2005, I was tempted to add. But no. I'd be accused of taking the mickey. 'Sorry?' I said, suddenly jolting out of my reverie.

'He's called "Mickey",' Mr Hargreaves was saying, giving me a funny look. But even then, I didn't escape lightly. He had with him an accompanying exotic for my perusal. His new batch of *Trituris vulgaris*. It took me several minutes of searching the tangle of weeds in his aquarium before I spotted the newts.

A few months later, he presented me with another challenge. In a cage, at one end of a perch, huddled some sort of parrot. Green-plumaged with bare, grey skin around the eyes.

'My *Ara nobilis*,' declared Mr Hargreaves.

'A conure?' I ventured to guess. Should have kept my mouth shut.

Mr Hargreaves tutted. 'No, sir. It's a macaw.'

'Bit on the small size.' Maybe that was what was wrong with the bird. Stunted growth. Undernourished.

There was another tut from Mr Hargreaves. Clearly, I wasn't impressing him. 'It's a Hahn's macaw. They're the smallest of the macaws. But I'm sure you knew that.'

I didn't. But Mr Hargreaves was sure telling me. 'And you can tell it's a Hahn's macaw from that prominent area of bare skin around his eyes. It leaves no doubt about its correct identification.'

Yes. Well, I wasn't going to utter another word.

Likewise, the Hahn's macaw. Seemed he had lost his voice. I suspected a touch of laryngitis and prescribed a short course of antibiotic in the drinking water. It seemed to do the trick.

The next parrot to be brought in was an attractive creature. It had a rich blue head and chest. The rest of the plumage was an iridescent green which gleamed in the July sunshine that was pouring in through the consulting room window and making the room as steamy as a South American jungle from where I assumed this parrot's forbearers had originated.

'What a nice blue-headed parrot,' I said.

'Ah, so you know a *Pionus menstruus* when you see one,' responded Mr Hargreaves enthusiastically.

No. Not at all. I'd been merely describing the parrot. The fact that I'd inadvertently given the correct name was just a fluke. But I wasn't going to let Mr Hargreaves know that, was I? After all, wasn't I supposed to be the parrot man of Prospect House? A fountain of information *(all pouring off the internet)*.

'Well, they are one of the best-known species in aviculture,' Mr Hargreaves went on, rather dampening the moment.

'And the problem?' I asked.

'It's his eye-ring. See?'

I could see. It was decidedly swollen. In fact, both rings were.

'A blockage of the nares, I'd say,' said Mr Hargreaves.

Once again, I didn't have to say another word. He was right.

'Antibiotic again?' queried Mr Hargreaves.

I nodded. *What next?* I wondered.

I didn't have to wonder for long.

Towards the end of July, a decidedly stressed African Grey was plonked on my consulting table.

'My *Psittacus erithacus* is very under the weather,' said an equally agitated Mr Hargreaves, his bony fingers stretching and curling in with concern. 'It's not at all like Polly to be so quiet.'

'Polly?' I said.

'Not a very original name for a *Psittacus erithacus,* I know,' replied Mr Hargreaves, looking red-faced. Very hot and bothered. And not just on account of the weather. 'I fear Polly's egg-bound. And that's despite giving her plenty of additional sources of calcium. You know. Cuttlefish and the like.'

Polly was showing the classical signs. She'd fluttered to the bottom of her cage. Her abdomen had dropped. She was straining.

'I haven't tried easing the egg out,' continued Mr Hargreaves. 'Too afraid it would break in her oviduct. Cause peritonitis.'

Clearly, Mr Hargreaves was well genned up on the condition. Fast broadband with good internet access, no doubt.

But one thing he hadn't tried was putting her in a heated cage.

'It might just do the trick,' I said, crossing my fingers discretely behind my back. I had such a cage down in the hospital. So, Polly was whisked down to the ward and carefully transferred across to the cage with its heated tray. An anxious half an hour ensued. Would she? Wouldn't she? Yes. She did. The egg shelled out without me having to intervene.

'You didn't have to egg her on then,' said Beryl, without the flicker of a smile. Had she intended the pun?

'The yolk would have been on me if I'd had to,' I replied with a grin.

A smile then did crack on her face.

A few weeks later, a new client turned up with a conure. He had an adoring owner who doted on him. And the parrot reciprocated.

'Jack lets me do anything with him,' murmured Sophie Hicks, a vivacious, slim-waisted woman in her mid-twenties with a halo of shimmering chestnut hair that cascaded down over her shoulders. She reached into the cage and ran a well-manicured nail down the conure's back. He gave a shiver of pleasure. 'He'll roll over in my hand and let me tickle his tummy,' she added. 'He simply adores it.'

I bet he does, I thought. *Who wouldn't?*

'It was love at first sight,' she went on. 'I saw him in the local garden centre, hunched over his seed bowl, looking thoroughly miserable.'

I momentarily thought of me in my student days, hunched over my bowl of cereal each morning. Yes, I knew the feeling.

But at that time, there was no young lady like this Sophie to cheer me up with a tummy tickle.

'My heart went out to him,' Sophie was saying, her full lips all of a quiver, a hand clasped to her bosom.

Yes... Yes... I've got the picture now. Thank you, Sophie.

'What's the problem with Jack?'

'I've found a lump on his shoulder,' said Sophie, leaning across the consulting table to give the parrot a look – blue-eyed flecked with gold – that was full of concern.

Jack was a Green Cheeked conure, sleek feathered, alert, fixing me with a dark, beady eye. 'Do you want me to get him out for you?' Sophie added.

'I'll be able to manage, thanks,' I replied. Picking up a towel, I opened the cage and before Jack had the chance to utter "Pieces of Eight", I'd pinned him down and winkled him out, his body wrapped, only his head showing.

'My, my,' purred Sophie. 'I can see you're an expert at handling birds.' She edged up to me. I was enveloped in her perfume – no doubt something with a name like *Desiree or Embolden.* Very distracting. I made an effort to concentrate on my examination of Jack, sliding the towel down to expose his left shoulder, where between the feathers over the upper part of his wing, I located the lump that Sophie had mentioned.

'Can you feel it?' she murmured in a husky breath that fanned my ear.

Boy. Too right. I could indeed feel it. And not just the lump I was holding between my thumb and forefinger. Phew. This Sophie certainly knew how to light my fire.

'So, what can you do about it?' she went on.

Douse it down with a cold hose, I thought. Out aloud I said, 'It's a feather cyst. Nothing too serious. I suggest we leave it alone. But if Jack starts pecking at it, then we'll consider surgery to remove it.'

I quickly bundled the conure back into his cage where he turned and lashed out at my retreating fingers.

'Now, now, Jack,' rebuked Sophie. 'Don't get so het up.'

I knew exactly how he felt.

It was several months before I was to see Sophie again. Months in which to get her out of my mind. But strange as it may seem – especially with having Lucy around – I just couldn't. That's to say the young lady would pop up in my dreams. I had this reoccurring one where I was an Amazon Green strutting up and down Sophie's shoulder, shoving regurgitated peanuts into her ear as a sign of affection. It was really absurd. Taking things too far – peanuts in particular.

So, I challenged Beryl when she informed me Miss Hicks was requesting a home visit.

'Come off it, Beryl,' I admonished. 'You know practice policy is to be seen by appointment.'

Beryl shrugged. 'I do realise that, Paul. And I did try. But she was insistent. And particularly asked for you.' I was given one of those laser-looks look of hers which spoke of sack-loads of peanuts.

It was with some trepidation that I found myself having to make that home visit to see Jack one sunny, sultry August afternoon. The sight of Sophie, in frayed denim shorts and the skimpiest of halter tops, made the temperature soar even higher.

'So good of you to come out,' purred Sophie. 'Being such a hot day, I didn't want Jack getting all hot and bothered in the car.'

Never mind me getting in the same state. Car or no car.

Sophie led me into a lounge, the walls and floor of which were painted white. All very minimalist. Jack's cage stood in one corner. He looked warily at me as I approached.

'So, what's up?' I asked.

'Jack's become so obsessive,' replied Sophie. 'He keeps freaking out.'

'And you can blame it on me,' said a voice over my shoulder.

I turned to see a sun-tanned, Italianate young man with designer-stubbled chin saunter in through the French windows. He was naked, save for a sarong slung low around narrow hips which showed off his toned physique. Ah, yes, I recognised him. The art-class model. Mandy's man.

'My boyfriend, Roberto,' said Sophie, by way of introduction. She slid an arm around his waist and ran a hand over his enviable taut six-pack abs and up through the dark curls on his chest. The reaction from Jack was startling. He leapt onto the bars of his cage and started to shriek and flap his wings.

'See what I mean?' said Sophie. 'I can't lay a finger on Roberto without Jack going into an absolute tizzy. He gets so jealous.'

Uhm… who could blame him? I thought.

'I've tried to make friends with Jack,' drawled Roberto. 'But it hasn't worked.' He held up his right hand, the index finger of which was strapped with Elastoplast.

'And when I let him out, he goes straight for Roberto,' said Sophie. 'My poor sweet. Just look at his back.'

Roberto swivelled to demonstrate the claw marks across his muscular shoulders. Sophie traced a finger over them. Roberto flinched.

'Careful, pet. They still hurt,' he said.

Another torrent of abuse streamed from Jack. My, what a spirited bird. I could almost sympathise with him.

'Have you any suggestions as to what we can do?' purred Sophie.

You could get rid of the boyfriend for a start, I thought. *Come off it, Paul. That's being ridiculous.* I'd be seen as a green-eyed monster. But as I watched Sophie smooth some after-sun lotion onto Roberto's ridiculously well-muscled chest, I did experience a twinge of jealousy. But in true professional style, I outlined an alternative strategy, one I'd previously tried on a crossdressing fireman's parrot. It was to be used in conjunction with covering Jack up at night and not putting him in situations where he was liable to become consumed with jealousy (no hanky-panky in his presence was implied if not spelt out). But it was the dabbing of Sophie's perfume on Roberto that was to be the key factor in reducing

Jack's temper tantrums. Confusing the parrot by the use of some common scents.

11
Finding It Hard to Swallow

I'd been having a problem with a bit of indigestion over the past couple of months. Nothing too serious. But I thought I'd have a quick dig around on the internet just to be on the safe side. And ended up worrying myself silly. From the symptoms described, which matched mine – belching, pain in the chest – it seems I was suffering from GORD – Gastro-oesophageal reflux disease.

'You'll just have to change your diet,' said Lucy. 'No great shakes.'

Hmm… no great sympathy from my fiancée then. Bless her.

Seems there is a whole range of foods unsuitable for people suffering from GORD: garlic, raw onions, minced beef, mashed potatoes, biscuits, crisps and chips.

'Chips. Why chips?' I moaned. I adored thick, crinkly oven chips. And the ban on biscuits evoked another moan. I loved a couple with my cup of tea first thing. But it seemed they were thought to be too fatty for delicate stomachs prone to acidic eruptions. Likewise, many fruits that are too acidic. Among them: oranges, lemons, cranberries, grapefruit and tomatoes.

Herbal tea in the form of camomile was supposed to soothe the stomach lining so I took a deep breath and stopped my favourite strong English breakfast brand in favour of a stewed mug of camomile. It smelt and tasted awful. Apparently, of all the teabags supplied to hotel bedrooms, the only ones that never get stolen are the camomile teas. I now knew why. Yuck.

'You've another problem which doesn't help,' said Lucy.
'Really?'
'You bolt your food down.' Lucy elaborated by printing off a couple of fact sheets from the internet entitled "Why Chewing Your Food Can Change Your Life" and thrust them in my hands. 'This will give you something to chew over.'

Ha, Ha, Lucy. Very funny. But I had to eat my words. Or rather the words in the fact sheets as many of them did make sense. Chewing food breaks it down into smaller particles. It allows the enzymes, amylase and lipase, found in saliva, to begin the digestion of fats and starches. Chewing also alerts the stomach that food is on its way and prepares it to make stomach acid; and having smaller particles to act on, there's a larger surface area for the digestive process to work on.

'Right,' I said as I started reading through the information, finding there was a lot to digest. 'So how many times should I be chewing my food?'

'It tells you at the end,' said Lucy.

I read on. It turned out that with soft foods such as fruit and soft vegetables, I should be chewing them five to ten times, whereas with more dense foods such as meats, that should increase up to 30 times. 'Thirty times!' I exclaimed. 'That's really making a meal of it.'

'It's no joke, Paul,' said Lucy, giving me a reprimanding look.

I did try to follow the advice given together with a change in diet. And yes, it did seem to ease the acid reflux, and avoided me having to make an appointment to see my GP, Dr

Merriweather. Having to wait in that bilious green waiting room would have been enough to make me want to throw up.

Being dietary-based, at least my condition was easily controlled. Not so some cases exhibiting similar symptoms.

Desmond was a case in point.

I was called out one evening to see him as an emergency at the hospital. He was a pug. So typical of his breed, I expected him to be all huff and puff. Full of himself. Big bulbous eyes forever on the lookout for what mischief he could get up to next. Only that evening, when he was brought in, he looked just the opposite. Downright miserable.

'Desmond keeps bringing up his dinner,' said one of the two burly guys that came in with him. Both were wearing grubby grey T-shirts and baggy shorts down to their knees. Both had every inch of exposed skin on necks, arms and legs covered in a forest of black tattoos which, together with heavily bearded jowls and shaven heads, presented a rather menacing gruff duo unlikely to sing your praises if you confronted them on a dark windy night. But this *was* a dark windy night and I was having to confront them and tune into their concerns about Desmond.

One introduced himself as Ken Butcher. Apt name. I could picture him cleaver in hand, ready to sever a side of beef, his own beefy tattooed joints poised, ready to swing into action.

'It's been going on for a couple of hours,' growled his mate, Oliver Robbins, whose stomach, protruding over the waistband of his shorts, suggested his brawn was more of the steak-pudding than the steroid-enhanced variety. 'He's getting quite distressed.' He looked across at Ken who was pounding his chest with a snake-tattooed arm, his face creased with concern, his lips a wobbling slit in the shaggy brown mat that framed them. 'Desmond, that is. But then so are we.'

Meanwhile, Desmond, standing between these two hefty guys, gave a loud snuffle and heaved up a puddle of foam, licking his lips as he deposited it on the consulting room floor.

'There. See? That's what we're talking about.' Oliver swiftly extracted a tissue from his shorts' pocket and bent down to wipe the deposit up before carefully folding the tissue and tiptoeing over to drop it in a nearby waste bin. 'We're *so so* worried about him, aren't we, Ken?'

Ken nodded, unable to speak, hairy fingers in his mouth.

Oliver emitted a little squeak before adding, 'We're frightened he might have got a blockage. That would be just catastrophic. A dreadful worry. Doesn't bear thinking about, does it, Ken?'

Ken couldn't reply, mouth still full of fingers.

I was worried too. But not for that reason. Another possibility topped it. I explained my plan of action to Ken and Oliver. 'I'm going to give Desmond an anti-spasmolytic injection to calm down his vomiting reflex. Okay?'

Both burley guys nodded.

'That should help to settle him,' I continued. 'And I'll keep him in overnight ready for some tests tomorrow. With your permission, of course.'

'Of course,' spluttered Ken, his mouth finally free of fingers.

'Whatever's best for our dear Desmond,' said Oliver, his voice catching with a sonorous sob.

They both bent down to kiss Desmond goodbye, reassuring him that they weren't abandoning him. He would be in safe hands. And not to fret. He'd soon be feeling better. He responded with a slobbery, vomit-flecked lick to each of their cheeks, leaving slivers of slime in their beards as several more kissy-kissy goodbyes were said.

Let's hope you do feel better soon, I thought, as having given Desmond his injection, I led him down to the kennels for his overnight stay. When I'd unclipped his lead and closed the kennel door on him, he looked up at me with those big bulbous eyes of his and gave a final, very loud, very frothy burp.

The next morning, Mandy had already been around, checking on in-patients before I arrived. All done in her customary efficient way. A way which she expected to be echoed by those she worked with. Lucy in particular. Poor Lucy, always did her upmost to comply with Mandy's exacting standards. Not always succeeding. Which occasionally caused tensions between the two of them.

'I see we've this pug in for a barium meal and X-ray,' stated Mandy, flicking through the case history notes I'd clipped to a board outside Desmond's kennel before leaving last night. She glanced at the watch pinned to her uniform breast pocket. 'Shall we make that for 11 o'clock after you've finished morning appointments?' I nodded meekly. 'I'll get Lucy to give him a dose of barium at 10.45. Twenty millilitres should be more than enough, wouldn't you say?'

I didn't say anything. Just another meek nod.

By 11.15, the barium contrast X-rays had been taken, developed and clipped up on the viewing screen, ready for me to study them. Only Mandy had already done so. 'A case of megaoesophagus by the looks of it,' she said as I studied the enlarged food tube on the X-rays, outlined in white by the barium that had been given earlier. Who was I to argue? The look in her damson eyes as she turned to me said it all. She was spot on. And she knew it.

I now had to explain the condition to his owners and tell them what the prognosis was likely to be.

I went on the internet to find out more information about megaoesophagus. Get genned up beforehand. But so had Ken and Oliver, and frankly, they seemed more genned up than me when they arrived to collect Desmond.

It was an effusive reunion.

'Our precious boy,' exclaimed Ken.

'Our sweetie pie,' squealed Oliver.

'Give your daddykins a kiss,' they said in unison as Desmond dashed between the two of them, giving excited little yelps, his curly tail in a constant spin.

'Congenital?' said Ken, raising his eyebrows when he learnt it was a case of megaoesophagus.

'Or idiopathic?' said Oliver, lowering his.

I creased mine together. 'Could be either.'

Whatever, such enlargement of the oesophagus couldn't be rectified. 'Only managed,' I stated. And that consisted of feeding Desmond in an upright position. Carefully. Food rolled up into little balls. Given over a 15-minute period, three to four times a day.

'Absolutely no problem,' declared Ken. 'We'll take it in turns to have him on our laps. Make sure his front legs are raised. Won't we, sweetie?' He turned to his partner.

'He's such a treasure,' said Oliver, looking at Ken.

I assumed they were both referring to Desmond.

He responded with another woof of delight.

I could see this was a dog who adored attention. His future would be secure in the caring hands of Ken and Oliver. A future he was bound to lap up whichever one he sat in.

My GORDS and Desmond's megaoesophagus were reminders of just how sensitive our digestive systems can be. So, it's a wonder that dogs can often eat the most obnoxious and most offensive things possible and yet, get away with it. Why do they do it? I'm often asked the question. But there's never a simple answer. Our adorable Welsh springer was a sweet-natured dog. Very friendly; always wagging the stump of her tail. A wonderful companion. Perfect in every way. Except in the way she made a beeline for any uncollected dog turd to devour it like a savoury sausage. One gulp and it was gone. A lick of the lips. Lovely. Any seconds? I've a mental picture of her out on the back lawn one frosty morning, a poo of her own making from the day before dangling from the side of her mouth as she chomped into its frozen contents. Thoroughly enjoying it.

And Bertie was no better.

There was an episode with slugs. We were being overrun with them. Great shoals? Herds? Battalions? Whatever you call a massive horde of slugs invading your garden in long mucoid trails, devouring everything in their path. I resorted to padding around the garden in flip flops at 6 o'clock of a June morning wearing only my boxer shorts, in one hand a pair of my veterinary forceps and in the other a large bucket of salt water into which I was dropping the slugs, one by one as I prised them up.

'One hundred and two,' I muttered, plucking yet another slimy brown creature from the leaf of a prize salvia.

With the bucket full, I sneaked out into the lane down the side of Willow Wren and tipped the contents into the hedge before anyone had a chance to see me.

Later that morning, the postman left the garden gate open. Never one to miss an opportunity to sneak out, Bertie did just that. He returned after about 30 minutes, looking a little sheepish as he trotted into the kitchen. There, in the middle, he came to a halt and, stretching his neck out, began to heave. One, two, then on the third, a massive gagging sound as he spewed out a foaming slime ball of molluscs onto the floor. My bucketful of slugs. Then, with a final hack and lick of his lips, he gave the pile a cursory sniff before walking over to his water bowl for a drink.

Dogs for you.

I suppose it could have been worse. Henry or Heidi, one of the two boxers owned by Sandra and John Coles over at Ashton Manor, could have been the recipients of my slug hunting endeavours. Least I had been able to keep it "in house" in every sense of the word.

But an intake of a different nature by Heidi presented me with a challenge a week later when Sandra and John turned up for an appointment at Prospect House with her.

Usually, she'd bound into my consulting room, her rump wagging in frenzied greeting, her shining brown eyes full of trust, forever seeking affection. I'd end up being shunted around the room, showered in saliva, licked to death. So that afternoon, in expectation of a similar effusive greeting, I was ready for the temperature in the consulting room to soar despite it being a rather chilly summer's day outside. But it wasn't the case.

The Coles arrived in an extreme state of agitation and with a very dejected Heidi. There was no friendly greeting from the boxer. Her eyes were dull and congested.

'She's not herself, as you can see,' said John.

'And she's been off her food these past couple of days. Which is not like her at all. Normally, she's an absolute gannet. Aren't you, pet?' Sandra crouched to give Heidi a hug, putting her arm around the boxer's neck. Heidi gave her a desultory lick in response.

'Any sickness?' I asked.

'Just a little. This morning,' replied John.

'No other symptoms?'

'Well, we think she might be in a bit of pain,' said Sandra. 'She does seem a bit sort of tucked up.'

I bent down and gave Heidi a reassuring pat on the head. She responded with a feeble lick of my hand. 'Okay, matey, let's see if we can find out what's going on.' Gently, I turned her around and checked her temperature. 'Well, that's normal for a start. Now, let's feel your tummy.'

With her still standing, but with a tremor in her legs, I began to gently knead her abdomen between my fingers, one hand each side of her. Liver, spleen, kidneys. They felt fine. No pain elicited. I gradually worked back towards her tail. It was when I pressed Heidi in her mid-abdominal area that she emitted a barely audible groan. 'Sorry, pet. Did that hurt?' Again, I carefully palpated the spot. Again, it elicited another faint grunt of pain.

In my mind, I swiftly checked the differential diagnoses. Of all on my list, there was one in particular that stood out.

I stood up. 'Heidi hasn't been up to her old tricks by any chance?'

I remembered John once telling me that Heidi had a habit of pinching things. 'That's not unusual,' I'd said at the time. 'Lots of dogs do it.' John went on to explain how it was only things off Sandra's dressing table. Seems Heidi would sneak into the bedroom and whip things off the table. Necklaces, bracelets and lipsticks would go missing, only to be found buried in her dog basket.

'And is there anything missing now?' I asked.

'Well... yes,' admitted Sandra. 'As a matter of fact, two days ago...' She took a deep breath before elaborating. 'But surely, you don't think...?'

I shrugged. 'There's a distinct possibility. The only way of knowing for sure is to get an X-ray and see what shows up.'

Several were taken of Heidi's abdomen and they confirmed my suspicions of a blockage. Something she'd swallowed. In contrast to the murky loops of bowel on the radiograph, there was, clearly visible, a different object: white, round and very distinct.

'There's our culprit,' I murmured, tapping the screen.

Mandy, alongside me, remained quiet for a change. On this occasion, I knew something she didn't. What that object was.

And if I didn't operate to remove it, the bowel could perforate and Heidi die from peritonitis. So really, there was no other option.

She was initially zapped with thiopentone in the prep room, intubated and her abdomen shaved before she was wheeled through to the ops room and slid onto the operating table. There she was connected to the anaesthetic machine, turned on her back, her legs tied to the sides of the table, her shaved area disinfected, ready for me to pin on the green drapes to surround the midline incision I would make. All this was carried out with ruthless efficiency by Mandy. Boy, did she know her stuff. Could never be faulted when it came to operational procedure. All very reassuring when I was wanting to concentrate on the laparotomy I was about to undertake.

'Right, here we go then,' I said, drawing a scalpel firmly down Heidi's midline. I was feeling a little more nervous than usual when about to start an operation. Probably because I knew Heidi so well, and the fact she belonged to good neighbours of ours. Once she was opened up, I slipped a gloved hand inside her. The impacted area of bowel was easily located and drawn out of the wound. I could feel the object through the grey shiny lining of the intestinal wall. Another incision and the object slid out. It was what I'd expected.

Heidi made an uneventful recovery from the operation. She went home to Ashton Manor with an Elizabethan collar just to make sure she didn't have a go at her stitches.

She returned in ten days' time to have them removed.

'You'll really have to be extra vigilant in the future,' I warned John and Sandra. 'You just can't afford the risk of Heidi swallowing something else off the dressing-table. So, let this be a timely reminder.'

I held up the object Heidi had swallowed and then handed it to Sandra. Her missing wristwatch.

Westcott being a seaside town, there was always going to be the potential for dogs to pick things up from the beach. Stuff washed in by the tide: dented plastic bottles, broken blocks of white polystyrene, the occasional flip flop and a variety of other items of dubious origin. Plus, the rubbish dropped by tourists. Even a genteel unpretentious resort like Westcott had its fair share of litterbugs. Certainly, back in the 18th century, the likes of Princess Amelia would not have been restrained in trashing the surrounds of her bathing hut when she came down from London for a dip; but then she would have had a court lacky at hand ready to scoop up any regal rubbish she let slip from her jewel-encrusted fingers.

The town's current faded gentility is summed up by its wide promenade, small white-painted pier and mile-long stretch of pleasure gardens in which is situated Westcott's Wonderland. The place where Tim and Anna Hutchinson were employed as guides, hopping/strutting around in their respective rabbit and chicken outfits. A two-acre site in a prime position right by the beach which was bequeathed to the borough by a local worthy, Sir Ezra Fetheringdale. He made his fortune in bird excrement – importing vast quantities of guano from South America to be used as fertiliser in this country. By all accounts, he had a magnificent pavilion designed and built to match anything seen at Kew. Stunning wrought iron work. A dome of stained-glass panes that reflected a rainbow of colour down into a vast interior. Here, he housed the spoils of his trips abroad. Not those of the culture trail through 19th century Italy and Greece – classical statues, Doric columns and the like. More elements of Peru and Ecuador through which he'd earnt his crust. So, visitors were faced with blocks moulded from impacted bird droppings, stuffed albatrosses, bleached skeletons of sea lions; and as a centrepiece, the monumental mummified carcass of a whale into which one could venture via its mouth providing one stooped to avoid its palate. These artefacts did initially attract public interest. But interest waned as people wearied at weaving through heaps of bird poo.

His pavilion fell victim to the shibboleth of the 70s – "concrete rules". It was demolished, its place taken by Westcott's Wonderland, a concrete assortment of paths meandering through a crazy golf course with concrete bunkers, a concrete-based paddling pool – forever slimy, causing many a tot to slip and split their heads open on the concrete edge. And a motley selection of rides to risk riding on: spinning teacups, revolving mushrooms, swirling pink ponies, all with the potential to throw you off onto their concrete bases. A case of falling on hard times if you weren't too careful.

It was from the Wonderland that a couple turned up on spec at Prospect House one Saturday afternoon when I was on standby, dog in tow on a lead, child of about three in a buggy. The child – I heard one parent call him Luke – looked very unhappy, sullen, disorientated. Maybe the result of being thrown around in a giant teacup too many times? Or dizzy from spinning on a monster mushroom? The dog, a crossbreed of some sort – tan-coated, whippet-thin with bulging eyes, quite ugly – didn't look much better. Though not from being spun around in a teacup, but more from the fact that a half-metre or so of blue plastic thread was sticking out from between his lips. Making him very down in the mouth, very uncomfortable. Head lowered, he slunk into my consulting room, stopping several times to claw at the protruding line. Lucy, on weekend duty with me, had taken details in reception. A James and Sarah Marchant, down from London for a few days with their son, Luke, and Clarence, their whippet-chihuahua cross. *(the mind boggled: a whippahua?)* It had been raining most of the morning. Not ideal weather for a trip to the seaside. I could picture brave souls battling the elements, determined to make the best of things in their pack-a-macs and rain hats, huddled on the promenade benches, forking through plastic trays of fish and chips, sipping lukewarm tea from polystyrene mugs. Welcome to sunny Westcott. It looked as if the Marchants had done battle and lost. Both parents were decidedly bedraggled. James's hair was plastered to his head, a drop of water suspended from the ring in his left earlobe. Sarah sported a very soggy sunhat. Both in T-shirts and shorts – items that were beginning to steam in the warmth of reception. As was Clarence's coat. Luke was the driest, protected by the plastic hood of his buggy.

It was James who hoisted Clarence – with his distinctive wet-dog smell – onto the table and stopped his paws from skating and skidding across the surface. 'You can see what's happened,' he said, holding the dog tightly. 'He came running back up the beach with that in his mouth. It's bit of fishing line, isn't it?'

I nodded. 'Looks very much it, I'm afraid.'

'We tried pulling it out,' said Sarah, standing back, rocking the buggy in which Luke was now falling asleep. 'But it seemed stuck.'

I grimaced. 'I hate to say it but that could well be because there's a fishhook the other end.'

James swung around to his wife. 'There, told you as much.'

'Okay... Okay... That's why we're here, isn't it? To get it sorted,' snapped Sarah in return, her hand starting to rock the buggy more violently. At which point, Luke was jerked awake and started to bawl.

'Now look what you've done,' she went on.

If steam hadn't been rising from their damp T-shirts, it certainly was beginning to now. I could almost see it curling up from their shoulders.

Shoulders squared for a fight.

'I didn't do it. You did,' retorted James, losing his grip on Clarence who seized the chance to leap off the table and charge around the room in a series of frenzied circuits. He too, seemed to be letting off steam.

Luke bawled louder.

'Now look what you've made me do,' cried James.

Luke bawled louder still.

'That's right, blame me,' screamed Sarah. 'Like you always do.'

Luke's howls reached bawling point. His face puckered. Puce.

Utter mayhem.

'Can I be of help?' A cool, calm, collected voice cut through that mayhem. Lucy's. It was as if a bucket of ice had been tossed into the room. The steaming subsided. The tension melted away. Clarence skidded to a halt and quivered. Luke gulped. And his parents fell silent.

'Thank you, Lucy,' I said. 'It's time to see what we can do for Clarence here.' With that, I picked up the lead still attached to Clarence, handed it to Lucy and the two of us took the dog down to the prep room; meanwhile telling the Marchants to wait in the waiting room or go for a walk in the grounds should they prefer, now that the rain seemed to have stopped. They chose the latter. If nothing else, it gave them the chance to let off more steam out there should they have wished to.

'Okay, Luce, let's have a look. See what's going on,' I said once we had Clarence in the prep room and on the counter. While she held him down, one arm over his shoulder, I gently prised open his mouth. There was little resistance.

'Good boy… good boy…' I murmured as I peered in. The nylon strand, with little lead weights attached, stretched over the back of his tongue to disappear out of sight down his throat. I pushed two fingers in and depressed his tongue. Still nothing could be seen. I had hoped to have found a hook caught up on Clarence's tongue or on the inside of his cheek. No such luck. The hook – and I was sure there was going to be one – had travelled down his throat and was caught up somewhere along his oesophagus. Or had even travelled down into his stomach. Only an X-ray would tell us exactly where it was.

With Clarence sedated and an X-ray taken, the position of the hook was clearly visible. Well down the gullet, just at the point where it entered the chest.

'Ouch... this is going to be difficult to get out,' I said to Lucy. 'I'll go and discuss it with the Marchants.'

I returned to tell her I'd been given the go-ahead to remove it if at all possible.

'So, Luce, how do you feel? Shall we give it a go?' The alternative was to leave it to Monday when fully staffed and get the op done by Crystal with Mandy's support.

'Doesn't seem fair to leave the poor chap that length of time,' said Lucy, stroking Clarence's sleepy head. 'It must be hurting him quite a bit.'

'I agree. So, we'll go for it then, yes?'

Lucy looked up. I gazed into her hazel eyes and a mutual bond of trust passed between us as she nodded.

I was nervous about the operation though I tried not to show it. But Lucy had been living with me long enough to sense my feelings. She patted my arm. 'It will be fine. Honest.'

The basics for setting up the op were no problem. There was a set of instruments ready in the steriliser. As with the op on the boxer, Heidi, giving Clarence an anaesthetic to enable intubation was easy. Clipping up his neck, carrying him through to the operating theatre, strapping him down on his back and attaching his tube to the anaesthetic machine was straightforward. Lucy knew what she was doing and did it well. More than a match for Mandy's efficiency.

It only remained to see what I could do. With the skin on Clarence's neck sterilised, I scrubbed up and fixed sterile drapes from an autoclaved pack around the operation site.

'Okay, Luce, here goes,' I said, making an incision through the skin over the spot where the hook was lodged as shown on the X-ray.

Dissecting down onto the oesophageal wall, I swabbed the area free of blood and took a look.

'Can you see it?' asked Lucy, sitting on a stool at Clarence's head, monitoring the level of his anaesthesia.

'Yep.' The black shaft of the hook was clearly visible. Not only was it visible but I could see that its barbed tip had pierced the oesophageal wall and curved around the vagus nerve and carotid artery, trapping them both. Great.

I clamped the hook with some artery forceps to hold it steady. Then picked up a pair of wire-cutters from the ops tray.

'Now for the tricky bit,' I muttered, glancing briefly at Lucy.

I began to saw through the shaft. Slowly. Carefully. Conscious of the carotid artery pulsating only millimetres away. Nick that and there'd be a blood bath. It seemed an eternity before the shaft was severed and it snapped in two. With the artery forceps still attached, I gently eased out the severed section of hook with its barb and dropped it on the table.

'Phew. We're getting there,' I murmured. 'Now, Luce, it's your turn. You're going to remove the other half of the hook by pulling on the nylon. As there's no barb on it now, it should come out easily enough.'

Lucy leaned over Clarence's neck and gripped the line still hanging out of his mouth. She pulled.

'Gently does it,' I said as she pulled a little harder when nothing had happened. Then suddenly, any further resistance disappeared and the nylon slid out with the remaining section of hook attached.

'Eureka,' she exclaimed, beaming broadly, as she held up the line in front of me, swinging it gently.

'Indeed... Indeed...' My grin matched hers.

Having packed the wound with sterile antibiotic powder, I stitched up the skin, though not the oesophageal wall. That was left un-sutured to allow any possible infection to seep out and subsequently be drained through the skin incision at a later date should it be necessary.

'Right. All done and dusted,' I declared as I sprinkled further antibiotic powder along the completed line of sutures.

Lucy and I carried the still unconscious Clarence back to the recovery kennel where we laid him out on a blanket and switched on the underfloor heating. I'd be reporting back to the Marchants, showing them the two halves of the hook – guessing they might like to keep them – a souvenir of their trip to Westcott. Clarence to be collected the next day. Stitches to be removed in ten days' time at their own vet's.

'Well, Luce. That seems to have gone okay.' I slid my hand into hers as we watched Clarence gave his first post-operative yawn and paddle of his paws. I took her other hand and pulled her around to me. 'Thanks for your help. Very much appreciated.' I pulled her closer and kissed her.

Clarence might now be free from his fishing line, but I was truly hooked.

12
Ticked Off

I had eased myself onto the chair in the doctor's consulting room, ready to be seen by the locum, who had waved me in without looking up from his computer screen.

'We've got the results back,' said the doctor, tapping the screen. 'No sugar. Ketones minimal. The tests are fine. I'm pleased to say your pregnancy's proceeding smoothly.'

I felt my lips crease into a thin line. 'I think there's been some mistake,' I began.

'No. No mistake, Mrs Jones. The lab results are all correct,' said the locum in a parsimonious voice. He was a middle-aged man, lean-framed, pinched-faced, with a weak chin edged with a sparse fringe of yellow-white stubble, the colour matching the random tufts sprouting from his head and nose. Given a nightshirt and fingerless gloves, he could have made a passable Scrooge – his ways being well in line with NHS policy for scrimping on medication whenever possible. He jabbed the screen again and then looked up. 'Ah, I see what you mean.' He peered over the top of large steel-framed spectacles.

I was tempted to say, 'Unless your Mrs Jones has a baritone voice and half-day's growth of beard then, no, I'm not her.' But then, in these days of transgenders, one could swing either way. And I guess a lot did, changing via the knife or an avalanche of bender-gender medication. So, choosing to tread carefully, I politely verified that I was indeed not the lady in question.

'Nor Mrs Dunwell by the looks of you,' continued the doctor, punching his keyboard. 'No. Of course not. She's rather... how can I put it without sounding sexist? A rather buxom young lady. Well stacked – plenty on her shelves. If you get what I mean.'

I did. And clearly so did he. His eyes bulged and a thin strand of saliva slid like a fishing line from the corner of his mouth. He flicked it away with a lecherous lick. 'Now let's see.' A new set of notes flashed up. 'Yes. Here we are. Mr Edwards. Right. So, how's the laryngitis?'

I was speechless.

'Still hurting then?' remarked the locum.

There was clearly a mix-up here. I cleared my throat and attempted to explain.

The doctor's fingers flew back across the keyboard. 'Okay. Okay. Mitchell, you say. Ah, yes. Here's a...' He stopped tapping and read the notes. 'Mitchell. Henry Mitchell.' His voice trailed off. Then softly, he added, 'My apologies, dear sir. I hadn't realised your prognosis was that bad.'

What? I was here to have my toenails checked. Nothing *that* serious. No deep, necrotic ulcers, brimming over with pus. Nothing Bubonic-plague-like liable to see me depart this world before you could say "Rats". Nothing too alarming. Nevertheless, with the locum's dire words echoing in my ears, I could feel the ground begin to shift below me. Maybe I would be six feet under before the day was out.

I leaned forward and attempted to explain to this idiot that he was supposed to be seeing Paul Mitchell. Not Henry Mitchell. Obviously, there had been a mix-up with the notes.

'Phew, I bet you're relieved you're not Henry Mitchell then,' commented the locum. 'He's only got three more months to live at the most. Approaching the final performance before the theatre of his life comes to an end.' The doctor paused to stare pensively up at the ceiling. 'Then it's curtains for him.'

Blimey. Sounded all very dramatic. Was this Henry Mitchell an actor? Someone who trod the boards in the West End? Or had played an inspirational Hamlet at Stratford? Seemed not.

'A branch manager at Lidl's,' the locum told me with apparent disregard for patient confidentiality. If not careful, Henry's history could soon be headlines in the Westcott Gazette. 'Makes you think though,' the doctor continued.

I did think. I needed something for supper. Just pray it wasn't going to be my last one. Lidl had a special offer on Butcher's Best sausages – buy one get one free. But it finished today. Must get in before it closed. That's providing I got out of this health centre alive. And the way this locum was behaving, I was beginning to wonder. I fidgeted in the chair. Glanced at my watch several times. Tapped my fingers on my knees.

But seemed he hadn't finished yet. Not by a long chalk. Though it wasn't actual chalk he was after. Rather pens. Freebie pens. Or similar.

For it seemed this buffoon now thought I was some sort of rep, with an appointment having been arranged through the practice manager. How on earth had that come about? We'd had similar visits to Prospect House. Beryl usually gave the reps short thrift especially if they turned up unannounced. But she was always keen to snaffle up any freebies the drug company concerned was offering.

'Freebies?' the locum asked me.
'Sorry?'
'Diaries?'

'Er... No.'

'Or matching notepads and pencils?'

'No, sorry.' *Goodness. Why was I apologising?*

'Pill dispensers?' Clearly, this man wasn't going to give up easily.

I shook my head.

The locum tutted. 'Shame. Last week, King Chemicals gave me a fountain pen that looked like a thermometer. Very nice. Only trouble is I keep sticking the nib in patients' mouths.'

Mmm... That reassured me no end.

Eventually, I managed to establish exactly who I was. Paul Mitchell. Here to have my toenails checked and not someone likely to be carried out feet first, though the state of my nails could have made them – or rather me – unbearable. I had onychomycosis of my toes. A fungal infection which had turned my nails thick, yellow and scabby. Quite embarrassing. Toe-curling in fact. The problem had already been diagnosed and treatment started some months back by my usual doctor, Graham Merriweather. I had been religiously applying the anti-fungal ointment prescribed by Graham for the last two months. And the appointment today was for a reappraisal of the condition with a view to carrying on the treatment. I was now worried as to whether this locum had managed to bring up my correct clinical history. I had visions he might ask me to drop my trousers, lie on the couch, on my side, knees up to my chest, while he rammed a lubricated finger stall up my rear, ignoring the protestations from me saying my prostate was in good working order.

I'll be buggered if I let him do that, I thought, wincing.

In the event, he only asked me to whip off my socks. Not my underpants. 'Uhm... Yes... I see...' he murmured as he inspected my line-up of mangled, mutilated discoloured toenails. 'They are rather mangy if you don't mind me saying so. You'll definitely need to continue the treatment. No question.'

I scrabbled out as fast as my crabby feet would let me, hoping those supermarket sausages were still on offer.

My next visit to the health centre was for a more serious concern I had. And this time I made sure Graham Merriweather was going to be on duty.

I never felt easy attending our health centre. It was the prospect of sitting cheek by jowl with a host of other patients, each potentially festering inwardly or outwardly with something that you could unwittingly pick up in your progression through the waiting room.

The strip lighting was as harsh as ever. Relentless fluorescent tubes that spot-lighted you, blanched your life. Made you more corpse-like than you actually felt. Join the line-up of cadavers in the morgue, folks. Ready and waiting. Grant you, there had been an effort to improve the décor. The ghastly green walls had been repainted. Still green. But a little less bilious in tone. Even so, staring at them for up to half an hour was still liable to initiate the slight twinge of a heave-ho if not the vomitus upheaval of a full-scale puke. And no real change in the pamphlets on display. The lumps and bumps to look out for. The bugs that could be ingested, inhaled or penetrate your innards via the various orifices on offer to them. With the heavy emphasis on prevention and cross contamination, I did wonder why we weren't all sitting in forensic white suits, masked, with over-boots and disposable gloves handed out by staff on arrival.

When the voice crackled overhead, requesting "Mr Mitchell for Dr Merriweather, room six", it jolted me from my reverie. I sprang to my feet and walked with what I hoped was a fit and purposeful stride down the nearest corridor. To discover that only led to rooms one to four. So, I had to tiptoe back out, skirt around the bodies still lying in wait and hope the adjacent corridor would correctly lead me to room six. It did. In it, Dr Merriweather was ready and waiting.

Unlike the last time I had an appointment with him, when he had a streaming cold and presented himself with leaden, red-rimmed eyes and sore nose, this time he was positively brimming with health. Bouncy to the point of leaping up from his chair to give me a hearty handshake, his pointy, beard-fringed face creased in a smile.

'Hello... Hello... Good to see you. Are you keeping well?' he cried.

Mmm... I wasn't too sure that was the most appropriate of greetings on entering a doctor's consulting room when it was odds-on likely you weren't keeping well at all. Hence, the reason for the appointment.

Still, he meant well even if you weren't.

I mumbled something about not being too bad, thank you. All things considered. Could be worse. That sort of thing. And suddenly realised I was almost talking myself better.

'Sit down, sit down,' said Graham, pointing to the swivel chair alongside his desk, while he plonked himself back in front of his computer screen. 'I take it the toes are on the mend now,' he went on, studying the screen on which no doubt my notes were displayed. I saw his brow crease. 'Strange. The locum has made a comment here. Seems you were showing anxiety symptoms. Something to do with half-price sausages. Suggests a course of Valium might be required. How do you feel about that?'

I gave what I hoped was a nonchalant, relaxed shrug. 'No, no. I'm fine now,' I reassured him. I was too. I'd managed to get to Lidl before they closed and bought up the last ten packs of Butchers Pride; still had six left in the freezer. So, I was well chilled out.

'So, what's the problem, Paul?'

I began to explain.

It had all come about through the acquisition of our two rescue dogs, Emily, the Welsh springer spaniel and Bertie, the tan and white crossbreed.

We were very fortunate to have access to some delightful woods and open countryside within a few minutes' walk from Willow Wren. Walks that had been enjoyed in the company of dear Nelson the Jack Russell before he sadly got run over. But now, with Emily and Bertie, they were again a source of joy to be shared.

There was a stile, only a hundred metres or so to the west of Willow Wren. The footpath took you along the southern boundary of Ashton Manor, the large timber-framed farmhouse where Sandra and John Coles and their two boxers lived.

The footpath meandered over to the far corner of the meadow where a metal field-gate gave access on to a farm track – bounded by hawthorn hedges – which zigzagged down into a lightly wooded area of oak and ash. There, the dappled shade created a welcome relief from the burning heat of summer days when, if ever, we were blessed with them. Nelson had loved that wood. So too did Emily and Bertie. Along its edge were towering mounds of brambles, intertwined with pink tresses of dog roses. In the autumn, large crops of blackberries ripened on those mounds. Succulent berries to be savoured on the grassy slopes below them. To be picked and passed between lips as Lucy and I lay there, our purple tongues exploring each other's mouths. Meanwhile, Emily and Bertie sat patiently waiting for the odd berry to be chucked their way. They didn't get many.

That wood, in late July, consisted of spent bluebell stalks and their yellowing spikes of leaves. A far cry from April's glade of trees, their dew-covered buds having just unfurled into a mantle of soft greens; while beneath, a misty blue sea – undulating eddies of bluebells – their heads nodding in the whispering breeze as it ran scented fingers between the trunks. Woven through the woods were many tracks. Exciting paths for Emily and Bertie to charge along, tails furiously wagging, pendulous ears flapping, as they picked up the scent of whatever animal had passed along them. Roe deer. Badgers. Many rabbits. Several of the latter could been seen out during the day, grazing at the edges of the meadow; only to rapidly retreat into the wood, their scuts up in alarm, exposing their white under-fur, as Emily and Bertie set off in hot pursuit. Their excited squeals would erupt from the brambles, accompanied by much crashing around in the undergrowth. But they never caught one.

At the far end of the wood, the land fell away across a rolling countryside dotted with a patchwork of maize and wheat, criss-crossed with acres of rapeseed already, this year, showing traces of the vibrant yellow with which those fields would soon be emblazoned. Far in the distance, you could just make out course of the River Avon. Evening time, the river caught and reflected the setting sun, turning its silver twists of water into meandering ribbons of orange. While above, a rich tapestry of cloud would wrap the sky in pink and purple folds.

The scene was one which made you want to stop and meditate – sit with one's back resting against the warm bark of an oak, and watch the evening melt into night. And I have to confess that's often what I did. Not me and Lucy. Me, Emily and Bertie. Dog time. Just the three of us.

There, we'd sit, them leaning into me, their hot doggy breaths on my face. My right arm over Emily's shoulder, my left-over Bertie's. Each hand caressing a neck, slipping up occasionally to tickle an ear as between us we put the world to rights, albeit it a one-sided conversation. But we were bonding nevertheless. And that togetherness certainly helped to reduce the tension in me and instil a sense of calmness and serenity. Not too sure about Emily and Bertie though. I've a feeling they might have preferred chasing after more rabbits rather than listen to me blather on.

'Maybe we can't put the world to rights,' I said on one such evening, looking from one to the other, my hands fondling their ears in the fading golden light. 'But we can have a damned good try.'

Both simultaneously turned and licked my face; and I couldn't help but smile as I felt their hot tongues on my cheeks. What great buddies we were.

So, yes, good company for each other. But sometimes came home with company we'd rather have done without.

'Hello, what's this?' exclaimed Lucy one summer's evening as we sat on the little patio to the back of the cottage, savouring the last of the sunset, pink ribbons of cloud above us, a warm, light breeze stirring the creamy heads of roses that arched over the French windows, filling the air with their delicate scent. A few bees still buzzed between them on late-evening pollen searches; while overhead, a tiny bat had appeared, to zigzag across the ever-darkening indigo sky. Lucy had reached over the side of her lounger and was running her hand down Emily's back; only to stop halfway down. She sat up and swung her legs off the lounger to take a closer look. 'Ah... Ah... thought as much. A tick.' She'd parted Emily's fur to reveal a small, grey, rounded object – the engorged body of a tick – one full of Emily's blood. Not the most romantic of things to see on a warm summer's evening when in the mood for a bit of canoodling but instead, having a blood-filled tick thrust in my face. Lucy had expertly pinched the underneath of the tick between finger and thumb, given it a twist and so managed to pull it free without leaving its head and pinchers buried in the dog's skin. When she flicked the tick onto the patio next to me, put her foot on it and squashed it, leaving a puddle of blood, any vestiges of romantic intent were also squashed. But that's Lucy for you. Might have a heart of gold, great empathy for the animals under her care. But also, very practical in nature. A tick was not to be tolerated.

She settled back down on her lounger. Me on mine. The dogs settled between us. We sipped our Proseccos and gazed up at the gathering darkness. Stars beginning to twinkle. The last rays of the dipping sun turning the dot of a passing plane into a diadem of silver with a lazy trail of white.

I sighed contentedly. Heaven. Sheer heaven. Truly romantic. A time to utter sweet nothings to each other.

'Remind me to order a tick remover tomorrow,' said Lucy.

Ticks – or *Ixodes ricinus* as Mr Hargreaves would have you say – are tiny spider-like creatures commonly found in woodland and heath areas. They feed on the blood of birds and mammals; and so, dogs on their outings in such areas, are liable to pick them up. As Lucy discovered on Emily.

And as I later discovered on myself – with the potential for dire consequences.

The spell of settled weather we'd been having continued, stretching into early August. Tempting many to take advantage of the balmy evenings to have suppers alfresco-style. Barbecues. We decided to do likewise. Well, at least Lucy did. 'We'll invite Sandra and John over,' she said.

'We will?'

'Well, why not? It would be good to see them.'

'Er... Yes, I suppose so.'

'You don't sound too keen.'

'No, really, its fine. And we haven't seen them since we did that bat count with them. Which was... what? Over two months ago?'

'Nearer three.'

That had been fun. Doing a head count of the Lesser Horseshoe bats that roosted in the Coles' barn-garage conversion. Fun because it turned out there were a lot of bats to count. And fun because we did it over several bottles of Prosecco. So, the final total was a bit hazy to say the least. Ninety – give or take a bat or two.

My apparent reluctance wasn't so much meeting up with Sandra and John. They were a nice enough couple. It was more the fact it would be over a barbecue. I'm not too keen on barbecues. Sweating over hot coals to dish up blackened offerings – charred pieces piled on plates often offered in semi-darkness and hence, requiring a bit of guesswork as to what was actually being offered. Still the invite went out. And the Coles turned up at 6.30 on the dot.

Sandra settled down on the one lounger that didn't have a wonky leg, glass of Prosecco in hand. 'Well, this is very pleasant,' she said at the precise moment a plume of black smoke rose from the barbecue and engulfed her.

As I battled to prevent the bangers and burgers from burning, the lamb kebabs from curling into cinders and the chicken pieces from roasting to ruin, conversation ebbed and flowed smoothly, aided by copious quantities of Prosecco. By the time I managed to serve up my offerings, we were so plastered every blackened misshapen morsel was swallowed with gusto even if it meant taking another swig of wine to wash it rapidly down.

'Delicious,' murmured John as he sank his teeth in what he thought was a sausage only to discover it was a fused length of crisped kebab when his teeth hit the skewer with a jaw-juddering crunch of tooth enamel against steel.

Our shared love of dogs, meant that each other's mutts got a mention. Especially the Coles' boxers. Henry and Heidi. They got a mention every time an inedible lump of meat was slipped into a doggy bag for them to chew over later. That turned out to be many mentions. As for Emily and Bertie. Well, they did their customary hovering, hoping to hoover up anything thrown their way. But they seemed reluctant to take up any more offerings after attempting to bolt down the first solid black balls of burnt flesh fired at them which they both promptly shot back up with much gagging and retching.

Good grief. Surely, my barbecue skills weren't that bad?

'Be like that, then,' was all I could say, somewhat miffed.

How the topic of ticks came about, I'm not too sure. I've a horrible feeling it was my fault. I've a memory that's associated with barbecues and dogs which makes for rather uneasy listening for some people, and so not one I'd generally share. But after a few glasses of Prosecco amongst friends, what the heck.

'You know, I had this Filipino friend, a vet,' I announced, standing by the remains of the meal, still smouldering on the barbecue, all offers of second helpings having been politely but firmly refused.

'Paul, don't,' hissed Lucy, sensing I was going to repeat a story she'd heard before.

'Anyway,' I continued, ignoring her, 'as you may know, they eat dogs out in the Philippines. And this vet friend of mine was at a barbecue where they were spit-roasting a dog – they're called apsos over there.'

'Paul,' hissed Lucy again. 'Stop it.'

I didn't. Seeing the Coles' eyes bulging, like those of rabbit just caught by a predator, just encouraged me to continue. 'As my friend was the honoured guest at this barbecue, he was offered a delicacy. A very special part of the dog.' I paused, swaying on the spot, and threw my left arm dramatically in the air before lurching forward a pace. 'Guess what it was.' The bulging eyes continued to bulge but not a word was spoken. 'Go on, have a guess.' Still not a word. 'Okay, I'll tell you then. Its ears.'

There was an audible intake of breath from both the Coles, though in the gathering gloom I couldn't really make out their features.

'Blimey, mate,' gasped John. 'For a moment I thought you were going to say its balls.'

'Ah, but I haven't finished yet,' I said, wagging a finger at his shadowy form. 'My friend, sitting like we are here, in semi-darkness, was handed one barbecued ear. Crisply cooked. Not able to properly see what he was eating, he started at one end and ran his teeth along the edge, feeling a whole series of crunchy bits drop into his mouth.' I struggled to stand upright for maximum dramatic delivery. 'Just what do you think those bits were, eh?'

John and Sandra remained silent.

'I'll tell you then. Ticks. Roasted ticks.'

The silence was broken by the sound of vomit splattering onto the patio. Within minutes, the Coles had excused themselves, thanking us for a delightful evening and vanished, heading speedily, if somewhat wobbly, back home to Ashton Manor.

'Why on earth did you have to bring that up?' demanded Lucy as Emily and Bertie busily mopped up what had been brought up on the patio. Evidently, in semi-digested form, my barbecued offerings became more palatable to them. Better that roasted ticks, dare I say?

Of course, I was well and truly in the doghouse for the next couple of days. Days in which, when not at work or on duty, I took Emily and Bertie for long walks over to the woods. There we'd settle down at the base of an oak for one of our chin wags – another man-to-his best-friend chat.

It was probably during one of those sessions that I got bitten. I'll never know for sure. But what I do know is that one morning a few weeks on, having showered, I discovered while towelling down, a large circular red rash a good eight inches or so in diameter, at waist level, just above my left buttock.

I stared down at it as I twisted sideways in front of the bathroom mirror. 'Bloody hell,' was my immediate reaction. 'What the fuck's this?' was my second. It didn't look good.

For a start, the rash was bright red. Not raised. No spots. And then there was its shape. A central blob. Then a circular area of normal skin. Then another circle of redness. It all screamed "bullseye". The sort of rash you got when bitten by a tick – though the culprit here had long since dropped off leaving no signs that it had bitten me. But even worse was the realisation that, for such a striking reaction to have occurred, the bugger must have been carrying *Borrelia burgdorferi*, the bacterium responsible for Lyme disease. Argh…

This much I already knew. Googling the condition, I soon printed out a pile of further information. It didn't make for happy reading.

'Seems you've missed out on the early symptoms,' commented Lucy as she scanned through the notes over coffee. 'Apart from the rash – the erythema migrans as it's called – you haven't had any flu-like symptoms. No headaches. Malaise. Fever.'

'I know… I know… But just look what I can go down with later if I don't get treatment right away.' The list went on and on, making me feel I was at death's door before I'd got halfway along the corridor to it. Rashes. Fatigue. Achy, stiff or swollen joints. Night sweats. Sleep disturbances. Cognitive decline. Just think if I couldn't find my way to work anymore. Calamity. Couldn't remember Beryl's name. Well, not so bad.

No wonder I was in Dr Merriweather's consulting room before you could say *Borrelia burgdorferi*. Not that I could say it. Nor could Graham. He just referred to it as that bloody bug. Mind you, it was said with great relish, 'You're my first case,' he announced, rubbing his hands together with great glee as he did so. 'Lyme disease. Just fancy that.'

Another unfortunate choice of words from my doctor. You'd have been hard pushed to find anyone *fancying* Lyme disease knowing what the dire consequences of picking it up could result in. But there was no denying Graham's thinly disguised enthusiasm. Any minute now, I expected him to ask my permission to take some photos of my lesions and have then blown up, poster-size, to display in the waiting room. Start a sort of rogues' gallery of interesting cases seen in the health centre. 'Well, well, well,' he continued. 'Who'd have thought, eh?' He gave his pointy chin a scratch. 'Lyme disease.' The latter two words were said with such reverence, with such awe, that I wondered whether he'd suddenly nip around his desk and give me a quick genuflexion. Me of the almighty Lyme. As to his "who'd have thought," I wasn't here to have him think. I was here to have him do. And be quick about it before all those secondary symptoms started settling in.

'Yes... Yes... of course,' he said when I curtly reminded him of the fact. 'No question.' Though I suspect he had many questions to judge from the way his fingers flew over his keyboard as he sought their answers on the internet before prescribing the high dose of antibiotic required for four weeks; and booking the blood test for Elisa, screening for antibodies to confirm the correct diagnosis. You see, I too had been busy Googling.

The prompt treatment with the correct antibiotic at the correct high dose for the correct length of time did the trick. I didn't succumb to any of the horrible conditions that characterised invasion of my internal organs with an armada of *Borrelia* bugs; and so, I sailed through unscathed and ship-ship. Not left a nervous wreck. But it did leave me with a tremendous respect for *Ixodes Ricinus*.

Lucy, ever efficient, demonstrated her practical approach immediately. A walk through the meadows over to the woods was no longer an amble done on impulse. But involved a stratagem of expediential proportions. As demonstrated by the checklist she pinned to the back door:

Boots. Yep.

Long-sleeved shirt (caveat – or similar to ensure arms covered). Yep.

Trousers tucked in socks. Yep.

Use insect repellent on exposed skin. No problem.

Stick to footpaths. Avoid long grass. Okay.

No romping in said long grass. Oh shame.

Lucy reminded me to check myself for ticks, especially after evening walks. Head. Neck. Waistband. Armpits.

'Groin too, I guess?' I said. 'You never know what you might find wriggling down there.' Lucy's sharp look soon wiped out the suggestive one I had in mind.

There was Emily and Bertie to consider as well of course. They'd already had the routine spot-on anti-flea/tick therapy. But with the discovery of that tick on Emily, Lucy felt more was required.

'These might do the trick,' she declared one morning, holding up two white plastic collars that had just arrived in the post. 'Ordered them online. Herbal anti-tick collars.'

And they did seem to work. Well, certainly we never discovered any more ticks on either of the dogs. And likewise, none on us. Lyme disease became a memory.

It was a memory that got prompted a few months later with the arrival of a new patient in the surgery.

'Know much about ferrets?' queried Beryl that afternoon.

'Er… well… no. Not actually, to tell you the truth,' I admitted, glancing down the list of appointments booked in for me. 'Why?'

'You've got one coming in at four o'clock.'

Ah… okay. A bit of a challenge ahead then. What little I did know could have been written on the back of an envelope. Correction. More likely on the back of a postage stamp. I did know that the ferret is the domesticated version of the European polecat and has been used for pest control and hunting for centuries. Not particularly helpful information. I also understood that they are engaging and friendly and extremely active. Hence, they are more and more often being kept purely as pets.

When the ferret landed on my consulting table, he was in a smart, chocolate-brown carrying box with his name – Hooligan – emblazoned across the top of the door. That should have been a warning. Cuddles or Sammikins would have been much more reassuring. The ferocious way

Hooligan was gnawing at the door's metal bars, his sharp pointed teeth working up and down each bar in turn, didn't help my reassurance levels to rise either.

'Don't worry,' said his owner, Mr Gardner. 'He's quite a friendly little fella really.' We both watched Hooligan continue to savage the bars in his attempts to open the cage door. 'Once you get to know him,' he added.

I did wonder how long bonding with a ferret might take. Certainly, longer than the ten-minute tête-à-tête he was going to get with me.

Mr Gardner grinned, displaying remarkably similar sharp incisors to his ferret. Though I doubted, he used them to open doors in a similar way.

But it wasn't just Mr Gardner's set of gnashers that were similar. His whole appearance and demeanour gave one the feeling that this chap was capable of shinning up drainpipes and whipping through sewers akin to the burrows and tunnels of any rabbit warren that Hooligan might frequent.

Not to put too fine a point on it, Mr Gardner looked the epitome of what one would imagine a ferret owner to look like even though there was the absence of a flat cap. Small. Wiry. Eyes close-set with a glint in them. And those teeth of course.

'I'll let him out then, shall I?' he said.

Well, I could hardly say "no", could I? So, I watched as Mr Gardner sprang back the door catch and Hooligan sprang out of the doorframe. Head weaving from side to side, he shot across the table like a jet-propelled caterpillar trying to escape becoming a blackbird's breakfast. I flapped a hand to stop him dive-bombing into a roll of cotton wool; whereupon, he twisted his lithesome body round and attempted to dart up the sleeve of my white coat at a speed worthy of any gold-medal sprinter. Mr Gardner eased him out for me.

'Slow down, boy,' he said with a chuckle. 'You're not going to find any rabbits up there.'

Apart from the scalpel-edged teeth, needle-pointed claws and a smell pungent enough to out-whiff a farting warthog, Hooligan was a smart-looking specimen. Soft, creamy-coloured coat, tipped brown, darker over legs and tail. Small, rounded pink ears. Pink snout. Button-black eyes. All very appealing. 'People often mistake him for a polecat,' said Mr Gardner, proudly. 'Very similar markings. 'It's this lump, here, over his left shoulder,' he added as Hooligan sailed over his hand and swooped under his wrist. 'Can you see?' Hooligan did another loop-the-loop around his arm. 'We'd been out ferreting a couple of days back,' Mr Gardner went on. 'And when we got back, my son noticed a tick on Hooligan's shoulder. He pulled it off. And now this.'

I nodded, knowing just what had happened. The tick had been pulled off, leaving the mouthparts in the skin. They had festered. And here was the result. A tick abscess.

'I'm afraid we'll have to have Hooligan in to get this sorted.'

'Serious stuff?'

'No... No... It can all be done under local anaesthetic. Just need to give him a small shot of sedative first. Calm him down a bit.' I went and got an ops gown which I bundled in a heap on the consulting table. Ever inquisitive, Hooligan weaved over to it and was soon burrowing under it. Sedative drawn up, hand clamped on his half-hidden body, rump still exposed, teeth thankfully not, I popped the sedative into his thigh. That evokes a series of angry hisses which slowly subsided as the sedative took effect. I slid the sleepy Hooligan back into his box and carried him down to the prep room, telling Mr Gardner to take a seat in the waiting room. 'Won't be long,' I reassured him. It was fortunate I had a gap before my next appointment. Time enough to see to the ferret.

'Oh gosh, a polecat,' said Mandy who had appeared to help.

'Ferret,' I said.

With local anaesthetic injected around the lump, I shaved and disinfected the area; and with a quick incision, excised the lump.

I was about to put in a couple of stitches when Eric popped his head around the door.

'Polecat?'

'Ferret,' said Mandy, knowingly.

Lucy appeared next.

'Ferret,' we all chorused.

Stitches in and back in his box, I was heading up to the consulting room with Hooligan as Crystal came down the corridor. She paused to peer in the box as I passed. 'Is that a...?'

'Ferret,' I interrupted, hurrying on.

During that short op, I had noticed an engorged tick hidden under Hooligan's right armpit; and decided it might be a good opportunity to demonstrate to Mr Gardner the best way to remove it should more appear in the future.

Summoning him in, I slid his still drowsy ferret out. 'Since the tick's mouthparts are buried in the skin, you need to use something to ensure the tick lets go. Or remove it with its mouthparts still intact.'

'A lighted cigarette?' suggested Mr Gardner.

I shook my head vigorously. 'Ouch, no. Potentially painful. Besides which, who smokes these days?'

I caught a whiff of tobacco-breath. But continued. 'Could try smothering it in butter. It would block up its breathing tubes.' I paused, not too sure whether ticks actually had breathing tubes as such.

'I'm vegetarian. Don't eat butter.'

My own tubes drew a sharp intake of air. *Calm, Paul. Keep calm.* 'Well, margarine would do. But even better would be a squirt of flea spray. It would then drop off dead.' I reached for a can I had on the adjacent counter.

'Not one for using chemicals.'

I replaced the can. 'Margarine then.'

'Stork?'

'Whatever.'

I was going to mention the use of a tick remover. But to be honest, Mr Gardner was beginning to get up my nose – regardless of what breathing tubes might be involved – and decided enough was enough before I found myself ticking him off.

I left him in reception settling his bill.

'Clover's on offer at Tesco,' I heard him tell Beryl. 'I might try that.'

13
Knowing Your Neighbour

There are plenty of things to worry about when moving house. Such are the concerns that it's reckoned to be the next down the list of major disruptions in one's life; the first being a death in the family. So, definitely a time of upheaval, if not quite in the same manner of losing a loved one, shedding tears over their grave. But still an earth-moving event nevertheless.

I was lucky in my post at the veterinary hospital since it came with a practice house – Willow Wren. A sweet, picture postcard cottage. Whitewashed, red tiled. End of a terrace of three nineteenth-century labourers' cottages – the other two now converted into one.

To the north of the property was a tiny square of lawn overlooked by the upstairs front bedroom. At the back, the kitchen door led onto a small, south facing patio, a great sun trap sheltered by the wooden panels of next door's fence. Here, Lucy and I were to enjoy many alfresco meals. Beyond the patio, a narrow lawn stretched down parallel to the wall. Alongside, a border crammed with cottage-garden-style plants. The yellow of forsythia. The sweet-smelling pink of daphnia. The striking red of japonica. And bowers of white and cream roses. Sheer delight.

As were the neighbours. Always a worry when one first moves into a new home. But Joan and Doug Spencer, our neighbours next door in Mill Cottage, were very welcoming. So, we were sad to learn of their moving when we ourselves had only moved into Willow Wren a couple of months before.

'To be nearer our daughter over in Gloucestershire,' Joan explained. 'And what with the two grandchildren growing up so fast, we felt it best to make the move now.'

So, we were to get new neighbours. But only one as happened, if you didn't count the cat.

'I'll think you'll like her,' said Joan, coming around to say her goodbyes as the removals van shunted its way out of the hard standing adjacent to their cottage and, with much grating of gears, pushed down through the tunnel of silver birch trees and out past Willow Wren. 'She's a widow whose son lives over in Chawcombe. He's the vicar of St Augustine's.'

'Oh, you mean Charles Venables,' I exclaimed.

'You know him?'

I did. Well, sort of. Having been coerced into judging the church's pet show last summer, I chose, as the winner, a lad with a well-behaved Labrador called Cindy, not realising the lad was Reverend Charles' son. Cindy was the family pet. Whoops.

From the front bedroom window, we watched, with interest, the unloading of the furniture van on its arrival next door.

A piano, small upright, nothing too grand. An elegant, oval table with pedestal legs. A chaise upholstered in red brocade. All suggesting a lady of culture, one with good taste.

Confirmed the next day when our new neighbour came around to introduce herself. Very much the sort who would own a piano and chaise.

'Hello, I'm Eleanor Venables,' she said when I opened the front door in response to the croaky creak of the doorbell.

Must get that oiled. 'Pleased to make your acquaintance.' She held out her hand and we exchanged a very firm handshake.

Here, we had a lady I judged to be in her early sixties. Well-preserved for her age. Pale moon-face. Dimpled-cheeks and just a wrinkle or two in the corners of her eyes which made her features quite alluring. But the effect spoilt by the deep line that ran down from each corner of her mouth. So deep were these lines it was if her chin was a separate entity, divorced from the rest of her face. A chin a ventriloquist's dummy would have been proud of. The impression reinforced when she spoke since it snapped up and down with every word uttered.

But the lady herself was no dummy. Well-cut heather tweed jacket and skirt. Smart. Finely embroidered white blouse. Classy. A thick sweep of platinum grey hair, tied back in a perfect chignon. Very stylish. President-of-the-local-Woman's-Institute material. No question. To run it with charm and decorum while ensuring everything got done the way she wanted. Exactly.

Over the next few months, we realised her greatest passion was for gardening. She was forever out in hers. Twice the size of ours, being formerly two plots before the pair of cottages was made into one. The Spencers had obviously spent a lot of time redesigning it with the incorporation of a screened-off vegetable plot and secluded patio. Right at the bottom of the plot, in one corner, they'd created a tiny wild patch, consisting of a pond, flanked by a clump of reeds, with a couple of water lilies on its surface and a bank of native plants – pink campion, bergamot and meadowsweet amongst them – which were allowed to grow unhindered.

I'd often see Eleanor when having a pee – me, that is, not her, God forbid – since our bathroom overlooked her back garden.

I'd watch as her tall, angular figure, drifted from herbaceous clump to herbaceous clump, flowed between shrubs, a snip here, a prune there. Her outfit season-sorted for the occasion. So, in spring and summer, green corduroy trousers, matching green waistcoat over a light green linen, short-sleeved shirt and soft green rubber wellies, complete with buckles at their tops. Come October, we discovered her outfits would change to match the autumnal hues surrounding her. Then russet-browns and ochres weaved through her clothing as she gathered fallen leaves with graceful, languid sweeps.

There was nothing graceful or languid when she swept around to Willow Wren one dreary, drizzly July morning.

Our doorbell gave its customary rattling ring – akin to the dying whirr of an eviscerated cricket. On answering it, I found Eleanor standing there, oozing agitation in the tremble of her legs, the crossing of arms over her bosoms. Her chin gearing up to go like the clappers.

'So sorry to trouble you, Paul.'

Uh… Uh… Not a good opening gambit. Trouble was about to brew. I felt sure of it.

'You haven't by any chance acquired a new addition to your…' There was a pause, her chin now in full throttle, up and down, as she searched to find the right word to use without giving undue offence. She came out with "collection". I suppose it was a fair summing-up of our motley menagerie of cats, dogs, chickens, rabbit and a goose called Gertie. A "collection" that was forever on the increase. So, her question was a reasonable one.

But, at that moment, our stock was stock-still. No additions. None planned. I told her so.

'Ah, in that case, I wonder what it was.'

'What was?' queried Lucy, having joined me at the door.

'I've no idea,' I replied, turning to her.

'Nor have I,' said Eleanor.

'What?' *(that was me)*

'What it was.' *(Eleanor again)*

'What are you talking about?' *(Lucy)*

It took a minute or so to sort out what was what and what Eleanor was on about. She'd been upstairs, just drawn back her bedroom curtains. Had wiped some condensation off the window when she saw it. 'It was padding down the garden behind the rhododendrons,' she informed us.

I stifled a "what?"

'It slipped between my *hymenanthes* and *ferrugineum*. *(what? what?)* Bit difficult to see exactly what it was in the drizzle. But it was definitely big.'

Both Lucy and I now had a string of "whats" dangling from the tips of our tongues.

'If you ask me, I'd say it was some sort of lion.'

Our 'WHATS?' exploded from our mouths.

'Not as big as an ordinary lion, mind you,' Eleanor went on.

I wasn't quite sure what she meant by an ordinary lion. Whatever its size, big or small, having a lion stalk through your garden made it far from an ordinary beast. In fact, something quite extraordinary.

'How large would you say it was?' stuttered Lucy.

Eleanor shrugged. 'Oh, I don't know. The size of an Alsatian, maybe.'

'Well, perhaps it was an Alsatian then,' I declared.

'Alsatians don't have manes. This creature did.' Eleanor looked nervously over her shoulder. 'So, what do you suggest we do?'

I grabbed her, pulled her in, while Lucy slammed the door shut behind her. 'That's what,' we cried as one.

There followed a crisis meeting, First, Lucy and I had to establish that Eleanor was not mistaken in what she'd seen. She was adamant that it was some sort of large beast, neither cat nor dog. Though she conceded it might not necessarily have been a lion. But certainly similar to what she'd seen on one of those David Attenborough TV documentaries. Apart from dashing out to buy a box set of the DVDs and fast-forwarding them in the hope of spotting a similar creature, that information was of little use.

The question of contacting the police arose.

'I think we should,' said Eleanor. 'Just think if we didn't and then someone got savaged. Torn to shreds over in St Mary's. Ripped to pieces between the gravestones, entrails everywhere. Rev. James would be very upset.'

So would the owner of the entrails, I thought.

'Yes... Yes... Okay. I see what you mean,' I interrupted, seeing the scene all too clearly. I could almost hear the crunch of jaws on bone. The tearing of flesh. I hastily reached for my mobile.

The police were quick to arrive. A car, with its blue lights flashing, screeched to a halt at the front of Willow Wren. Three officers sprang out, looked nervously around and then belted down the side to hammer on our cranky-cricket doorbell. I'd barely opened it before they pushed their way in, the last one kicking it closed as the three of them ground to a breathless halt in the hallway.

'We understand there's a lion on the loose,' said the first one in, extracting a notepad and pen. As did the other two. 'Who's seen it?'

'I did,' said Eleanor.

'And you are?'

'Eleanor Venables.'

The first officer started scribbling. 'Venables. Is that spelt with a "balls" at the end?' There was a snigger from the second policeman. And a snort from the third. 'It's no laughing matter, lads,' said the first sternly, turning to them. 'Cadets. Training,' he added, by way of explanation, turning back to us.

Interesting, I thought. Work experience here. How to catch a lion in five easy moves? First, establish its true identity. 'Like one on Planet Earth,' I heard the first officer mutter as he scribbled down Eleanor's answer to his question. Location? In the garden. More scribbling.

'Better take a look, lads,' barked the officer. One cadet scurried over to the front window, the second to the side one. Both looked nervously out.

'Nothing, sir,' reported the one from the side.

'But something in the bushes out there,' said the one at the front. 'Looks suspicious.' We all crowded around to look for ourselves.

There was a wail from Eleanor as a tortoiseshell cat sprang onto the front lawn and padded swiftly across in the direction of next door.

'Oh, Tammy,' she cried, hand flying to her chest. 'My poor puss.'

'I take it that wasn't what you saw earlier?' queried the officer.

Snigger from first cadet. Snort from second. Large "Nos" scribbled on their pads as Eleanor shook her head vehemently.

'I should go and see that's she safe,' she said, squeezing past us all, heading to the hall.

The officer put out a restraining hand. 'I don't think that's advisable, ma'am. Under the circumstances. Not until we've established the whereabouts of purported lion.' The two cadets nodded in agreement, writing an emphatic "Stay put" on their pads. In capital letters. Underlined. I noticed one of them then slip out a mobile from his jacket pocket and start to deftly tap away at the keypad, looking up briefly to wink at his mate.

Hello… Hello… I thought. *This could be going viral.*

It did.

Barely minutes later, my mobile rang. It was Westcott FM, our local radio station. 'Hello,' said the voice down the line. 'I'm Vicky Dixon, presenter on "Westcott Ways", our daily morning show. I understand you've a lion on the loose over your way. Would you like to give us an update as to what's going on?'

What could I say? A creature akin to something from Planet Earth had apparently been seen? But the only thing spotted since was next door's cat padding across the front lawn?

Vicky sounded rather disappointed when she received that information. Guts on the gravestones would have been more to her liking.

'Sir… sir…' exclaimed the first cadet, having finished his texting to alert the world to the unfolding drama here in this usually quiet corner of Sussex. 'There's movement on the right flank.'

I assume he was referring to the path that ran down past the side window of the cottage; and down which was now hurrying the cassocked figure of Rev. James. The garrotted cricket announced his arrival.

'My dear boy,' he gasped as I opened the door to him. 'What in heaven's name is going on?' He pointed up the path at the police car. 'I saw the proximity of the constabulary to your residence and thought it prudent of me to see if I could be of assistance in whatever matter that has brought officers of the law to your domicile.'

In other words, you're being a nosy git, I thought a little uncharitably. Out loud, I cut to the chase. 'There's a lion on the loose.'

'Holy shit,' squealed Rev. James and flung himself over the doorsill and into the hall where he crossed himself three times whilst slamming the door shut behind him with his heel.

'Join the club,' I murmured.

The club expanded when the sighting by second cadet of two dumpy figures accompanied by two boxers was confirmed by the vocally impaired cricket to be those of Sandra and John Coles from Ashton Manor.

'What's afoot?' they queried when I answered the bell.

'Lion on the loose.'

Their feet leapt in the air and two 'Bloody hells' exploded from them as they and their boxers hurled themselves into the hall. They now stood nervously in the middle of Willow Wren's sitting room while Henry and Heidi played chase with Emily and Bertie around the kitchen table.

'Hey, Paul, take a look at this.' Lucy had turned on the telly and tuned to South Sussex news. And there was Eric's face looming large on the screen, full of concern.

'Should you be watching this, Paul, don't worry,' he was saying. 'We're right behind you. Ready to back you up should the lion attack. And if you do get mauled to death, we appreciate the good service you've provided to the local community.'

'Amen,' murmured Rev. James. 'Whoops, sorry, Paul,' he added, seeing me grimace. 'Force of habit.'

Eric's face faded to be replaced by the newsreader who stated that police had warned all residents of Ashton to stay indoors. My grimace grew grimmer.

'Well, that's settled then,' declared Lucy, clapping her hands together. 'Before any of us get mauled to death, who's for coffee?'

'Tea please,' said the cadets.

'Milk, two sugars,' said one.

'Milk, one sugar,' said two.

'Well, this is all rather jolly,' said Rev. James as he was handed his mug of coffee. 'Nothing like a crisis to bring the community together.' He beamed benignly around at us, crowded together, mugs in hands, sipping nervously, crunching on the ginger biscuits Lucy had managed to unearth from the back of the cupboard.

The "jolly" had barely been spoken when a roar rent the room. A muted roar admittedly. And not that close. But loud enough and near enough to make coffees (and two teas) spill from mugs and biscuit crumbs splutter from mouths.

'Did you hear that?' said Eleanor, blanching.

'I did indeed, ma'am,' said the officer, baulking.

So did the two cadets, scribbling.

I didn't say a word, still nibbling.

The two cadets sprang back to their respective window positions and scanned the lawn, the drive, the pathway across to St Mary's, tombstones still free of entrails. Nothing to report, they stated as another roar rolled out. As one, we went rigid. Fixed to the spot. Anxiety feeding its way through us like snake venom through veins. *Could it be…?*

John Coles was the first to break ranks. He coughed. 'It's a cow in labour, over on the farm.'

"Cow" appeared on two notepads. Coffee (and two teas) was resumed.

The accompanying conversation was strained. Stilted. But flowed. Touched on the weather. Cool for July. But no rain. Mentioned Ashton's pageant. Next Saturday. Should be fun. Providing it stayed dry. And providing no lion was still on the prowl. Conversation stopped abruptly.

The rasping incessant rattle of the garrotted cricket brought me to my senses. *Who on earth...? Why no sighting by the cadets?*

'I'll go,' I said to Lucy, wondering who it could possibly be. I cautiously levered the door open an inch or so and peered out. I was confronted by a bush. Not of the rhododendron variety, mark you. But a bush all the same.

'Hi,' it said, extending a leafy branch *(arm)*.

I shook the offered twig *(hand)*.

'I'm Russell Baxter.' *(not a real tree then)*. 'I expect you're wondering what this is all about.'

Well, yes, I *was* rather curious. After all, one didn't often have a talking tree turn up on one's doorstep.

'The Westcott vet practice got in contact with Highdown Safari Park. Someone by the name of Beryl. Said you were under attack by a lion? Needed a trained marksman with a tranquillising gun. Well, that's me. So here I am. In my camouflage gear. Good, isn't it?'

I must admit it did look quite effective. Green leaves sprouting from arms, legs and torso. With even a bunch piled on his head, from which dangled folds of green netting. Obviously, Russell was proud of his arboreal appearance – he did blend in with his surroundings – and had obviously fooled the two cadets in slipping down to the cottage undetected – possibly by ducking down along the hedgerow. But was that pride sufficient to fool a lion? I suspected not.

The tree *(marksman)* pulled out a rifle he'd had under the cover of his canopy *(combat fatigues)*. 'Now, just fill me in first and then I can get on with it. Track the lion down and dart it. The back-up team are on standby just down the road.'

Once armed with the Planet Earth details, the name of Eleanor's cat and had been informed that a cow was in labour nearby, he set off; and despite the useless information he'd been given, there was a determined quiver to his foliage.

Of course, I had a deluge of questions to answer when I returned to the sitting room; the cadets' note-taking went into overdrive. Everyone jostled to get the best view of the tree as it swept around to the front of the cottage, only to judder to a halt in the middle of the front lawn as if suddenly rooted to the spot.

'Must have seen something,' said Sandra Coles in a brisk tone of voice.

'The lion?' said Eleanor, in a sharp tone of voice.

'Bearing in mind we have been made aware of a creature such as that witnessed by the likes of David Attenborough, there is a distinct probability that the sighting of such an animal has been the chief reason for the marksman's decision to become stationery,' said Rev. James in his customary long drawn-out obtuse, rambling tone of voice.

Heads crowded the window, straining to see.

What we did see was a large golden retriever come lolloping over from the churchyard – tombs still bloodless. Rather less golden than he should have been. His lower legs brown, splattered with mud. Likewise, his neck. Brown, thickly covered in mud. Very mane-like. Very lion-like.

As the dog sniffed the tree before cocking his leg against it, we all turned to stare at Eleanor. And a chorus of 'Wells?' welled in our throats.

Eleanor's garden became the focus of attention again just a month or so later.

'You won't believe what I've just seen,' I said to Lucy, having just been to the bathroom for my first pee of the day. 'Eleanor's back lawn. Total devastation. She's going to go bananas. Take a look.'

Lucy hopped out of bed, returning to declare me right. Eleanor would be livid.

The term "lawn" could no longer be applied to what had been neat closely mown grass. So well-manicured by Eleanor that it looked as if every blade had been subjected to a thorough clipping and polishing. But not now. Now it was a sea of churned up turves. Ashton's junior football team couldn't have done a better job in their muddier moments of play.

We both knew how much our neighbour adored her garden. The hours she spent tending to it since moving in next door a year back. She had replanted the Spencers' borders. There were now two of them which were a pleasure to peer down on from our bedroom or from the bathroom when I was standing at the toilet pan or towelling myself down after a shower. Small plants to the front. I spotted purple asters, eryngium, pale blue salvias. Larger to the back. Splashed of yellow daisy-like rudbeckia, pink phlox and veronica. Some I didn't recognise and looked them up on Google. Clumps of colour, blended and coordinated to please the eye. As one flowered and faded, another nearby took its place. And between those two borders was a lawn worthy of any bowls club.

As Eleanor told me whenever I poked my head over the dividing fence – which was often – 'A lawn is so important to set off borders, don't you think? So, I've made sure mine's extra special.' She went on to tell me she'd revamped the lawn, seeding it with a top-quality mix. Several types of fescue and some crested dog's-tail. 'No ryegrass mixture. Too coarse. Besides, I don't need it as my lawn's never going to be subjected to heavy wear and tear.'

Mmm... Heavy wear, maybe not. But tear... Well, that was going to be a different story. One that unfolded like her rolled back turves later that Sunday morning.

As I let Gertie, our goose, out and fed the chickens, I could hear Eleanor muttering to herself the other side of the dividing fence and stood on the small pile of bricks adjacent to the fence – kept there for moments like this when a tête-à-tête was likely to occur – to pop my head over.

'So, you've had visitors,' I said.

'Dreadful. Simply dreadful.' Eleanor approached me, tiptoeing through the tufts of torn up grass. Her moon face, normally tranquil, was eclipsed with rage. Her grey-brown eyes flecked with fury. And an unseen hand was yanking her strings so violently from behind that it made her ventriloquist's dummy-like chin work up and down at a rate of knots. 'Utter devastation. What could have done it?'

In answer to her question, I pointed to a hole in her hedge that ran down the other side of her garden and which separated it from adjacent fields. 'I'm pretty sure it's a badger.'

'Why my lawn?'

'Perfect place to dig up some nice juicy worms.'

Eleanor squared her shoulders, the thick sweep of her platinum-grey chignon quivered, and in her cultured voice said, 'Well, I wish he would damned well find somewhere else. Bloody pest.'

Her use of the vernacular continued most of the morning as she set to work with a trowel, on her knees, shuffling back and forth across her lawn, rolling back each uprooted sod and uttering similar in the 'You sod,' said loudly every few minutes to vent her displeasure at the culprit.

I did pop my head over the fence again later to see how she was getting on. Give a few words of encouragement. Buck her up a bit as she continued to knee-shunt across her mangled sward. Many of the holes being filled in were round, elliptical.

'They're called snuffle-holes,' I told her. 'It's where the badger had pushed his snout down into the ground so he can suck up a juicy worm without it snapping in two.'

I half-expected another swear word or two. But clearly, Eleanor was getting out of puff and just responded with a nasally snuffle of her own as she continued to plug the plethora of holes.

I knew badgers have a large territory which they patrol every night and that they have several feeding areas. Maybe Eleanor's lawn was a one-off stop for a snack before moving on to pastures new?

I did suggest that to her later in the day, once her lawn was patched up.

'We can only hope,' said Eleanor. 'But I'll certainly put some wire netting across that hole in my hedge just in case he tries coming back.'

He did try. And did succeed in getting through. A messed-up lawn greeted Eleanor the next morning.

Brock had found a rich supply of worms in her lawn. A yummy feeding area. Very yummy. So yummy that he made a determined effort to tunnel under Eleanor's netting night after night. Her re-ravished lawn became a daily sighting to accompany my morning pee.

'Have you any other suggestions as to how we can stop him?' she asked the following Saturday after a week's worth of lawn-mauling. She looked across to where I was on my brick-pile, looking over the fence.

'Well, there are those ultrasonic devices. They emit a high-pitched sound when triggered by the movement of an animal.'

'Oh, good gracious, no. It might upset Tammy. And I couldn't be doing with that. She's a nervous enough cat as it is.'

Good point, I thought. Besides, it might encourage the cat to pop into our garden to poo. So, definitely not a good idea.

A trawl of the internet came up with a few other options. Sprinkling chopped chilli peppers around the lawn. Eleanor wasn't keen. Strips of cloth soaked in Citronella or Olbas Oil, hung across the lawn. She did try that one. The evening aroma that wafted over our garden was quite refreshing. But didn't deter brock.

When Rev. James learnt of the problems Eleanor had been having with her rogue badger, he came up with another suggestion: and spelt it out to us in his customary expansive manner – a way with words that had seen a gradual decline in church attendances due to Rev. James's interminably lengthy and waffly sermons, boring his congregation to death in this life. *(If not hastening them to pass on to the next one.)*

'As I understand it, the complexities of dealing with said badger means there has to be a comprehension of the dealings of said creature's mind,' he began.

Both Eleanor and I were lost instantly. 'Sorry?' we exclaimed.

'I quite understand it is difficult to comprehend the nature of things that Nature puts before us.'

'Very.' *(me, puzzled)*
'Absolutely.' *(Eleanor, perplexed)*

There was an enthusiastic nod from Rev. James. 'That's the precise reason why one has to explore the avenues that lie open to us in our attempts to walk a course that will bring a satisfactory end to our endeavours to end said badger's perambulations across said lawn, if you see what I mean.'

I didn't.

Nor did Eleanor. 'What's the daft old bat wittering on about?' she whispered in my ear.

'Don't ask me. Ask him.'

'I daren't. We'd be here for hours.' She giggled.

'Now,' said Rev. James, giving Eleanor a reprimanding look, 'you should be getting down to basics, if you don't mind me saying.'

I did mind him saying but couldn't say. Nor could Eleanor, her fingers pressed tightly to her lips in her attempt to stop giggling.

'I feel it's incumbent on me to offer my assistance since as I understand it, the incursions of this creature have, as yet, not been thwarted by the efforts of your good selves to bring about closure to the activities of said creature, whereby your lawns have been made the object of his attention in the need for him to find sustenance. Am I correct in that assumption?'

Eleanor nodded, her shoulders heaving.

I, too, was wordless. What was the point? Any forthcoming would have been buried under the avalanche from Rev. James.

He clapped his hands. 'I've had an inspiration. Not exactly having been guided by the hand of God but set on a pathway that may take us in a direction that could evolve into a solution.'

I inwardly groaned. Oh gawd. Back on avenues and pathways again. All I could see ahead was being led up a blind alley.

'Actions speak louder than words,' said Rev. James, suddenly becoming very lucid.

Eleanor and I exchanged looks. We could be in for a whole heap of action then. Rev. James asked if we wouldn't mind waiting awhile. He'd be back in a jiff with something that just might deter the badger once and for all. We were intrigued enough to wait as he hurried back over to St Mary's. And it wasn't for long.

'Oh, for Christ's sake,' exclaimed Eleanor, 'what on earth is he up to?' Rev. James had re-emerged from the church at a slower pace than when he'd entered, his shoulders stooped. The reason, the large wooden crucifix he was dragging behind him. He trailed it across the communal drive and around the side of Eleanor's cottage, propping it up against the sidewall by her back garden gate. He was a little out of breath and excused himself while he recovered. Then he was in full flow again.

'It's been languishing in the back of the vestry for ages, its virtues hidden from the likes of those who may wish to contemplate the sacrifices that one may have to make to find inner contentment.' The reverend paused to smile benignly at the crucifix. 'I suddenly thought it may provide the necessary means by which you could find such contentment if we stuck it in your garden, Eleanor.'

You should have seen Eleanor's face. It was more than a little cross as she stared at the big one in front of her. That was a bog-standard crucifix with a somewhat battered wooden Jesus, in traditional white loin cloth, arms outstretched, in full writhe; though his facial features expressed more agony than may have been intended due to wood worm having powdered his right eye and dry rot having splintered his lips, to leave a gaping hole worthy of "The Scream".

I knew badgers got used to the layout of a certain area and that by changing things around or adding items could be off-putting to them. So, a scarecrow wearing a rustling nylon mac could work but might need repositioning daily. Highly reflective strips of aluminized plastic, wind chimes and toy windmills could make brock think twice about using Eleanor's lawn as an eatery. There is the theory that the vibrations from windmills will drive the grubs deeper in the lawn making them more inaccessible. I think brock would just dig deeper, make more mess. But a crucifix? I just couldn't see that working. But then they say God works in mysterious ways; so perhaps there was a way he was going to stop badgers in their tracks. Or at least the track that led into Eleanor's garden.

Certainly, being creatures of habit, badgers can be very determined in their efforts to keep to traditional pathways once they've been established. As demonstrated with this brock. Eleanor had tried to plug the track coming in from the field with plastic netting weaved through the base of the hedge. To no avail. Then chicken wire. Equally unsuccessful. Weld mesh laid flat to stop brock digging under it was a further failure. I knew of someone who used a large boulder that he and his mate heaved with great difficulty across a badger run that came into his garden through a hole in his fence. The next day, he found the boulder had been rolled to one side. That all smacked of the Garden of Gethsemane, so I didn't think it was worthy of a mention. We had enough of a cross to bear as it was.

Once Rev. James had excused himself to write up his sermon for Sunday – said in so many, many words – Eleanor and I had a brief pow-wow as to our next course of action.

'I really don't think I can cope with waking up each morning to a dying Jesus on my lawn,' declared Eleanor, with a shudder. 'But then I don't want to offend Rev. James. He is, after all, trying to be helpful.'

I agreed. 'Well, how about giving it a go for just a few days? At least then, we'll have shown willing and be able to sleep easy in our graves.'

I saw the look Eleanor gave me and grinned. 'Sorry. Couldn't resist that one. But you know what I mean.'

After much discussion, it was decided that the most effective position for the cross would be right in the middle of the badger run through the hedge, facing out to the field from where brock would come.

It didn't take too much effort to erect the cross, the ground in the herbaceous border next to the hole in the hedge being well worked over by Eleanor in the past.

'I'll be amazed if it has any effect,' said Eleanor, jamming a spade in the mound of earth we'd excavated and standing back to survey our handiwork.

The cross rose above the line of beech hedging, Jesus facing west, his chipped body caught in the rays of the setting sun, a halo of orange light around his head. If I'd had the slightest element of religion in me, I could have almost convinced myself that it might work. But it would be a miracle if it did.

Eleanor sniffed. 'I suppose we can be thankful it's not a statue of St Francis of Assisi, otherwise we'd be welcoming in all the bloody badgers in West Sussex.'

Much to our surprise, we had no visit by brock that night. Hence, no tearing up of the lawn. Eleanor was delighted. 'God works in mysterious ways,' she said.

'It's early days,' I warned.

I was rebuked with a 'Ye of little faith.'

We actually did enjoy a week free from the roaming of brock; and so, Eleanor was happy to put up with the cross in her hedge. 'Grin and bear,' she said.

The following Sunday changed all that. It was mid-morning. I was hoeing the vegetable plot when I heard what appeared to be chanting over the fence. I sprang onto my pile of bricks and looked over. Eleanor was standing by her back door, hands clasped tightly together at bosom-level, staring towards the cross, clearly agitated. It was from that direction the chanting was coming; more specifically from over the hedge in the field.

I decided I'd get a better view from the back-bedroom window as to what was going on, and ran indoors and up the stairs, leaving a startled Lucy preparing Sunday lunch in the kitchen. And what a sight I saw.

There must have been at least 20 or so white-habited nuns crouched in the field to the front of the crucifix, palms together under their chins, eyes closed, fervently chanting, in unison, some homily to God which I couldn't quite catch. I saw Eleanor storm up to the cross and peer over the hedge, her face full of fury. 'What the hell's going on?' she thundered.

There was a ripple of startled 'Hail Marys', before the nuns scrambled to their feet, rapidly crossed hands over bosoms and with a bow to the crucifix, hurried out of the field, heading for the church.

Rev. James was later to explain loquaciously. A charabanc-load of nuns had stopped off to visit St Mary's on their way to an afternoon service over in Brigstock. Many had been caught short and slipped into the field to obey urgent calls of Nature, the most convenient place being in front of Eleanor's crucifix. So, what we had been witnessing was not nuns earnestly praying but rather a bunch of nuns earnestly peeing, giving thanks to Jesus for their blessed relief. Whatever the reason, the crucifix had to go. But not before brock returned, so making Rev. James's trudge back to the church with his crucifix all the more of a cross to bear.

So, Eleanor's battle with brock continued. No resolution in sight.

It was during one of my bathroom visits – having succumbed to the aftereffects of a particularly potent vindaloo – that it struck me. Sense of smell. Mine at that moment being under attack.

Most animals have a good sense of smell.

We might be able to smell that there's a teaspoonful of sugar in our mug of coffee. But it seems a dog, for instance, can sense that teaspoonful in two Olympic-sized swimming pools. I felt sure it was the same for badgers. After all, part of the skill of badger-watching is to make sure you are sitting downwind of the set. Otherwise, your scent can be carried by an eddy of breeze and be detected underground. Result? The about-to-emerge badger gets wind of you and decides on a no-show.

Here could be the answer to deterring Eleanor's rogue badger. Well, at least a possibility. Put him off with human scent.

I saw Lucy's puzzled look when I suggested it.

'So, what are you going to do? Tell Eleanor to roll around on her lawn?'

I shook my head. 'No, pee on it.'

You should have seen her face. Her look of incredulity. 'You're joking, surely?' She gave me a long, hard stare. 'No, you're not, are you?'

I shook my head again.

Lucy continued: 'I really can't see Eleanor stooping to doing that.'

To be truthful, I couldn't either. The sight of Eleanor squatting on her sward didn't conjure up a pretty picture, no matter how genteelly she conducted her sanitary movements. 'Well, I could do it, I suppose.'

'Oh, come off it, Paul. I can't see Eleanor allowing you to wander around her lawn squirting urine everywhere.'

'She doesn't have to know. I can do it under the cover of night.'

'And risk being exposed if she happened to spot you? I'm not sure her heart would stand being flashed at.'

But I wasn't to be deterred. 'I'll fill one of our empty cleaner sprayers. That should do the job.' And that's what I did that night. Under the cover of dark, I sneaked over the fence for a quick piss… piss… across Eleanor's lawn.

Looking down at her lawn from the bathroom the next morning, I was delighted to discover it had been left untouched. Boy, was I relieved.

So too was Eleanor, though puzzled as to why brock had stopped turning up. 'Perhaps he just got pissed off,' she suggested to me later.

Ah, Eleanor, if only you knew. So close to the truth. So close.

14
A Colourful Life

'Goodness, Beryl, you look like...' the words faltered on Eric's lips as the laser-look she gave him stunned him into silence. I too had been rendered speechless on arrival at the hospital that August morning. We both stood there like lemons, while the indrawn cheeks and tight lips on Beryl's face suggested she was sucking on one.

'So, what do you think?' she queried, her good eye swivelling from me to Eric and back again, while her glass one stared blankly between us. Always an unnerving sight. But it wasn't this that had drawn our eyes to her. It was what she was wearing. 'So?' she repeated, raising her arms and twirling around. 'Makes a change, doesn't it?'

She was obviously fishing for a complimentary comment. But not the likes of what Eric landed her with. 'Strewth, Beryl, you look like a squashed satsuma.'

Ouch, Eric, that's not very tactful, I thought and hastened to make amends. 'Very cheerful, Beryl. Helps brighten up the place.'

The object of our attention was what encased Beryl's torso. Almost swamping her in a vast ball of wool. A very voluminous sweater in vivid orange. Far removed from the black polo neck and black cardigan with matching black trousers that made up her usual daily office outfit.

'Thanks, Paul,' replied Beryl, glaring at Eric who turned scarlet and sped out of reception. She plucked at one of the shapeless sleeves, pulling it up from where it had slipped down over her hand. 'Orange is associated with improved concentration,' she went on. 'Helps overcome feelings of dread.' She gave me a cheery smile. 'Perhaps I should knit you one.'

What a dreadful idea, I thought as I swiftly followed Eric.

Mandy remarked on Beryl's buoyant mood, while I checked on the routine ops booked in for me to do that morning. 'Must be that orange sweater.'

'More likely this.' I tapped the ops' list. Ernie Entwhistle's collie, Bess, was down to be spayed. He and Beryl had become close friends since the death of his previous collie, Ben, last summer. The bouquet of flowers from him last Valentine's Day proof of their closeness even if it did have that frog in it.

'Well, Bess, my pet,' I said as Mandy brought the collie through from the ward. 'Sleepy time for you.' Between us, we levered her onto the prep table where she sat good as gold while her right foreleg was shaved and thiopentone injected slowly into her vein until she sank into unconsciousness. At that point, an orange blob loomed up at the prep door window.

'All's well, Beryl,' I called out. 'I'm just going to start spaying her.' The orange blob faded from the aperture. It reappeared in the corridor as Bess was wheeled out of the operating theatre 20 minutes later, sporting six stitches that closed a midline incision. I reassured Beryl that the op had been straightforward.

'I'll let Ernie know then,' she replied, pulling her orange woolly sleeves up as she bobbed back up to reception. Rolling along the corridor, Eric's analogy to a "satsuma" took on a certain element of truth.

The usual routine with standard operations was for the owners to phone up later in the day to see what time they should collect their pets. They would then be met by Mandy or Lucy with any instructions for follow-up appointments if required. In the case of spays, an appointment for removal of stitches in ten days' time would be booked.

An exception had been made for Ernie Entwhistle at Beryl's request. I was to see him and hand over Bess. 'Would that be okay?' How could I possibly refuse?

Beryl's jumper bristled with expectation as five o'clock approached, the agreed time for the handover. By then, Bess had recovered from her op and, though a little woozy, was on her feet and ready to go. 'Ernie's arrived in the car park,' said an excited Beryl, dashing down to the office to let me know, then speeding on down to the ward in a blur of orange to bring Bess up. I made my way to reception just as the front door opened and Ernie Entwhistle entered. I was expecting the usual nattily dressed gent in navy blazer but Ernie appeared encased in a huge sweater that hung down over his wrists and sloped in a jagged edge around his hips. And the colour? Bright orange.

When Bess appeared, there were frenzied wags of her tail, while Ernie and Beryl embraced in what could only be described as an orange squash.

Whatever, it certainly made for a colourful end to that particular day.

As it turned out, it wasn't just that day. Colour in its many variations proved to be a topic that constantly reared its head in the ensuing weeks, on account of Beryl's new-found fascination for its influence on our lives. A subject that came to colour her life more and more; and in doing so, coloured ours as well. We might have been forewarned the morning Eric was flicking through the latest edition of the Westcott Gazette. Seems that since last month's meeting of the Chawcombe and Ashton Ladies' Afternoon Tea Group when their guest speaker, Cecil Groper, had shown slides of near-naked young tribesmen dancing around a blazing fire, there had been a surge in new members.

Eric chortled. 'Bet that caused a few red cheeks,' he commented, reading the news item out to us.

Beryl jumped on it immediately. 'Good example that.'

'In what way?' asked Eric.

'How such a thing can affect you.'

Eric screwed up his lips, the corners of his eyes creased. 'I'm not so sure I follow you. I mean it's not every day you're going to get a bunch of naked young men war-dancing around Westcott's shopping precinct, pounding through the Pound Shop, is it? For one thing, Health and Safety wouldn't permit it.'

'I'm not talking about the young men. It's those ladies. Their flushed cheeks. An indication of what they were feeling.'

An image of what they might have been feeling sprang up in my mind. A horny image. Porn-in-a-teacup. That sort of thing. I quickly dismissed it.

Beryl elaborated. Seemed she'd recently become interested in chromotherapy.

Eric and I looked blank.

'Colour psychology,' she explained.

We were none the wiser. Though it did seem to be linked to the Chawcombe and Aston Ladies' Afternoon Tea Group's cheeks and the genitalia of those tribesmen. Beryl attempted to explain more fully. And by the time I had finished my coffee, I had a vague inkling of what she was on about. But very vague.

It all hinged on the colour red. It seems chromotherapy practitioners believe every colour relates to an area of your body. Red and pink are linked to your blood circulation and breathing. Hence, when you see it, it means the pulse has quickened, breathing's more rapid and blood pressure's risen in that part of the body.

'In what part?' whispered Eric, leaning across to me. 'Cheeks or those guys ding dongs.'

'Eric,' snapped Beryl. 'Enough of that.'

It was enough too, for the time being, with coffee break finished. But not Beryl's discourse on colours. Much more was to come later. And all prompted by the arrival of a new client.

A Miss Veronica Springfield.

'A nice name,' I commented, running a finger down the list of appointments booked in for that afternoon. 'Conjures up pastures full of meadowsweet, poppies and nodding heads of golden wheat.' My, what a romantic mood I was in. From the withering look thrown at me by Beryl, she clearly thought I was high on something. Or had succumbed to too many whiffs of nitrous oxide during the morning's ops.

'Can't go by names,' she muttered curtly, probably thinking more in terms of fields full of ragwort, dandelions and prickly heads of thistles.

However, when Miss Springfield did step lightly into reception, she actually summed up her name. There was a spring in her step. And she did field an exceptionally tall and willowy frame. The sort of frame a wicker man, given the chance, would have been keen to weave his hands around. Her hair was buttercup yellow. Her eyes forget-me-not blue. And her lips the pink of wild roses. Her grace and charm set off by the folds of cream cotton blouse and flowing cream trousers, over which she wore a soft cashmere coat that Joseph would have been proud of. A coat of many colours, but colours that were subdued. A wash of indigo and pale green, delicate swirls of light blue, the merest hint of cerise. Colour-coordinated? Veronica Springfield certainly was.

In sharp contrast to Beryl, perched on her computer stool. Back in her normal black garb. And now with a black look to go with it. Clearly rattled by this radiant creature that had materialised in front of her. Even if her mind might have progressed to a desire for a meadow choked with brambles and nettles, she managed to crack her lips into a semblance of a smile when Miss Springfield verified that she had an appointment to see a Mr Mitchell at 4.00 pm.

'That will be this gentleman,' said Beryl, pointing a talon at me.

Miss Springfield's eyes blazed with all the azure intensity of cornflowers on a hot summer's day as she extended a well-manicured hand to shake mine. 'I'll go and fetch the clan,' she said. 'You may have to excuse their behaviour as they are rather a boisterous bunch. And can get a little out of hand.'

Like me in a field of wheat with the likes of you, I thought, dreamily watching her drift out of reception. I was soon jerked out of my reverie by a cacophony of barks that exploded from the car park. 'Good grief, Beryl. What am I booked to see?'

She peered down at the appointments' book. 'A French bulldog by the looks of it.' She peered closer. 'Sorry, French bulldogs. Doesn't say how many, though.'

I was soon to find out.

First, one head appeared around the bottom of the reception door. A heavy brown, massive square head, medium eyes set wide apart, rounded upright ears. A second brown head snuffled up alongside it. Both took one look at me, growled and backed out, still growling.

'Oh, stop it, boys. Don't be so silly,' Veronica Springwell's voice – not quite so melodious as before. 'Go on, get in there.'

The two dogs reappeared. Powerful, muscular little dogs. Brindle-coated. Short stubby-tailed. Their nails skittered and scrabbled on the vinyl as they reluctantly ventured in, all of a huff and puff. Veronica followed, holding their two leads in one hand. In her other were three more, stretched and strained behind her. 'Come on, you lot,' she said, turning to pull at them. 'There's nothing to be afraid of.' Three more heads appeared. Three more brown, muscular square heads that instantly emitted a series of deep growls as Veronica dragged in three more French bulldogs almost identical to the first two.

'Meet my cheri amours,' she gasped as the five of them milled around the reception, sniffing and snorted with cocking of legs by two, and a squat from one of the other three. No comment from Beryl. She just cocked her eye and adjusted the numbers in the appointments' book.

In a whirl of leads and legs and lolling tongues, her cheris were hustled and bustled along the corridor into my consulting room. Here, more formal introductions were made via each individual dog being hauled onto the table – his or her name announced and for him or her to be given a general check-over by me. Victor and Hugo, the two males – father and son. Zephine, Fantine and Cosette, the three females – a mother, daughter and a half-cousin. *(Not clear how the latter had appeared on the family tree – something to do with a randy uncle on her aunt's side, said Veronica.)* Whatever, her cheris had evidently expressed plenty of amour in their lives to date. And the fact that Victor and Hugo were still entire, there was potentially much more amour to come. Clearly nothing "miserables" about that lot. Oo la la.

I'm not sure how the subject of chromatology arose. I think it was during my examination of the fourth bulldog – Fantine, I think it was. I have to admit that by then, I was getting a bit wound up listening to my fourth heart, checking my fourth set of lungs, my fourth set of teeth, looking down my fourth couple of ear canals; conscious time was ticking on and that other appointments would be piling up in the waiting room.

'It must be stressful at times,' said Veronica, as I gave Fantine a clean bill of health and she was hauled off the table to be replaced by an identical-looking bitch – Cossette – the half-cousin. Fifth heart, fifth set of lungs, etc. coming up. 'Being a vet,' she added as I rammed my auriscope down my ninth ear canal. Just one more to go.

'Maybe you should try a bit of this.' A card was slid across the table as I popped my auriscope out of its last lughole.

I snatched it up and quickly glanced at it. Dr Veronica Springfield. Chromotherapist. Let me bring colour into your life. A mobile phone number and website were detailed. 'Thank you, yes. Certainly worth considering.'

'You might find it does you good,' said Veronica, gathering up her cheris' leads. 'Take you out of yourself.'

Could well do, I mused as I watched Veronica Springfield glide serenely back down to reception with her pack in tow. New horizons. Fresh pastures. Yes, those pastures in particular could do me good especially with the likes of

Veronica to lend me a guiding hand as she plunged through shafts of ripening wheat.

I coloured at the thought.

*

Colour cropped up during another of Eric's perusals of the Western Gazette. This time as we were having our afternoon tea break. If he'd been looking for the latest activities of the Chawcombe and Ashton Ladies' Afternoon Tea Group, then he wasn't disappointed. He learnt that they had invited Cecil Groper back for another lengthy exposé on the Papua New Guinea tribesmen, having ascertained there'd be plenty more revealing pictures to accompany it.

He also learnt about a case that appeared at Westcott's magistrates' court. And it had him in fits of giggles. Of course, I had to ask what he'd found so funny. It seems that last week, a horse and cart driver was given a 12-month conditional discharge for taking his Clydesdale, Connor, through red traffic lights. In his defence, the owner of Connor, Mickey O'Flynn, claimed his horse was colour-blind.

'Seems that's not the case,' remarked Eric, reading on. 'Horses can see red and blue but are unable to tell green from grey. So, seeing red at the lights, Connor should have stopped. He didn't and saw blue instead. The flashing light on the police car. That soon brought him to a halt.' He chuckled again. 'Great story, eh?'

I nodded and smiled.

Even Beryl permitted her lips to curve up in semblance of one, before telling us that Mickey O'Flynn was quite a well-known local character, often seen busking in Westcott's shopping precinct with his horse.

I didn't realise how relevant the item on Connor the Clydesdale would become in just a couple of days' time.

Meanwhile, Beryl's burgeoning interest in chromotherapy continued. And we weren't spared that interest.

'What are all these colour charts doing in here?' demanded Crystal one lunchtime, Beryl being absent over at

Bert's, buying baguettes. She waved one of the cards at Eric and me.

'It's Beryl,' said Eric hesitantly. 'She's thinking we might be better off with a change of colour scheme in the waiting room.'

'Why, what's wrong with what we've got? I thought we all decided that something neutral was best. Hence, we went for magnolia. A safe bet.'

'It's one of Beryl's latest fads,' explained Eric. 'Chromotherapy.'

'What?'

'Chromotherapy,' repeated her husband. 'The science of using colour for health benefits.'

'I know what it means,' said Crystal, a little impatiently. 'I'm just wondering what makes her think she can dictate what colour schemes we go for – not that it's necessary to redecorate as we only had it done last year.'

'I'm sure she means well,' said Eric.

'Well, you tell her from me that it's our decision. Not hers. I'll tell her myself if necessary when I get back from my afternoon visits.' With that, Crystal about-turned smartly and marched out. Clearly in a bit of a strop. And that was unlike her. Usually, she was cool, calm, collected. Maybe there was more to it. Something on the home front causing a bit of friction between her and Eric? Something more than a pot of paint could put, right?

Eric gave me a sheepish look just as Beryl bustled in brandishing our baguettes. Oh Lordy. Were we now going to bite off more than we could chew?

With the baguettes eaten and coffee nearly finished without mention of colour charts, we thought we'd got away with it. Not so.

'So, what do you think?' said Beryl, picking a sliver of ham out from between her incisors with a long red talon. 'Blue?'

Eric pretended to feign puzzlement, but it didn't work.

'The waiting room,' continued Beryl. 'A nice shade of cornflower?'

'Uh... well... maybe a bit on the cool side,' Eric risked saying.

An eye was swivelled on him.

'Green?'

'A touch sickly perhaps.'

An iris contracted and a pupil constricted.

'Yellow then.'

'I'm not sure we really...'

There was a whirl of an eyeball. The click of a false one. Laser beam on standby. Focused. All systems ready to go.

I went. Hastily springing to my feet, excusing myself.

Disappearing before Beryl, all fired up, saw red.

But I was to see red later that afternoon while working through my appointments list, though the patient in question couldn't. I already knew that, thanks to last week's feature in the Western Gazette about the court case involving the horse and cart, Connor being the horse that got trapped. Going through a red light.

'You've done what, Beryl?' I fumed.

'Booked you in to see Connor,' she repeated.

She saw my stunned look. 'Connor the Clydesdale,' she said as if that would make it any clearer.

It didn't. 'But, Beryl, I'm in the middle of appointments here in the hospital. I can't suddenly go galloping off to see a horse somewhere, can I?'

'You won't have to be galloping off anywhere. He's coming in.'

I was even more flummoxed, picturing Connor cantering up through the carpark to sit in the waiting room before trotting in to see me. I would bridle even if he didn't.

Beryl tutted. 'I can't see why you're getting on your high horse, so.'

'Beryl, that's not funny.' I glared at her, getting redder by the minute. Did I notice a slight twitch at the corners of her mouth? The briefest of smiles cracking her pancaked cheeks? Whatever, she reigned it in well. Oh, blimey. Now, I was at it. Next, she'd be telling me straight from the horse's mouth.

Which is exactly what she did. Putting the cart before the...
Stop it, Paul. Stop it.

She went on to explain.

Mickey O'Flynn, Connor's owner, had phoned through asking if someone could check over his Clydesdale. He'd suggested bringing the horse over rather than having the vet visit. 'Guess it's because he hasn't got a home address,' said Beryl in an aside. 'Being a traveller and all that.' She thought it a little unusual, but rather than not see Connor at all, had arranged for him to be here in the carpark at 4.00 pm.

I was still fuming. 'You could have said.'

Beryl shrugged. 'You didn't ask.'

'Come off it, Beryl. That's no answer. It's not every day one has a horse clumping up for an appointment, is it?'

'I know that, Paul. All the more reason you should be pleased rather than annoyed. Something out of the ordinary. A bit of a challenge. And I've given you a half an hour slot. Should be time enough.'

'It's not for you to say what you consider a bit of a challenge. Besides which, how do you know I can work out what's wrong in 30 minutes?

Beryl began to quiver. The ends of her raven-wings began to tremble. All tell-tale signs of a spat's beginnings.

Mine were well under way. The tic in my forehead had started to throb. My heart was thumping. Teeth grinding.

The appearance of Crystal stopped a mini-war from breaking out.

'Beryl, I've just seen a horse and cart out in the carpark.'

'It's an appointment booked in for Paul.'

Crystal swivelled to me. 'Well, aren't you a lucky lad. Having something out of the ordinary. Nothing like a bit of a challenge, is there?' she said, her blue eyes blazing.

'That's just what I was saying,' said Beryl, her one eye lasering.

'Er, no...' I said, both mine glazing.

'I've given him a 30-minute slot.'

'That sounds about right. Time enough to find out what's wrong, eh?' Another flash of the blue eyes and Crystal was gone.

Beryl scratched the mole on her chin. 'Now, what were you saying, Paul?'

Perhaps I was being a bit OTT. A bit stressed. But in part that may have been my wariness of all things equine. I'm not really horse-vet material. And they, being the canny creatures they are, can easily sense that. A case of eying me up as I approach. The prick of ears. The snort as they look down their nose at me. The pawing of the ground. Then a kick in the nuts if they can.

As to riding the wretched creatures, I had given it a go – taking some riding lessons along the way – in the hope it would enable me to have a better understanding as to what made them move. Only to discover I was the one being taken for a ride.

Nancy was a knackered nag – one of the more elderly residents of the riding school. A fat, frumpish mare whose arthritic plods around the sand school suggested she was fast approaching the time when she should be shuffling towards the great Knacker's Yard in the sky.

I desperately sought to obey the instructions given. Clenched heels, calves, knees, thighs and buttocks as needed to move Nancy on. Invariably such clenching failed. The only movement induced was in Nancy's bowels; the result of which she'd shudder to a halt, raise her tail and emit a series of explosive farts worthy of the cannon fire that ripped out at Waterloo.

Not that I had to worry about my riding capabilities on meeting Connor. Here we had a horse of the draft variety – a dray for pulling carts, not producing farts. A Clydesdale. A gentle giant. His shoulder a good foot or so above mine. Chestnut-bay. A white blaze running down his forehead. White sockings running down his elbows and knees, merging into the long white feathering over fetlocks and hooves. The coat finely brushed, the feathering finely teased out. Immaculate grooming all over. Complimenting the multitude of straps and their shining brass attachments that made up his harness: head band, breast strap, belly band, back band, girth strap, nose band and several more. A criss-cross display of gleaming polished leather. Of particular note were the two large circular leather blinkers, one to each side of the head, preventing rear and side vision. It meant I had to step in front of Connor, face to face, so that he could see me and I could say hello eye to eye. There was no response as I reached up and stroked his nose. He remained stationary, front left leg slightly bent, tip of hoof on the ground in resting position; his rump between the bars of the grey-painted trailer that stretched out behind him, on which were a large open carrier bag full of hay, a fleece jacket and a rucksack. The owner of the last two items was standing alongside: Mickey O'Flynn.

In comparison to his well-turned-out horse, Mickey resembled a half-empty bag of horse nuts that had been sitting in the sun too long. Crumpled. Creased. In faded, baggy, grey tracksuit bottoms and matching hooded, grey sweatshirt, equally shapeless. But two things made him stand out. First, the hat rammed down over his forehead. Black with fur-lined flaps that curled out from each ear like a couple of dead chinchillas. Second, a bright red guitar looped over his shoulder and which he was strumming. He looked up, sharp-nosed, steely-eyed and stopped strumming as I approached

With a name like Mickey O'Flynn, I expected a 'Top of the mornin' to ya' or similar as it was actually afternoon. Instead of which, I got a 'Pleased to meet you. Thanks for agreeing to see Connor here.' Though it *was* said with a thick Irish brogue.

'That's no problem,' I replied, lying through my teeth. Of course, there was a problem. If not with me, then certainly with Connor. That's why he was here, wasn't it? Whatever the problem, to be on the safe side, I had changed into a brown coat and brought out my canvas bag of various instruments – hoof picks and the like – that I usually took on farm visits.

'Connor's gone a bit lame on his nearside front foot. The one he's resting now,' Mickey informed me, swinging his guitar off his shoulder and sliding it onto the trailer. 'Not noticeable on hard ground, roads, pavements and the like. But on soft ground like grass, there's a definite favouring of that leg.'

I let out an almighty inward groan. Just as I feared. Here we had something that needed a proper workout. A thorough assessment of the degree of lameness and where it was originating from. And that required having Connor walked up and down. Trotted. Put through his paces. On soft ground. Hard ground. How the hell was I going to do that with him so heavily harnessed to the cart? Besides which, where would I do it? In and out between the parked cars? A quick trot over to the Green to weave through the bedding plants? Curses on Beryl for landing me with this.

'I did think it might be his frog,' Mickey was saying.

'Sorry, what?' I said, snatched from my thoughts of Connor padding through the town council's petunias.

'A bruised sole. May have trodden on a stone. The frog only touches the ground on soft going. So, it would hurt more than when on hard ground where the shoe would raise the hoof, wouldn't it?'

Well, actually, yes, it would. Mickey was making sense. Could well be something as simple as that. Just needed me to take a look. Get the hoof raised and check for any damage to the frog and sole. And if there was, then no need to put Connor through his paces. The Green's petunias and marigolds could rest easy. Phew. But I had forgotten one thing. Connor's sizeable feet. It wasn't going to be easy to get a good look.

'No problem,' declared Mickey as if reading my mind. 'Connor be a fine fella. He'll let me lift his foot. Then you can have a good poke around for sure.'

And that's exactly what we did. With the foot lifted, I began my good poke around. <u>Using</u> a hoof pick, I carefully scraped out bits of compacted straw and mud from the inner edges of the shoe and from around the frog. But found nothing. No tissue damage.

'It ain't a bruise then,' said Mickey as he gently released Connor's foot.

I began to panic a little. More complicated reasons for the lameness started to surface. Navicular disease. Damage to the coffin bone. All rather misty, distant diagnoses discussed at veterinary school but never seen in practice. All needing a much more thorough investigation, one involving X-rays and the expert opinion of someone who knew what they were looking for. Not me, for sure.

'Do you think this may have any bearing?' Mickey continued. He'd run his hand up Connor's leg and was smoothing an area on the lateral side of the horse's shoulder, just below the scapula. 'It does seem a little bit puffy here. A bit painful?'

Connor shifted his stance slightly, pulling to one side with a twitch of his upper leg muscles.

I gently followed the contours of those muscles and got a similar reaction from Connor. Nothing too obvious. But a reaction, nevertheless.

'Steady, boy, steady,' I murmured, turning to Mickey and adding, 'Could be we've a pulled muscle here. Perhaps a sharp turn with the cart? It would certainly account for the lameness you've seen.'

Mickey nodded. 'A course of Bute then? Reduce the inflammation?'

My turn to nod. 'I'll get one of the nurses to make up a prescription for you. Five days' worth of powders, one daily in a bowl of pony mix. And plenty of rest. That will probably do the trick. If not, give us a shout.'

'To be sure, I will,' said Mickey. 'Now how much do I owe you?' He thrust his hand in one of his hoodie's pockets and pulled out a roll of notes.

'Settle up with Beryl in reception,' I said as a phone started ringing in Mickey's other pocket. That was also pulled out to reveal a smart, slimline iPhone. 'Excuse me if I answer this. It's the wife,' Mickey said. 'Asking after Connor.'

Seemed our traveller was a man of means, running a thriving busker business. Connor undoubtedly being the big draw. But then, there was also the guitar playing. Good playing and good singing to go with it?

To be sure, yes. As shown by the session Mickey treated us to before he took to the road again. Infectious Irish jigs that had Beryl rocking in reception while colour surged in her cheeks.

I thought Beryl's interest in all things coloured would wane in due course. But no, it didn't.

'What the heck have we got here?' exclaimed Eric one coffee break, having found a booklet in his favourite chair. I, too, had one in mine and several were spread out on the office table.

'Looks like some sort of colouring book,' he went on, picking his up and thumbing through it.

'That's exactly what it is,' said Beryl, bustling in with a tray of coffees. We each had our own mug. Eric had a bulldog on his. Crystal's a smart French poodle. My mug had a rather sickly rabbit on it that looked like it was suffering from a severe case of myxomatosis. Enough to put you off drinking the contents.

I also picked up my copy. The title – "It's Cool to Colour". Inside, page after page of line drawings ready to be coloured in. All depicting animals: cat, dog, horse, pig and many more.

'The idea is to colour them in,' Beryl explained. 'It helps to calm you down. All part of mindfulness therapy.'

'Mind your what?' queried Eric.

'Mindfulness, Eric.'

'Don't know if I need that sort of thing,' he replied. 'My mind's full of enough stuff as it is. The next dog castrate. Mrs Belling's peke with the eye ulcers.'

'Ah, but that's precisely where this can be of help.' Beryl had picked up one of the booklets on the desk and was waving it at Eric. 'Colouring enables negative thoughts to be expelled. Allows you to take in positivity.'

The way that Eric was glowering at Beryl, it would have taken many colouring sessions to expel his current negative thoughts about her.

'Your brain experiences relief by entering a meditative state,' she went on, obliviously of his dark looks.

Eric snorted. 'I can do that by having a tumbler of whisky. Without the need to colour in a pig or the like.' He had been flicking through the booklet and had stopped at the drawing of a large spider. 'Especially something like that.' He raised the page to show Beryl. 'Surely, colouring that in is more likely to raise your stress levels rather than lower them?'

Oh, dear. I could see the stress levels between the two of them beginning to rise. Maybe both of them should start colouring straightaway.

Beryl was undeterred. 'It's a chance to unplug from technology,' she said, staring him in the eye with her one good one. 'Switch off the TV.'

'What? And miss out on EastEnders?'

Whoa, Eric. Don't wind Beryl up too much. I knew he and Crystal never watched EastEnders.

She took a sip of her coffee, both her and her mug steaming. But Beryl was determined to push her point and said, 'It promotes creativity over consumption,' before adding rather cuttingly, 'especially if there's a tendency to hit the bottle.'

Ouch, Beryl. You're flying rather too close to the wind here. We all knew of her disapproval of alcohol. On the rare occasions Eric and I had popped down to the Woolpack for a quick beer and ploughman's lunch, we'd return to the hospital with a couple of peppermints stuffed in our mouths. Even then, there'd be a glare and sniff from Beryl. And once, a withering remark aimed at Eric after he'd had an extra half-pint, when she said, 'With breath like that, you could anaesthetise a Great Dane at 20 paces.' No holding back our Beryl when she wanted to speak her mind.

The reference to alcohol, albeit it an oblique one, clearly rankled with Eric. 'Well, if you think that colouring in spots on a leopard or stripes on a zebra is going to make you feel better, bully for you,' he said. 'It's certainly not my cup of tea.' He slammed his copy of the colouring book on the desk, slurped down the last of his coffee and stormed out.

'Wonder what's got into him all of a sudden?' queried Beryl, her false eye glinting. She turned to me. 'So, what about you, Paul? You might find it beneficial to have a go as you do get stressed quite a bit. And colouring can be done by anyone, you know. Not just artists or creative types.'

Whoops, Beryl was at it again. Tact in short supply today. I muttered my thanks, held on to my book, and promised to give it a try *(oh, really?)*, colouring profusely as I sped out of the door.

It was my half-day off and, Lucy had also managed to get herself a free afternoon. And since it turned out to be a glorious, warm summery one, I decided it was a good opportunity to go for a ramble up on the Downs. We'd enjoy it. As would Emily and Bertie for certain.

Lucy flicked through the colouring book as we first drove back to Willow Wren to have a spot of lunch and collect the dogs.

'One of Beryl's latest fads,' I remarked. 'Surprised she hasn't got you and Mandy up for it yet.'

'Just give her time,' replied Lucy. 'Knowing her, that won't be too long.' She closed the book. 'Could be she's onto something, though.' I saw her briefly glance at me. 'After all, you do get a bit uptight occasionally.'

'Well, so do you,' I retorted.

'Yes, yes. I know, I do. In fact, we all do. One of the hazards of the job.'

I braked to a halt on the hard standing in front of the cottage without another word, deciding it best to drop the subject for fear of getting into a slanging match similar to that I'd witnessed starting up between Eric and Beryl earlier. Fortunately, the exuberant greetings from Emily and Bertie, with much squealing and tail wagging, dissipated the tension that had started to surface. But Lucy was right of course. There were plenty of stresses and strains involved in our dealings with animals. The responsibility to diagnose and treat their medical problems. Care for them to the best of our ability. So, it was important to find ways to manage and control those stresses and strains to avoid falling apart at the seams. Not go over the edge. Not crack up. Perhaps it might not be such a bad idea to look into mindfulness a bit more.

Perhaps colouring a donkey or two to avoid making a complete ass of myself.

After some soup and some crusty bread and cheese, I was feeling a bit less edgy. Looking forward to the walk I'd planned.

'Okay, let's be off,' I said, bundling the dogs into the back of the car.

'You haven't said where we're going yet,' said Lucy, belting herself in.

'A surprise,' I said, enigmatically. Goodness, I was sounding just like Beryl.

The surprise involved a three-mile drive that took us parallel to the northern slopes of the South Downs, from where we turned into a small car park tucked into the side of a hill. From here, a chalky track winds to the top. Emily and Bertie raced ahead of us as we hauled ourselves up the path.

This is a corner of Sussex that shall forever hold a place in my heart. Below us now, nestling beneath the Downs, flanked by the silent rush of the Arun, and wrapped in bowers of trees, is a place called Bury. I feel as if I know each blade of grass in its banks, each flint in its cottage walls and each tile on its red-capped roofs. For I was born there.

My parents' cottage was set back, half-hidden by a steep bank which, in spring, was carpeted in daffodils and framed by pink clouds of cherry blossom. It had black, timbered walls with sandstone infill and a huge thatch of grey that drooped over the eaves like a shawl on an old lady's shoulders. I can remember April days, skipping down the lane in front of the cottage, past scented drifts of primroses and dog violets to enter the dark tunnel of Church Lane with its towering walls of flint and canopy of ivy-clad trees. Sun filtered through emerald buds, dappling the lane with shadows that danced with me past Jasmine and Ferry Cottages, once home to the ferry workers, and on down to the banks of the river Arun.

I could see it now. A sliding, tidal river to the front; dark and dangerous, it glides past in murmuring ripples to cut through the gap in the Downs and flow swiftly out to sea. Banks lined with paper-brown reeds, a breeze rustling through their tousle-headed ranks, now peppered with fresh spears of green. Beyond, lie brook pastures, grid-lined by silver fingers of water, between which, black beef cattle snort and graze. This flat expanse of meadows is dotted with scrubby pockets of grey-green willow and alder. In May, clumps of hawthorn grow heavy with blossom and pencil-edge the meadows in white.

But it was August now. A sun beating down from a bleached blue sky. The chalky path we'd zigzagged up cracked like crockery, the grass to each side flopped and faded, hedgerows powdered white with dust. The only sound's the muted zeep-zeep of a yellowhammer deep in a sea of shimmering corn and the excited yaps of Emily and Bertie, coursing through it.

'Breath-taking, don't you think?' I said to Lucy as we took in the sweeping view.

'I couldn't agree more,' she murmured, slipping her hand in mine. 'Thank you for bringing me here. It's truly beautiful.'

It seemed only yesterday that I was here as a boy. Here in this corner of Sussex, beneath the Downs. Yet only a day's needed, one precious memory of the years spent in Bury, for my heart, like the lark in the meadow, to soar and soar with the love that stands beside me now.

I don't need a colouring book.

I have Lucy. My perfect picture.

Together, we'll share future memories.

Memories that are bound to be colourful in the best possible ways.